After Paradise

After Paradise

Robley Wilson

Black
Lawrence
Press

Black
Lawrence
Press

www.blacklawrence.com

Executive Editor: Diane Goettel
Book and Cover Design: Amy Freels

Copyright © Blue Garage Co. 2017
ISBN: 978-1-62557-978-2

Published 2017 by Black Lawrence Press.
Printed in the United States.

Acknowledgments

A portion of this book appeared originally as a short story, "Dancing for Men," in the collection of that title, published by the University of Pittsburgh Press (1983).

"For a man and a woman. For one plant divided
Into masculine and feminine which longed for each other."
—Czeslaw Milosz: "After Paradise"
Tr. Robert Hass

1.

Thursday. Early September. On a field in Maine, the outskirts of a small town called Scoggin, here are three men. One of them holds a flashlight; the other two are toting armloads of wooden stakes and short, heavy hammers. The man with the torch is wearing a light jacket, khaki pants, and a grease-stained fedora; he is smoking an unfiltered cigarette. The others wear overalls and denim shirts. All three wear army boots.

The man with the flashlight, who is the layout man in charge of this activity, indicates a spot on the ground, and one of his crew promptly sets a stake and hammers it into the earth. The layout man takes a number of paces away from that stake and signals a new location with his light. A new stake is set, and the process continues.

The field—the locals call it "The Meadows"—covers a fair-sized area, perhaps thirty acres or more, and its grasses in this late summertime, ordinarily knee-high, barely reach the men's ankles. The men are here before dawn, and though at this early hour the grasses are damp with dew, the morning sun will burn the dampness away and the dry and yellowed grasses will be brittle underfoot. No rain has fallen here—at least none of any consequence—since June, and when the leader has finished with his smoke he won't simply toss it away. First he will kneel to stub the burning tip into the dirt; then, when he is sure the cigarette is dead, he will field-strip it, splitting the paper by running his thumbnail the length of the butt and scattering the loose tobacco to whatever winds there are.

The three men make their way roughly around the perimeter of The Meadows, moving counter-clockwise. Sites are chosen, stakes are set, the noise of the pounding rings against the hush of the morning—wood-notes, hammer-songs. The trio continue the circle until they are nearly to the place where they began.

Now the movement is in the interior of the field, where yet more stakes are hammered into the ground. By the time the work is finished, an edge of orange light has appeared on the eastern rim of the world, and the sky has begun to lighten upward. It is 4:30. The men have established the layout for a traveling carnival whose vanguard—the trucks and trailers loaded with tents and platforms and rides and the gaudy signage of the trade—is already laboring up the long hill past Goodwin Memorial Hospital.

What the three men have made—and it is what they make in every town where the show pitches its tents and its concessions—is a real-size map of the carnival, whose three dimensions will be erected by the crews to follow. From the main entrance, which is at the front of the carnival, the tents and concessions as one travels counter-clockwise are first those designed to appeal to families and to children, then those for older patrons, et cetera, so that shows at the back of the carnival and down the left perimeter are increasingly "adult." The concessions: popcorn, cotton candy, and drinks—but no beer, because the county doesn't permit selling alcohol by the drink—are interspersed.

Their work done for the morning, the men leave the field, climb into the dusty Ford station wagon parked at the side of the highway, and drive into town for coffee and safer cigarettes—and perhaps enough conversation to establish for them Scoggin's samenesses to, and differences from, the dozen other northeastern towns they have platted this arid second summer after the war.

* * *

The first of the carnival vehicles is already at the crest of the hill, already turning in to The Meadows, finding by rote its place on the map of the empty field—each new truck arriving at its pre-plotted place, and each one disgorging one or two or three men or women who set themselves to the business of unloading their trucks, setting their platforms and stages, putting up their tents like nomads arriving—how apt this is—at a temporary oasis in the desert.

From the foot to the top of Hospital Hill, the train of vehicles comes on. Vans, ten-wheelers, pickups dragging closed trailers—here is a mile or more of equipment, displays, performers.

Far back from the earliest arrivals, a green Chevy pickup truck towing a silver Airstream trailer is moving along a deserted street—River Street, so called because it parallels the Scoggin River—following a ten-wheeler with the words *World of Pleasures* elaborately inscribed across its rear doors. The script is overburdened with serifs and curlicues, and its colors, even in the weak morning light, are vividly red and yellow. *World of Pleasures* is what this carnival is pleased to call itself.

In the cab of the pickup: Frank Coggio, driving; the passenger beside him: Sherrie Adams, an exotic dancer known professionally as *Sharita*.

How to describe Coggio? He is small, dark, a man whose appearance and demeanor are entirely out of key with the pleasures of this or any other world. He wears a narrow snap-brimmed hat encircled by a stained grosgrain band. He is smoking; one might infer from the pale-olive cast of his skin that he chain-smokes, that his fingers—also yellowed—are rarely if ever empty of a Lucky Strike tapped from the pack in his shirt pocket.

The name, Coggio, is what? Italian? Then one might imagine he came from South Boston, a nineteen-forties Italian ghetto of a thousand men as small, as dark, as fond of nicotine. Imagine, too, that he plays checkers—a hustler adept at contriving *twofers* and *threefers* as he collects his winnings from any poor mark who challenges his board-game skills; that he plays the ponies—Rockingham, Narragansett when he is in this neck of the woods—that certainly his hands are dirty from handling the kind of paper money spent on the World of Pleasures grounds.

But Coggio is not himself a carnival gambler. He stammers, forcing out his hard consonants only over two or three attempts, and the stammer seems intrinsic to his entire body: he has no aptitude for the shell game, or three-card monte, or any other con whose success depends on the dexterity of the concessionaire's fingers. Coggio's fingers are clumsy; like his speech, they stumble over small objects.

Coggio is a sideshow talker.

Which seems paradoxical. A talker draws the crowds, sells and takes the tickets, makes his success or failure by the effectiveness of his spiel. A man who stammers, who finds himself blocked on the wrong side of letters like *p* and *b*, and *m* and *n* (to name the worst of them), whose attempts to express himself are painful and patience-testing to normal hearers—how can he summon the eloquence to gather an audience?

But Coggio can, and does. It is a trick of some queer biological circumstance that when he is doing his job on a carnival stage, his stammer disappears. Standing in front of the gaudy banner that proclaims Sharita's name to the world, Frank Coggio is as eloquent as a Bryan, a Roosevelt, or—to reach back to his distant Mediterranean ancestry—Cicero himself berating Cataline.

That eloquence may only be a quirk of Nature, though it might also have to do with Coggio's passenger. It might be that Sherrie—Sharita—is the inspiration that lifts him out of his flawed self, remakes him, gives him the smooth tongue that helps make a living for both of them. Frank and Sherrie are not married—they are rarely lovers—but they are a couple, dependent on each other, protective of each other, inseparable for more years than they might care to remember. And they are fond, one of the other, a fondness not always fathomable to the strangers among whom they move.

Not that Sharita is past her prime. She claims to be in her late thirties; one could reasonably add five years and not be far wrong. But she is still attractive, in the hard way of women who have never lived comfortably, never known a settled domestic situation, never confronted the world without the embellishment of stage cosmetics to convey expression to the farthest row of the house. And she is—ask Frank—"a good person", who suffers and forgives the day-to-day humiliations of the responses to her dancing: the innuendos and catcalls, the indecent proposals, the sweaty hands that reach across the line that is supposed to divide performer from audience.

Perhaps she forgives them because she deliberately courts such negative—say "lascivious"—attentions. As the years have made their marks on Sharita, and as she is more and more distant from the days when she was part of the Jazz Age marathon-dance madness, Coggio has watched her raise the temperature of her performances: fewer clothes, more suggestive movements, an obscene act or two to swell the crowds of men who supply the wolf whistles, the rhythmic clapping, the atmosphere that eggs the dancer on to show more, do more, allow more. Now the icebox in the trailer behind them holds a newly added part of the act: a three-foot rat snake, coiled inside the ice compartment.

Why a snake? Only a month earlier, in a small town in western Massachusetts, the local police closed Sharita down for "obscene and vulgar acts" involving a novel way of holding a lighted cigarette in not her proper lips. Next day, Coggio bought the snake at a pet shop in Worcester as an alternative and an embellishment to the cigarette routine. Sherrie rehearses with the snake—a safe and not impressively long creature—but she has danced with it in public only once, a week ago in Bangor. "I can't do this," she told Coggio afterward. "It scares the shit out of me; what if it really gets inside me?" "We'll t-talk about it," Coggio had said. "N-not every copper's so t-touchy." Now they're back to the original act, where she feels comfortable. They only use the snake out front, to draw the crowds.

The snake sleeps in the icebox, where the cold keeps it sluggish and tractable. It gives Sherrie a start whenever she opens the icebox door: that creature half coiled around the diminishing block of ice that keeps cold the milk and tonic, the vegetables and wax-wrapped slices of meat on the shelves. When Coggio lugs in a new chunk of ice, a 25-cent block every other day, Sherrie holds the snake, then resettles it around the new ice. Before the next show, she has to brush the damp sawdust off the snake's skin.

None of this—the obscene performances, the erotic costumes, the suggestive and vulgar content of her dancing—is to suggest that Sharita is an evil person. Sharita is still Sherrie Adams, a persona not only "good", but God-fearing as well. Sherrie attends church, when she can and where there is Christian Science, and she wears an anklet bearing the inscription *Love*. The word is probably wasted on Sharita's audiences, but as a reminder to Sherrie, no doubt it reassures her—and never mind the audience.

* * *

Sherrie has slept off and on for most of the trip—the night drive down from Waterville to Scoggin, Coggio slouched over the wheel, his eyes fixed on the shoulder of the two-lane blacktop roads—and now, the truck and trailer halfway through the town, she wakes up and looks out the window.

"Is this it?" she says. What she sees through sleepy eyes are drab tenements, a storefront or two, a filling station featuring Cities Service products.

"B-b-big city of Scoggin, Maine," Coggio tells her. "The n-next three days of your l-l-life."

Sherrie sighs and stretches. "You get any sleep at all?"

"S-stopped outside P-p-portland. Caught forty winks in the p-parking lot of the train s-station."

"Good for you." She rests her head against the window, watching the town slide past. "Looks like nowhere," she says.

Coggio smiles, showing yellow teeth. "Your h-hometown."

"Funny," Sherrie says."Just watch out for that kid on the bicycle."

"P-paper boy."

"I don't see any papers."

"He's f-finished for the d-day."

Sherrie sits straighter, fiddles with the truck radio until she finds music. What she finds is a rendition of Duke Ellington's "Caravan." She snaps it off angrily.

"Christ, I hate that music." She says it with startling vehemence.

2.

Across the highway from The Meadows, a teenaged boy sits on a blue bicycle and watches the carnival being assembled. The sun is barely above the horizon; ranks of thin clouds have taken on colors that range from orange, at the land's edge, to a shade of yellow, half-way up the eastern sky, that might be called peach. The morning is cool, but that swath of orange suggests the day will turn hot, yet another in the hundred-odd parade of days without rain, and the sooner the shows and concessions are in place, the better for the men doing the work.

The blue bike is trimmed in off-white: painstaking triangles at the front tips of the fenders, a less careful striping along the frame; a bullet-shaped chrome headlight is mounted at the front, a nippled red reflector at the back. The boy—his name is David Willard—painted the bicycle himself, the body color *Royal Blue*, the trim *Eggshell*. He has been up since four o'clock, and though he did not arrive at the carnival site until after the three men had positioned their stakes and gone off to find coffee, he was in time to watch the first trucks unload and the first tent rise over the first stage.

A lot of work remains to be done—the cook tent with its stoves and tables and benches isn't settled yet, the merry-go-round and its ponies aren't put together, and half the attractions are still mere stakes scattered across the beaten-down grasses of the field—but David consults his wristwatch and pushes off in the direction of town, pedaling hard until he is at the crest of the hill, then coasting down it, almost the whole distance into Scoggin.

His destination is Kate Meredith's house.

Kate is not quite his girlfriend. They don't go steady, they don't wear each other's jewelry, they aren't even in the same class at the local high school. David is a senior; Kate is a sophomore. They pass each other in the school corridors sometimes, exchange an occasional glance in the cafeteria. What they share—what brings them together—is the neighborhood, their white-collar fathers in this blue-collar town, and their membership in the Scoggin High School drama club, Thespis. At Thespis meetings, the two of them read together, play with or against each other in—so far—three school productions; David is a whiz at memorizing. The two of them often sit by themselves in far corners of the gym, heads almost touching, talking and laughing like a pair of happy conspirators. Someday their respective yearbooks will likely call them "most popular" and—quite possibly—"class clown".

Today, Kate has agreed to go with David to watch the carnival set up. She didn't ask her mother if it was all right, this early morning adventure, because she was afraid Mother would say no. She would have asked her father—the parent far more likely to say yes—but he has been away on business for nearly two weeks. She thinks it likely that at five a.m., the time David has appointed, her mother will be sound asleep, a book or a magazine butterflied open across her stomach.

The clock on the stand beside her bed already reads 5:15. She's running late, but then, so is David. In the dimness from a hall night-light, she moves about, dressing, being careful—never mind trusting the depth of her mother's sleep—not to make any unnecessary noise. Kate is fifteen, a naturally pretty girl with solemn brown eyes and a full lower lip; she can skip such refinements as makeup, and she is in the final stages of getting ready to tiptoe out when there is a noise at the window, a sharp clatter like small hail.

Going to the window, Kate sees David looking up at her from the gravel driveway, grinning and waving like a ninny. Annoyed, she goes to the window, slides it half open and kneels to speak to him in a voice the play books call *sotto voce*.

"What do you think you're doing? You want the whole world to wake up?" She frowns at him over the windowsill. "My gosh," she says. Boys have no sense of decorum; she thinks she has known this all her life.

David doesn't bother to talk softly. He is breathless from pedaling hard across town, excited by seeing Kate, in a hurry to lead her to the World of Pleasures.

"I've already been over at The Meadows," he tells her. "Hurry up, will you?"

"Would you *please*? My mother's asleep." This in a hoarse whisper.

"They're already unloading. They're putting up the sideshow tents."

"I'm hurrying. I'll meet you out front."

"If I get a ladder, you can climb out the window."

"We don't have a ladder, and I'm not climbing out any window anyway. What is the matter with you?"

"We could pretend we're eloping."

If this isn't the silliest thing Kate has ever heard, it comes pretty darned close. "David—" she begins, and then realizes she is speechless.

But David is not, and he plays it out. "Honeybun?" he says, "did you pack a suitcase? I'll hold the ladder for you."

"—will you please GO!" Not a whisper. She closes the window, almost too hard, and turns away.

* * *

David shrugs, but he is sure Kate isn't truly angry at what he said. He knows she makes allowances for his awkward affection.

He takes up the bike and wheels it around to the front porch of the Meredith house. Once there, he lays the bike on its side and sits on the next-to-the-bottom step. Kate's bike is nearby, chained to the railing.

David thinks his worst fault, or one of his worst faults anyway, is pushing his jokes one step too far. His father, the minister of the Congregational Church, is forever chiding him. "You just don't know when to quit, do you?" his father says—daily, it seems. "You always have to take it one step further, and cross over the line of common sense and decency." His mother puts it differently. "David, why must you always have to have the last word?"

But he likes to think that the "last word" in this present instance, the scenario in which he elopes with Kate Meredith, isn't really a crossing of the line. Elopement isn't going to happen in the next four or five years—or maybe further off than that—but it's a thing he wants to see happen. He so much wants it that he has just now amazed himself by joking about it with the object of his desire. Not that Kate *knows* she is such an object. In Mr. Clifford's English class last year, there was a line of poetry David knew he would never forget. It went, "Never seek to tell thy love, love that never told can be." It fits his case exactly, which is why Kate thinks he is trying to be funny, and that's all. If she knew the painful truth. . . .

While he waits, he considers his near future. The plan to watch the carnival build itself has long been arranged—since mid-summer, in fact, a scorcher of an afternoon in August, when Kate came home from the YWCA camp in Winthrop and he bumped into her at a Twilight League baseball game, Genest Concrete against Allied Shoe. He was by himself, on a bench behind the home dugout; Kate was with her father, sitting in the first-base bleachers. David was watching her—it was between innings—when she looked in his direction and waved. After the next inning, he climbed up to talk with her.

"Hi, Katie."

"Hi, Dave. You know my dad." She turned to her father and touched David on the shoulder. "Daddy? You remember David? His father runs the Congo church."

"He's the minister," David had said. "Nobody *runs* a church." Not that he'd meant to belittle his father's importance, but the touch of Kate's hand through his shirtsleeve had thrown him somewhat off stride.

"Good to see you again, David," her father said. "How are you enjoying the game?"

"It's a good one, sir. I like it when they're close."

"So do I—though I thought Grimes should have held on to that line drive in the third. That would have changed the whole complexion of the game."

"Yes, sir. It certainly would have."

It had been awkward, making conversation with Mr. Meredith, feeling the sweat trickle down his side, when he'd rather have been talking with Kate. Even looking at his own feet—because he wasn't sure how directly he should look at her father—what he saw was Kate, her white ankle socks, her penny loafers with actual pennies tucked into both of them. The embarrassment was really getting to him, but then Mr. Meredith rescued him.

"I feel like a hot dog," he'd announced to no one in particular. He stood on the bench and sidled around Kate on his way to the end of the row. "Either of you two want anything?"

"I'd like a tonic," Katie said. "Anything but Moxie."

"Nothing for me," David said. "Thank you for asking."

"You're sure?"

"Yes, sir. I had a big lunch."

What a jerk he'd been, to say a dumb thing like that. What difference did lunch make at four in the afternoon? Katie's father must have had him sized up as some kind of nitwit. "What do you see in that Willard boy?" he'd probably said to Katie when they got home. "He sure as hell didn't inherit his father's gift of gab." But would Mr. Meredith have said "hell"? Yes, probably. He'd been in the war, in the Air Corps; he hardly ever went to church. He'd have called David a moron in no uncertain terms.

But the afternoon ended well. He was able to talk with Kate—her father was at the concession stand for*ever*—and agree with her how lousy it was that summer was going by so fast, school already on the horizon, but Thespis would start up and they'd be in plays together, and hey, there was a carnival coming, Labor Day weekend. No, Kate wasn't sure she could go, but she'd try to get up early the first day, to watch the shows set up. That had been David's idea, his fall-back in case she turned him down for an after-dark date. "It won't be as big as the circus," David said, "but it'll still be like going behind the scenes—if we get there early enough."

So here he was, plenty early enough, but stuck waiting for Katie to finish whatever she was doing. His father must be right. Once, when he'd been waiting to take the family to the movies, he'd said to David, "If God had intended women to be on time, he wouldn't have invented mirrors." Mother had overheard him, and she made them wait even longer.

* * *

Upstairs in her room, Kate takes a thin blue jacket from the closet and shrugs into it. From the top shelf of the closet she brings down the pink cap she wore for softball at the YW camp and carries it with her across the dark hallway to the bathroom. She closes the bathroom door and turns on the light. Brushing her hair—it is chestnut colored and falls to the middle of her back—she ponders it, wonders if it needs washing.

She is of two minds about her hair. She knows boys like girls with long hair, that it is the first thing they notice about a girl and, usually, the first thing they praise. She knows Daddy likes it, because whenever she raises the possibility of getting it cut, he is eloquent in protest. "It's your crowning glory," he says. "It's the artistic frame for your pretty face." Trained as an engineer, he isn't usually so flowery, but something about her long hair inspires him.

Mother sees the matter differently. She seems to be neither for nor against Kate's long, straight hair. Her own hair, after all, is as long as Kate's, though she wears it up most of the time—sometimes in a bun, sometimes in one or two braids bobby-pinned upward, once in a while in something called a French twist. Her attitude toward her daughter's hair is often wary. She agrees that men like long hair, "but that's the problem," she tells Kate. What is she worried about? "Men like to touch a woman's hair," she says. "The silkiness, the softness, it pleases them. But some of them like the pleasure too much; they get carried away."

When Kate wants to know what her mother means by "carried away," she gets vague answers, or no answer at all. She remembers a Robert Browning poem in her freshman English class, about a man so afraid of losing the woman he loves that he strangles her with her own hair. It's not likely her mother is worried about *that*, is it? The poem didn't make sense anyway. Why would you kill somebody you were in love with? If you were afraid of losing her, why would you turn right around and do the one thing that would lose her forever? On the other hand, another poem they read in the same class said, "Each man kills the thing he loves." So there you were. Or maybe it was a thing that only made sense to men, that men simply did things that were incomprehensible to women.

Or it all might have something to do with Miss Folsom, the teacher of that class. Miss Folsom is a spinster, and that fact probably colors her outlook on love. It isn't that Miss Folsom doesn't have a sense of humor, but that she has a tendency to dwell on the dark side of life. "Gallows humor," she'd told the class one day. "The real purpose of being alive is: you die. You might as well laugh on your way to the cemetery." When Kate reported this, her mother gave a small smile. "She might not feel that way if she had a man in her life." Which probably meant that you wouldn't so much look forward to dying if you were leaving someone behind.

As for long hair, Kate considers it a mixed blessing. It's a pain to care for. It snarls. Her glasses—she is near-sighted—get tangled in it. When she washes it, it takes forever to dry. Worse—and upsetting— it attracts, in a scary way, boys she doesn't know, boys who pass her in the street and make comments; boys who drive by in cars that are deliberately made to draw attention, like mid-nineteen-thirties Chevrolets and DeSotos and Fords painted garish colors; boys who think they are God's gift to womankind, and so you are supposed to forgive them for being rude to you—shouting things, tooting their car horns. Wolves. Make-out artists. The kind of boys her mother is picturing when she says no to Kate in response to the simplest, most innocent request. What is it about long hair, the soft frame for her face, the graceful fall to her shoulders? What attraction? What promise? What secret danger in someone so young? Why is what is all right for Daddy all wrong for other males? Maybe Miss Folsom knows something important after all.

In front of the bathroom mirror she puts on the cap, pushing her long, dark hair up under it so that she looks almost boyish, as if that will foreclose all the hair questions.

As she turns out the light and crosses the hall to make sure her bedroom door is shut, her mother's voice arrests her.

"Kathryn?"

The name is couched as a question that needs to be answered, and so Kate goes down the hall to her parents' bedroom. The nightstand light is on and she is surprised to realize that Mother has been awake all along, reading a book. The book isn't a surprise; Mother is studying to renew her teaching certificate, and it's rare to see her without a textbook in her hands.

"Mother," Kate says. "It's five in the morning."

"Your father isn't home. I couldn't sleep." Mother picks up the alarm clock on the nightstand and looks at it. "And what are you doing up at this hour, young lady?"

"I didn't dream you'd be awake. Where's Daddy?"

"He called from Cleveland. You didn't answer my question."

Kate comes into the room and sits at the foot of her mother's bed. Daddy has been away on business, looking at sites for a new

General Electric plant—a job he has been doing ever since he came home from the war. A week ago he flew on a company plane to Wright-Patterson, and from there he drove to Toledo, and then on to Cleveland, sizing up factories that are standing empty because whatever they used to manufacture isn't needed any longer. Sometimes it's cheaper for GE to renovate existing buildings than it is to put up new ones, which certainly makes sense in terms of managing money, but makes life unpleasant for Mother.

"I promised David," Kate says, "that I'd go with him to watch them set up the carnival. Up at The Meadows."

"David Willard?"

"I don't know any other Davids." It's her mother's habit to confirm information she already knows, a carryover from Kate's bad old days, when she was continually being cross-examined about where she was going, who with, how late. It's Kate's habit—her own carryover—to respond with sarcasm, though nowadays the sarcasm is mild.

"And at this ungodly hour?"

"I guess that's when the show arrives. I'm late already." A lock of hair has fallen across her left eye, and she tucks it up under the cap. "Will Daddy be home today?"

Her mother sighs. The sigh means that whatever she might like to happen, the chances are it won't. "They want him to fly down to St. Louis, and then go on to Tulsa. He thinks he'll be back by the middle of the week."

"That's awful," Kate says. "Don't they know he has a family?"

"Of course they do." She rests the book face-down on her lap and looks at her daughter in what Kate considers to be her maternal pose. "Did you fix yourself some breakfast?"

Kate shakes her head—didn't Mother hear her say she was late? "I'll grab a doughnut on the way out." She gives her mother a hasty kiss on the forehead. "I've got to go. David's waiting."

"Be careful, dear. You know I worry."

Kate pauses in the bedroom doorway. "You don't have to worry about David," she says. "I'll be fine."

She descends the front stairs, and detours through the kitchen. She takes a small white pastry bag out of the breadbox. In the bag are two jelly doughnuts, left over from the half-dozen her mother bought day before yesterday at the bakery on Washington Street.

Outside, she shows the bag to David. "I stole breakfast," she says. "What is it?"

"Jelly doughnuts. Want one?" She doesn't see any harm in the two of them sitting on the front steps for a few minutes, sharing the pastries. As usual, she has to get on David's wavelength, to gauge his mood. She never knows whether he'll be somber or giddy.

"Come on, Kat," he says. "We can eat anytime."

It's only in the last couple of weeks that David has taken to calling her "Kat," and it makes her wonder if he considers her to be some sort of pet, a possession of his, or even a familiar—the kind of animal witches keep with them as identifiers. Does he think he can't be David without Kate beside him? That makes hardly any sense, but she wishes he would stick with "Kate" and not pretend she's especially his. She isn't a cat; she doesn't even especially *like* cats. Daddy calls her "kitten" sometimes, but that's different, and she doesn't even care for that.

Anyway, it's clear that David's mood is impatience and bad temper—that the funny fellow who pretended they were eloping has disappeared. There's nothing to do but unlock her bike and follow him to The Meadows.

* * *

"My dad says that when the circus used to come to town, when he was a kid, they had elephants to put up the Big Top," Kate says. The two of them are sitting across the road from The Meadows, watching the activity at the carnival and sharing the doughnuts, which are only slightly stale. The steady drone of generators forces Kate to raise her voice to be heard. "That's what they call it: 'the Big Top.' He's got pictures he took—these monster elephants with their heads up against the tent poles, pushing, and all these bare-chested men pounding stakes to anchor the ropes that hold the poles in place."

"Your dad's hardly ever around," David says. "I didn't know he cared about that stuff."

"There's a lot you don't know about him." Now that she thinks about it, there's a lot *she* doesn't know about him, and a lot more she doesn't understand about her parents' marriage. Her father is gone so often, he's away for so long at a time, and yet her mother seems not to be upset about being left alone. Sometimes—like today—she can't sleep, but her insomnia isn't because she misses Daddy. She's a restless person; even when Daddy is home, Kate often wakes up in the middle of the night and hears Mother going into the bathroom and closing the door, so she can turn on a light and read without disturbing him.

"Like for example, you probably don't know that he's a big railroad buff—they call them 'buffs'; don't ask me why." Kate wonders if David really cares about what her father's hobbies are, but she plunges on. "Before he went off to the army, he used to have this model train layout in the attic where we lived when we had the big house on Grove Street. He'd be up there all day, Sundays. Even in the summer. It'd be like a hundred degrees up there, and you'd be downstairs hearing these toy trains running around the ceiling over your head."

"I collect stuff," David says.

He has to bring the talk back to himself, doesn't he? All right; let him. "Like what?" she says.

"It depends when you ask me. I used to collect coins, but I'm changeable. My dad says I lack focus."

"So what are you collecting now?" Kate is honestly curious. It might help her understand him.

"Right now it's stamps."

"What kind?"

"Not the whole world. Just the United States." He brushes sugar off his hands, crumples the doughnut's tissue-paper wrapper and pushes it into the bakery bag. "I'm specializing in plate blocks."

"What are plate blocks?"

David acts annoyed. "You know," he says.

"If I did," Kate says, "I wouldn't have to ask."

"Stamps are printed in big sheets, and they put the number of the printing plate at each corner of the sheet. What you do is buy a block of four stamps from the corner that has the number. I just bought the Utah Centennial stamp a couple of weeks ago; I could show you. Some people buy blocks of six and some of them collect position blocks, which means they try to get the number from all four corners of the plate."

"Sounds complicated."

"And it can get expensive. If the stamp has more than one color, there's a plate number for every color." David looks at his hands, which are slender and slim-fingered. Kate thinks it's as if he doesn't know what to do with them. "My dad's the real collector in the family," he says. "Right now he's back to butterflies. The house smells of ether all the time."

"Why ether?"

"That's how you kill them. And then you pin them on a board so they look like they're alive."

Kate shivers. "Poor butterflies."

"I know," David says. "It's such a big thing with him, it's like an obsession. Ma says that before I was born the two of them would take a week every summer and go to a different part of the country, just to chase butterflies."

"That's some hobby."

"I don't know how he can do it—breathe that ether stuff. It makes me dizzy."

"It sounds kind of childish. Especially for a minister. Sticking pins in bugs."

"Playing with trains isn't childish?"

That takes Kate by surprise. It isn't like David to go on the attack, but the attack is so just, it makes her feel sheepish. "Maybe a little," she admits.

David studies Kate, looking wistful, his hands again nervous. He acts as if he is thinking of doing something, she's not sure what. Touching her? That would be upsetting. Pointing across the road toward the carnival activity? There isn't much to see after all; tents are going up, men in undershirts are lifting and carrying. And the Ferris wheel—first a vertical and then, section by triangular section, a circle. It looks too delicate to ride on.

"How come you're wearing that silly cap?" David says.

Not a question she had expected, but it makes her take off the cap and shake her hair free. "I was too tired to wash my hair last night," she says, "so I decided to keep it out of sight." Then she says, "I didn't want to disillusion you."

It is a teasing thing to say, almost flirty, and if David responds to it the way some boys would, Kate doesn't know how she'll unsay it. She puts the cap back on; her hair is to her shoulders. She crumples up the bakery bag and stuffs it into a pocket of her jacket.

"I can't believe I'm doing this," she says. "I can't believe I'm sitting here at dawn, watching a bunch of half-naked men putting up tents."

"I thought you wanted to."

"I did." Now what has she done? She has gone from flirting with him to injuring his pride. "It seemed like a keen idea at the time," she says, which probably makes matters worse.

She stands, stretches, then reaches down to take David's hand and pull him to his feet.

"Come on. I'll buy you a cup of coffee."

"I don't drink coffee."

"I'll teach you," Kate says.

3.

Across the road, Frank Coggio is in conversation with two men handling an enormous signboard that features a fanciful rendering of Sharita—half uncovered, balloon-like breasts, belly bare to well below the navel, thighs parted suggestively—under a banner that reads *Garden of Paradise*. Both the signboard and the banner are products of Coggio's lively imagination. The overall setting is meant to represent Eden, with a large and elaborately-drawn serpent gliding out of a tree to tempt the dancer, and Sharita's name at the top of the sign in garish red letters outlined with yellow. As an example of art influencing life, it is the signboard serpent that gave Coggio the idea of adding to Sherrie's act the snake presently dormant in the Airstream's icebox. With any luck the local law won't object to Sherrie's performance with the cigarette, and the snake can dream on. Maine is not Massachusetts. The worst that could happen is that the local authorities might call the act a fire hazard.

Finally, after considerable swearing, pointing, nodding, and repositioning, Coggio and the workmen seem to arrive at a compromise. The Sharita sign is prominently in place beside the tent entrance; Coggio is satisfied that his celebrity is displayed to best effect; the men mutter their way to other assignments.

Coggio doesn't rejoin Sherrie in the trailer. As usually happens when they arrive in a new town, Sherrie is hard to get along with—irritable, short-tempered. She doesn't sleep well during the drive between towns; that's part of the problem. New places represent a fresh set of unknowns; that's another. And then there is the ongoing problem of the act: Sherrie hates it, and in some way Coggio can't explain she manages to turn the hatred back on herself. What would she rather be doing? How many times has he asked that question, and how often has she reacted with angry tears? No sensible alternative offers itself. "You know how things stand with me," she will say. "You know what's out there."

Frank Coggio knows exactly what's out there.

When he first met Sherrie Adams, she was tending bar in upstate New York, a town called Chittenango, and he was driving a delivery truck for Railway Express. The bar was the Two-Spot, taking its name from the fact that it was built in the angle where two state roads met to form one. Situated as it was, the building was coffin-shaped, a deep and narrow space fitted into the vee of its lot. Its interior was rustic—unfinished pine walls, oak table tops, electric light fixtures disguised as kerosene lanterns; wooden flooring, narrow windows only on each side of the entrance. It was a place that never saw daylight.

This was a dozen years ago, when Frank Coggio and Sherrie Adams were both in their early thirties. Sherrie had grown up in Utica, Coggio in Boston. By the time the two of them met, Sherrie had been laid off from her last steady job, as a PBX operator in Schenectady, and had worked at the Two-Spot for nearly five years. Coggio had knocked around the Northeast doing this and that—gas station attendant, car salesman, carpenter—before he ended up in Syracuse. The Depression was at its worst; people worked whenever and wherever they could.

The instant connection that formed between the two is hard to define. Love? Possibly. Certainly they liked each other from the beginning, shared secrets and ambitions, were protective of each other. Once only, shortly after Pearl Harbor, was marriage mentioned. The fact of war—the perilousness of the "Yellow Peril"—pushed many couples to the wedding chapel, but Sherrie and Coggio backed off. When Coggio bought her a zircon ring to wear, it was for him no more than a wistful joke. For her part, Sherrie was wise enough to treat the cheap ring as a token of serious affection, even if it couldn't be a solemn promise of love everlasting. At the least, it helped her deflect the advances of the men—not the regulars—who dropped in at the Two-Spot. It pleased Coggio that so cheap a gift could protect an object genuinely precious to him.

On his time off, Coggio would sit at the bar, nursing a 7 and 7, perhaps hoping to take Sherrie to a movie in Syracuse. In those early days he indulged his dislike of the men she served drinks to, ready to put himself between them and her—if necessary, if the zircon might finally fail in its effectiveness. How she put up with them—the leering banter, the innuendo—he could scarcely understand, and yet she suffered everything with smiles and easy graces that made her imagine he truly loved her.

"I'm all right," she would tell him. "You don't realize how lonely they are."

As if she didn't recognize Coggio's loneliness. But he didn't kid himself. He knew she'd had a life before him, and that long before she fell back on tending a switchboard for a chemical company in Syracuse, she'd been a famous dancer, traipsing around America, winning prizes at marathon dances when that fad was at its height. Oh, yes; she knew about life and the limelight, and she certainly knew about men.

And so, when he saw a salesman twist the wedding band off his finger and slip it into a jacket pocket, he kept his mouth shut and gritted his teeth. When a young college student had one drink too many and tried to catch her hand in his across the counter, Coggio stayed in his seat and stared hard into his own drink. ("Oh, my," Sherrie said to the salesman, "your fingers are starting to lose their nice even tan.")

Coggio thought she was a marvel.

* * *

When she got married, it seemed the end of the world for Coggio. One day he was worshipping Sherrie from afar, and the next she was gone, so distant that the word "afar" had no force. He never laid eyes on her husband, had no idea what he did or where Sherrie had met him. It wasn't until years later that he found out her old dance partner had reappeared and swept her off her feet. "I thought he was bringing back the old glamour," she's told Coggio. "Little did I know."

The war progressed. Nearly forty, Coggio was too old to be drafted, too short to enlist. He quit Railway Express—or was "let go"—and went back to New England, worked in Maine at the Bath Iron Works, where he was attached to the paint crews that put the finishing gray touches on destroyers destined for anti-submarine duty in the North Atlantic. When it occurred to him that the job was doing some indefinable hurt to his lungs, he turned in his time card.

He planned to stay at his boarding house in Brunswick only until BIW cut his final paycheck. As it turned out, it was lucky he did. Sherrie Adams found him and phoned him.

Three years had gone by since her marriage, and in all that time Coggio hadn't had a word from her—no postcard, no letter, no nothing. And now here she was, that familiar voice, that way she had of pronouncing his name as if the *a* in *Frank* had some sort of fancy dictionary mark over it.

"You have to help me," she said. "You have to."

"How did you t-track me down?" he wanted to know.

"I have to get away," she said.

"Where are you?"

"In Hartford." A hesitation. "Avon," she said. "It's just outside Hartford."

"What's the m-matter?" he said. "What's wrong?"

"Everything. Everything's wrong."

"What c-c-can I d-do?"

"Come and get me. Please. Come and take me away with you."

"I'm a l-long way from H-Hartford," Coggio said.

There was a clatter at Sherrie's end of the connection, and a man's voice—a big voice, as from a big and angry man—said, "Not too fucking far away to please me."

"Joe," Sherrie said, "get off the line."

"The hell," Joe said.

"Frank, don't hang up." And then Sherrie said, "Joe, I'm having a conversation. Hang up. We'll talk when I'm finished." And to Coggio, "It's all right, Frank. He's just got this jealous streak."

Coggio was thinking her husband would have plenty of reason if he knew how much Coggio had cared for Sherrie, and for just a few seconds he wanted to tell him, "You don't know the half, you can't even imagine how much I'd give you to be jealous of."

But in fact what he finally said was to Sherrie herself, after her husband had screamed into the extension and then—apparently, from the sound of it—flung the phone onto the floor.

"T-t-tell me how to f-find you."

She told him what routes to take, told him to travel on 44 west out of Hartford, told him where to find the bus station in Avon and what time tomorrow she'd be there. He'd found a pencil and written everything down on the margins of the day's Boston *Post* sports page.

"Will you b-be all right?" was the last thing he said.

What Coggio meant was: Will your husband beat you? Out of anger, or shame, or drunkenness, will he hurt you?

She didn't hear him say it; she'd hung up the downstairs phone as soon as she finished her instructions. For fifteen or twenty seconds Coggio heard nothing but the echo of his own question, then the upstairs phone clicked and the dial tone sang in his ear. He fretted about the notion of Sherrie at the mercy of her crazed husband, but as soon as he tried to imagine her exquisite face bruised and raw he realized—remembering how adroitly and firmly she dealt with the men at the Two-Spot all those years ago—he was wrong to be afraid for her. He should better have said, "Remember how lonely he is. Take care of him; make him understand that you don't deserve bad treatment. You know. You know how." But how little he knew.

* * *

Today, having settled matters with the crew setting up the Garden of Paradise artwork and after stopping by the kitchen tent for a cup of strong java, Coggio makes his way back to the trailer. Maybe Sherrie will be awake, and, if he's lucky, she may even be in a good mood. Not that it really matters.

It's too easy to forgive Sherrie her shortness of temper—especially easy for Coggio—for one thing, because she lives her life in the shadow of Joe Connors, the man she married, the man Frank

Coggio rescued her from; for another, the disguise she has adopted—
the road dancer she's become—is hard on her pride. Tending bar
would be more acceptable, but when Joe comes looking for her, as
someday he surely will, that's the first occupation he'll think of.
That Joe will find her and drag her back into his harsh idea of marriage—it is Sherrie's worst and constant fear. Better to do what she's
doing, which has the advantage of anonymity, the virtue of being
an unlikely job, the fact of constant movement from town to town
and state to state.

When he comes into the trailer, Sherrie is still lying on one of
the narrow beds, but she is awake, eyes open, looking straight at him
as he shuts the door behind him. Her head is propped against an
orange pillow, her hands are folded across her stomach, the chenille
robe she wears is open only far enough to expose one bare leg.

"How was your n-n-nap," Coggio wants to know.

"I haven't slept," she says. "I had that dream again, the one
where Joe has the knife and fork."

Coggio has heard her tell this dream a dozen times at least.
Connors is sitting at a table, a dinner table, and Sherrie is lying
naked in front of him while he cuts chunks of flesh from her tits and
wolfs them down like a starving man. Sometimes there is wine on
the table, a bottle of red, and Connors guzzles it between mouthfuls
of Sherrie. It's a dream that infuriates Coggio because he can't figure
out how to respond to it. On the one hand he is angry at what Connors is doing; it shows the man's contempt for the woman—that she
is no more to him than a cut of meat, like a brisket or a pot roast.
On the other he envies the man in the dream, because Sherrie is
spread before him in her womanly glory, open and passive, available
in ways she is not to Coggio. It isn't that Coggio has never taken

Sherrie to bed, but that when they do have sex it's because she is drunk, or exhausted, or sunk so deep in despair she'd fuck anything that had a heartbeat.

"I'd like to k-kill that bastard."

"He'd kill you first," Sherrie says. "You know he would."

Coggio wonders. He's never seen Connors, and only has Sherrie's word for the man's ruthlessness. It seems to Coggio that this Joe Connors is the kind that likes to beat up on women for no good reason, and that his imagination for hurting them is fed by their weakness, their availability as victims. How he would deal with a man, especially a man like Coggio, whose rage would make him larger than life and stronger than any normal opponent, is another story. Connors would have to reckon with him in ways that Sherrie doesn't realize.

"L-let's hope he g-gets the chance," Coggio says.

"Let's hope he doesn't, for both our sakes."

4.

The coffee shop is on Longfellow Avenue, in a building that used to be a jewelry store. It still has two display windows designed to show off the watches and necklaces and diamond rings that are the stock in trade of every jeweler who ever lived, but now the windows are empty.

The man who owned the jewelry store was named Roger Krauss. He was of German ancestry, but he was born in Boston and moved with his family to Maine in the nineteen-thirties, when he opened the store. Mrs. Krauss—Sandra—was from Ohio; she married Roger in Haverhill, in the Lutheran Church, in the mid-twenties. The Krausses had one son, Karl, who was drafted into the army in 1943 and was killed at Anzio. Karl is buried in Oakdale Cemetery, across Main Street and a couple of miles down Ridge Road on the back road to Kennebunk. His parents closed the store and moved to North Carolina shortly after the end of the war.

David knows all this useless history, about the coffee shop before it became a coffee shop, because his father was acquainted with the Krauss family—not a friend exactly, but a counselor to them after their son's death. There was no Lutheran church in Scoggin—still isn't—but Roger and Sandra turned to the First Congregational Church, and its minister, because it was Protestant and trinitarian, and stood only two blocks from the store. Reverend Willard read the burial service for Karl, and later accepted a cash donation from Roger Krauss to install a memorial window in the Congo church remembering

Karl Krauss, Beloved Son, 1926–1944

In those already-forgotten days the Krausses had lived in the small apartment above the store, but no one lives there now, the space apparently given over to storage of who knows what.

The coffee shop is so new, its name—*Coffee And*—is not yet painted on the front windows, and it has become a game among the patrons to devise alternative logos for the shop. The current favorite is "The Holy Doughnut," though the origin of that name is obscure, there being no church nearby. Other wags have proposed "Mom's Place," "The Wakeup Call," and "Scissors and Pastry"—to name only a few.

Kate and David lean their bikes against the chain-link fence between the coffee shop and the yard of the Longfellow School next door. Longfellow is where David attended, kindergarten through sixth. Kate went to Edison, on the other side of town. It still surprises David to remember that Kate existed all those years before he first saw her in junior high, and yet he never knew it.

When the two of them come in, the shop is already crowded, but after a few minutes they capture a booth in the far corner near the restrooms. When the waitress arrives, Kate orders coffee regular. David orders cocoa.

"It really isn't cocoa weather," Kate says.

"What *is* cocoa weather?" David asks.

"You know. Snow. Freezing temperatures. Winter in general."

"That's when I order ice cream," David says.

"Just to be contrary."

"Just to be me."

Kate smiles. David takes that to be a sign of approval, which is a good thing because it means he can relax a little. He doesn't understand why being with Kate is so difficult, why the chemistry between them is so changeable, so unmanageable. One minute they're almost lovey-dovey, the next they're on the verge of a fight. He knows he can be a real pain in the neck, and he knows his moods get in the way of what he feels deep down, but Kate usually matches him, pain for pain, mood for mood. If they actually get married someday, what kind of cat-fight will it be? And yet, he tells himself, and yet he wants it.

When the coffee and cocoa arrive, Kate puts out her hand and prevents him from raising his cup to his mouth.

"No," she says. "First you have to try my coffee."

He shakes his head. "I don't like coffee."

"How do you know?"

"I just do." Not much of an answer, he has to admit. He doesn't *know*, but he thinks he knows, and the knowledge has a lot to do with the people he sees drinking coffee. Mr. Godwin, the editor of the Scoggin *Tribune*, where David works part-time, is a coffee drinker, and Mr. Godwin is a sour man—unsmiling, disapproving. He can't say this to Kate; she'll laugh in his face.

"Come on," she insists. "Try it." She has pushed her cup and saucer across the table so they sit beside his cocoa. The coffee regular is a pale yellowish-brown color, like the long stockings he used to wear with his corduroy knickerbockers when he went to grade school. It is an unpleasant brown—not like the dark, strong brown of cocoa. Worse, the coffee has a *smell*, while the cocoa has an *aroma*.

At any other time, in any other place, David would stick to his guns and refuse until the coffee was withdrawn. But this is Kate; something else is involved besides stubbornness and his pride. Here is a situation where firmness may very well be a weakness. What is he afraid of? That a sip of coffee—and coffee with cream, at that—will transform him into Marcus Godwin?

So he relents. "If it means so much to you," he says, and he lifts the coffee to his lips and drinks—enough to taste the coffee-ness and earn Kate's smile.

"You see?" she says. "Not so bad, is it?"

"But I prefer my cocoa," he says. He slides her cup back to her. "If coffee is so wonderful, why do you put cream in it?"

"That's just me," Kate says. "Usually I put a lot of sugar in it too. My mom says that when I drink a cup of coffee, it's a full meal."

"My dad says coffee stunts your growth." Why he said such a thing is beyond him. It's true that his father has made that statement, but why is David repeating it now? Is Kate's growth stunted? No. Then what is happening inside his head?

But Kate saves him. "My dad says smoking stunts your growth," she says, and he realizes that she has accepted his stupidity as her cue to take part in an absurd dialogue, the kind of comedy act they might invent at the end of a Thespis rehearsal or while the cast is striking the set on the last night of the annual play.

Now he is obliged to keep up the dialogue, but in what direction shall he steer it? Coffee, cigarettes—what vice should he turn to?

"The Boy Scouts say that playing with yourself stunts your growth." Even as he says it, this declaration seems to him so uncalled for, so ridiculous, that he begins laughing. First out of embarrassment, and then, as he sees Kate's amusement, out of a sense that he has somehow struck just the right note. It's as if the two of them are in a Marx Brothers movie, in which nothing they say is too foolish.

Kate calms down first. "Maybe," she says. "Maybe everything adults tell you you're not supposed to do stunts your growth."

She has grown serious so abruptly, David has to force himself to be serious too. For a moment, the pair of them sit in a silence so solemn, an onlooker would be worried for them: two attractive young people who ought to be happier than they seem. Then Kate breaks the spell.

"I'm surprised there aren't a lot more midgets in the world," she says.

At this they both break up, giggling so loudly that everybody in the coffee shop turns to look at them. But David isn't embarrassed any longer. Instead, he is thinking how smart Kate is, how quick, how clever, how funny—and most of all, how much he likes her and wants her to be in his life in every way possible. For her part, Kate is marveling at how naturally David responds to her prompts, as if the two of them were on stage without books, making up one *ad lib* after another. She can almost hear the applause.

They subside slowly. The other customers lose interest—no applause from them. For a few minutes Kate and David sit quietly, sipping from their cups, grinning at each other over their performance.

"I didn't tell you," David says at last. "I get to keep my summer job after school starts."

"I didn't know you had a summer job," Kate says. "Where?" In a way she is disappointed. They were having fun, and now David has brought them down to matters of fact.

"At the *Tribune*," he says. "I read proof and help with deliveries."

"You have to be a good speller to be a proofreader," she says.

"I am a good speller."

She takes this in. "They say that kind of close reading can ruin your eyesight," she says.

"That's true," David says. He giggles. "And stunt your growth."

This time when Kate laughs, she makes a snorting noise that would mortify her mother. But never mind; David has redeemed himself by bringing both of them onstage for an encore. She has to pull herself together and deliver her next line.

"Not getting enough sleep can stunt your growth," she says.

"Especially if you sleep in a short bed," David says.

Kate can't stop laughing. "Wait," she says, "I've got coffee up my nose."

Then she notices that David has gone straight-faced, that he is suddenly less concerned with joking around, with being a hilarious twosome, than with focusing on something happening behind her back. When she half turns in her seat she sees through the shop's front window two people standing on the sidewalk outside. She recognizes Tom Gowen and Shirley Kostas, classmates of David's. That's it, Kate thinks; now David will act as if she's not even here with him—or he will try so hard to pretend she *is* here, he'll embarrass her and she will have to leave without finishing her coffee.

They've talked about Tom and Shirley, not because Kate is interested in them but because David often brings them up in the middle of otherwise sensible conversations. She knows why, though she doesn't entirely understand what she knows. David fancies that Tom and Shirley are an ideal couple, and he talks about them as if he wishes David and Kate were like them. Which, so far as Kate is concerned, is too far-fetched to be worth considering. Tom is the school paragon: smooth-talking, good-looking, smart, and on top of everything else he's a terrific basketball player. His father runs Gowen's hardware, on the corner of Main and Kimball. The worst thing Kate has ever heard about Tom Gowen is the rumor among her girlfriends that he marcels his hair.

She doesn't know that much about Shirley. She knows Shirley lives with her mother, who is divorced. She knows Shirley's uncle owns Tony's, a hole-in-the-wall store next to the Capitol Theater where kids on their way to and from school stop to buy penny candies and tonic, and where adults buy fruits and vegetables and cigarettes and magazines when going all the way to the A&P is too much trouble. She knows Shirley's brother George was killed in the war; people say he was shot by a sniper in the center of the town in Greece where his great-grandfather was born. "That's irony," was Kate's father's reaction. Kate had thought, *No, it's just bad luck.*

Finally, she knows Shirley Kostas isn't very bright. That fact all by itself is enough to keep the girl off Kate's good books. She wonders why a smooth boy like Tom would lower himself to go steady with a dumb blond like Shirley. She supposes it has something to do with sex.

David knows what Kate knows, but his imagination makes it seem that he has far more knowledge than she does. And that apparent knowledge indeed has to do with sex. Tom has let it be known that he and Shirley sleep together; as far as David knows, they are the only two people in the entire high school who are doing it, and that fact he finds stunning. If it *is* a fact—though why would Tom lie about it? That would be a terrible thing to do to Shirley, to give her that reputation.

So David believes, and when he is by himself he sometimes tries to picture the two of them together, in the same way he used to study kissing on the movie posters outside the Capitol: which way were the heads tilted, where were the man's hands, where were the woman's, did it look as if their mouths were open, Frenching? But studying his image of Tom and Shirley is a greater pleasure; he knows them, they are a perfect match: her blond beauty, his dark handsomeness. What must they look like, naked? He doesn't dwell on it, but once in a while he suspects that the reality falls short of what he pictures. Who could live up to a Romantic Ideal?

One day in cafeteria, Tom and Shirley sat at his table, directly across from him. When Tom got up to fetch a straw for Shirley's milk, David talked with her.

"Hi," he said. "I'm David. A friend of Tom's."

"I know," Shirley said. She turned her head away, looking for Tom.

"How's your uncle?" David said. "How's Tony?"

She had given him a look that dismantled him, then put him back together in somewhat shabbier condition. "My uncle's name is Anthony," she said, "and he's fine."

Then Tom arrived. David had mumbled something about English class and fled.

* * *

Tom and Shirley, "the ideal couple," have taken a booth at the front of the coffee shop, where David can continue to admire them and Kate can be petulant. She is extremely good at petulant.

"She thinks she's so-o-o-o special," Kate says.

"She's all right." David tries to be matter-of-fact, even disinterested.

"Just because Tommy's a friend of yours."

"What's that got to do with anything?"

"I think she's a dunce," Kate says. She twists to take in the lovers, who are sitting side-by-side, not across from each other like normal people. "Look at them. He's all hands."

David looks down into his cocoa. He is thinking of Tom's hands, seeing them in his mind's eye. Under Shirley's skirt. Inside her blouse. Everywhere.

"They sleep together," he says.

Kate acts offended. "That's nobody's business," she says. "And probably it isn't true."

"Tom wouldn't lie to me."

She gives him a long and pitying look. "Yes, he would," she says. "That's what boys do."

An awkward silence follows this pronouncement. Finally Kate says, "We'd better go. My mom will be fretting."

"Yeah," David says. He looks at his wristwatch. "Mine too."

He digs in his pants pocket and brings out some coins. He counts out a dime and two nickels onto the table. Kate counts with him, to herself. When he starts to slide out of the booth, she reaches to touch the back of his hand.

"You should leave something for the waitress," she says.

David finds another nickel and adds it to the coins before him. "Okay?" he says.

She gets up with him. "It's something," she says.

Their way out of the coffee shop takes them past the booth where Tom and Shirley are sitting. That the two of them are sitting side by side is an arrangement that annoys Kate—though she isn't sure whether it's because she thinks it's improper, or because it wouldn't have occurred to David to try and sit beside *her*.

David taps Tom's shoulder as they pass. It's a light touch, but enough to make Tom look up.

"Hey, Tom," David says. "Hi, Shirl."

"David," Tom says. He tilts his head to look past David at Kate. "Hi, Kate."

Kate nods. Shirley doesn't acknowledge anything, just sits looking straight ahead, rotating the table's cream pitcher between her hands. Tom's left hand is resting, palm up, in her lap. A gray, pleated skirt, Kate notices.

David holds the door open and lets Kate go out first. Once they're on the street and walking their bicycles in the direction of Kate's house, David reaches out to squeeze her hand. It's an odd gesture that presses her hand hard against the handlebar grip.

"Are you and Tom really close?" she asks him. "I mean are you good friends?"

"We know each other," David says. "Why?"

"I wondered," she says. "He didn't have a lot to say to you."

"He's with his girl," David says, as if that explains everything. As if a boy could be that focused.

"She didn't even open her mouth," Kate says, but she knows she's mostly talking to herself. David's hand feels dry and dead on top of hers; she slips her hand out from under his and raises herself onto the bike seat.

David does the same, and for the length of a block they pedal in single file down the empty sidewalk. At the first intersection, Kate takes to the street; David draws alongside and they go two abreast.

"I don't think people have to always be pawing each other, do you?" she says. "To prove they care about each other?"

"No, I don't," David says. "Unless they're especially close. Like engaged."

Kate is startled by this suggestion. "Are they eng

Shirley?"

"All but. She's wearing his i.d. bracelet."

Kate laughs. "Oh," is all she says.

She can't tell which of them David is more smitten by: Tom or Shirley. "Smitten" is one of her mother's words, and it means liking someone whether they're likable or not. In other words, David is blind to Tom's and Shirley's flaws, whatever they might be. She imagines that he admires Tom because Tom could prob-ably go steady with any girl in the entire high school, if he wanted to, and she thinks David is much too impressed by the fact—if it *is* a fact—that Tom and Shirley are doing it. For David, the sex part of it makes Shirley desirable, but for Kate, it makes Shirley a tramp. How fascinating that two people can look at the same set of circumstances and arrive at opposite opinions. How can anyone—even David—not see the difference between an i.d. bracelet and an engagement ring?

When they arrive at Kate's house, it's obvious that David isn't in any hurry to leave her. He must feel—as Kate feels—that something between them is wrong and needs to be put right. It's likely that the problem has something to do with her unwillingness to put their handlebars together so David can hold her hand as they steer in unison. He would see that as Romantic—capital *R*—because, she thinks, he is still under the Tom-and-Shirley spell.

* * *

"When was the first time you noticed me?"

They are sitting on the front steps, Kate's bike leaning against the railing, David's lying on the grass between the sidewalk and the curb. She's not sure why she is asking the question, except that

David doesn't seem ready to go home, and perhaps she thinks that steering him to focus on her will purge Shirley Kostas, that tramp, from her thoughts.

"You mean the first time *ever?*" David says.

"Well, the first time you noticed it was me, different from some other girl. The first time you really saw Kate Meredith."

David is looking at his hands again, as if they hold an answer to the question. He shrugs. "I don't know," he says. "I guess it was at a basketball game, my junior year."

"Which game was that?"

"I think maybe it was the Thornton Academy game. The one we lost by two points."

Thornton is the traditional rival, the annual big game in both football and basketball, probably because Scoggin is a public school and Thornton is private. It's some kind of class war, Kate thinks; a struggle between haves and have-nots, rich and poor.

"That was a heartbreaker," she says. "I remember."

"You cried," David reminds her. "Toward the end of the game you were cheering and crying at the same time. I especially noticed that."

Kate is sorry David remembers *that*. It makes her seem silly and weak to be someone who takes a game so seriously that she weeps over it. "I cry very easily," she says. "But not very often. Sometimes an emotion can make you stop being sensible."

"There's nothing wrong with showing emotion," David says. "I think that's one of the reasons we both joined Thespis."

"What are the other reasons?" Kate says. Fishing.

He looks up from his hands and grins at her. "You mean besides my deep love for the theater?"

"Yes. Besides that."

"You want me to say I joined because of you," he says.

"Not if you didn't." What is the matter with him? Or better still, what is the matter with her—as if she needed flattery. "Never mind," Kate says. "I was only joking."

Now there is an awkward silence, which Kate feels it is up to her to break.

"So tell me," she says brightly, "are you going to take me to that carnival?"

"Do you really want to go?"

"Well, I don't know." She rests her elbows on her knees and her chin in her hands, pretending to consider the question of whether she *really* wants to go. "Maybe because you got me up at five in the morning and we watched them unload the shows and things— Maybe you feel as if you've already taken me? Is that what you're saying?"

David takes the cue.

"You mean you want me to buy you a ticket and take you on the rides, and that kind of stuff?"

His tone is teasing, which is a relief to Kate. It means they are back to normal. It means she isn't some catty girl, acting jealous of Shirley Kostas. It means David isn't mooning about how Tom is having sex and he isn't.

"That kind of stuff," she agrees.

"I suppose I could do that," he says. "I suppose I could take you to The Meadows some night this week." He leans back against the railing and makes believe he is reading a list written on the palm of one hand, like cheating on a test. "I suppose I could get an advance on my allowance and squander it on you. I suppose I could try to win you a kewpie doll. I suppose—"

Kate interrupts. He's got her giggling. She punches him on the arm and runs up the steps.

"Hey," he says, "I haven't got to the cotton candy. I haven't bought the popcorn."

"You idiot," she says. "I don't know if you're a smart person or a dumb one." Meaning why is he so slow to realize she needs entertaining, so slow to give her an exit line, so slow to focus all his attention on *her*?

"What if I'm dumb?" he says. "What then?"

"Then my father won't let me go anywhere with you. He wants me to be an intellectual."

"How do you know?" David says. "He's never home."

"Don't be fresh," Kate says, and she runs into the house, closing the door too hard behind her and leaving David standing on the sidewalk. It's like a slap across the mouth, this reminder that she might as well not have a father, even though she has said almost the same words to her mother a hundred times.

From the hallway, she has a last glimpse of David through the sheer curtain over the front-door glass. He pulls his bike up from the lawn, but before he climbs onto its seat to ride off, Kate takes an odd satisfaction from the forlorn way he stands looking toward the door she has shut between them.

5.

Sherrie is still trying to close her eyes for an afternoon nap—never mind the risk of more bad dreams—but the noise of generators outside the open windows of the trailer, not to mention the slow buildup of heat inside, are working against her. There are no matinee performances on the first day in a new town, and she needs lying flat in bed to undo the discomfort of sitting all night in Frank's pickup. And more and more lately she feels a mix of fatigue and inner turmoil that not only keeps her awake, but breaks into her sleep even when she has succeeded in dozing off.

She's beginning to think something is ailing her, and she wonders what it could be: she is always tired, she is serene one minute, irritable the next; she has days when she is impatient with everybody and everything, and she is especially short with Frank. Poor Frank, who, when you come right down to it, is her knight in shining armor, her rescuer, her genuine savior—in this world if not in God's. And he's a good listener when she needs someone to be sympathetic, like listening to her bad dreams and putting up with her fears.

She thinks, though, that she might be some kind of Jekyll and Hyde character, going from one mood to another without rhyme or reason. A half-hour ago he'd helped himself to a beer out of the icebox—no harm in that, he bought it, he's entitled—but when he uncapped the bottle and sat heavily on one of the dinette benches to drink, Sherrie had exploded.

"Christ almighty," she'd said, "can't a body have some privacy once in a while? Can't you guzzle your beer somewhere else?"

He'd looked at her, her sprawled against the headboard of the Hollywood bed, wearing the chenille robe she'd had forever, probably putting on display all God gave her, and what must he have thought? He'd looked, taken a slug from the bottle and raised it in her direction like a salute.

"Fuck you, Sh-Shara," he said, "and f-fuck your p-p-privacy." And out he'd gone, slamming the door behind him so hard that the metal skin of the trailer shimmered over her head.

She'd get a lecture from him later on. "Next time you've got the r-rag on, let me know," he'd say, "and I'll k-k-keep my distance."

Nice of him, she thinks now, always blaming something out of her control, never blaming her. It's another way she gauges his feelings for her: even when he's angry, and she deserves it, he absolves her.

But what is it that's making her into such a pain in the neck? She has her health, she has a job—such as it is—and she has a man who dotes on her even when he doesn't comprehend her. She ought to thank her stars for her place in the world.

She unbelts the robe and opens it to survey herself. It's been more than two years since she's seen Joe Connors. The bruises on her arms and shoulders have long since faded, the cigarette burns are healed—nothing left but tiny rose-colored welts alongside her darker nipples. All that mars her body is the appendectomy scar, a relic from fourth grade.

Lying so, the pink robe fanned out from her like a butterfly's wings, she thinks how she doesn't look bad for a forty-one-year-old woman, all things taken into account. Men still find her desirable; she's had her share. Though she shares the bed with Frank—and now and then they make a kind of animal love, it's true—she's not above having another man, some man singled out at the last show, some man clean and clean-cut, who appreciates experience. None of them stay the whole night; Frank wouldn't put up with that—him sitting outside, smoking and drinking beer, waiting to go back to the bed that's properly his. "I never get used to their smell on the sheets," he said to her once, and it's the only complaint he's ever uttered on that subject.

* * *

But none of her virtues can quite put down the hard knot of uneasiness in her chest, which, as it does now, corrupts the well-being she ought to be enjoying. That unease always begins with her imagining that some person in one of her audiences calls out her name: "Sherrie Connors"—the married name she dropped on the day she ran away with Frank. And then what? In one waking nightmare, the namer drives home to Avon and rings up old Joe. "Guess who I saw in Wherever. Your wife. And guess what she's doing for a living." In another, the namer is Joe himself, who then shoulders his way through the rest of the men fronting the stage and hauls her down into the pit; what happens to her there is unspeakable, a compendium of all the ways that men have humiliated her, one by one over time. All the nightmares have the same ending: she is back in her marriage to Joe, and her life is over.

Where is Frank Coggio when this black destiny smothers her? Having a beer, a smoke, a loud chat with a crony—sitting outside the trailer, where she has sent him because she craved quiet time.

She knows this is work she ought to be grateful for, this dancing for men whose profane comments on her performance are weak versions of the brutalizing they'd prefer—this is what she thinks of as an accidental occupation. If it hadn't been for Joe Connors, twenty years ago—Joe with his dapper way of dressing, his talented feet in their fancy wingtips, his glib line of patter that always got him fresh jobs—she'd be doing something else today. Who knew what? Probably she'd be bartending right now, except that's the first thing Joe would have thought of. It wouldn't be his first guess that she'd gone back to dancing; where was the living in that? Marathon dances died out long before the war, and even when they were most popular there wasn't much money to be made.

But she remembers the best of those days, especially the rich people who came to watch. They were the ones who put up the prize money, and the management would seat them in boxes by the side of the dance floor. There they'd be in their fancy dress clothes, the men in tuxedos and white silk scarves, and the ladies with no bosoms in shiny gowns with glittery necklaces and white gloves that came up to their elbows. You didn't see people dress up like that anymore, and you didn't see the big motorcars, the LaSalles and Cadillacs, the Packards and Lincolns with chauffeurs they arrived in and went away in. It was some swell stuff, but under the surface it was all hand to mouth.

Oh, she and Joe were as good as anybody, and in the beginning they both had the stamina to go along with the talent. One day, two days, a week—nobody could outlast them, and that's where the money was: in the surviving. Sometimes it was cash, sometimes it was donated merchandise you could sell for cash; either way, it was a living.

Then came the Depression—hard times, the end of the dance craze and all sorts of other silliness. She and Joe split up. Just as well;

he'd gotten a bum knee after a too-fancy Tango step he'd tried in Cleveland, and Sherrie'd had just about enough of the marathons anyway. What was the future in sleeping on your feet, five minutes here, ten there, counting on your partner to hold you up? How long was she going to put up with the heartburn, eating cold burgers and fries to music?

But Joe wouldn't stay out of her life, dance or no dance. When he walked into the bar in Chittenango after the years since she'd seen him—or thought of him, for that matter—she didn't recognize him at first. He was heavier, broader in the chest, coarser than when they'd danced together. She supposed it was because of the knee, that he couldn't exercise, but so what? He wasn't dancing, so he didn't need to keep in shape.

Anyway, none of that seemed to matter to the new Joe. He was still full of himself, but more confident than she'd ever seen him. He had the Pratt & Whitney job in Connecticut, he was making good money, and he claimed he'd been carrying the torch for her ever since their partnership broke up. When he proposed, she was swept away. Oh, she kicked herself now for not taking a deep breath, counting to ten, giving more consideration to what she was getting into. But at the time Joe Connors seemed just the star to hitch her wagon to, and she almost jumped to say yes. No more long hours behind the bar; no more fighting off God's gifts to women. She'd have a home, companionship, maybe she'd still have a chance at a kid.

Poor Frank. He'd had to stand by and watch it happen—saw Sherrie Adams walk out of his life on the arm of Joe Connors, a man he'd imagined as a slick-haired gigolo with swivel hips and a fairy's mincing walk. Far from it. More likely this new big lummox would make mincemeat out of Frank if their paths ever crossed. It was one thing to pick her up at a bus station in Connecticut, with Joe not yet realizing she'd packed up and honest-to-God gone, but it would be something else to meet the man face-to-face. Yet whatever might happen, she'd always love that Frank had rescued her, that he'd stuck by her, that he swore to fight for her if he had to. Not every woman had a body she could count on like that.

She turns, restless, in the small bed and reverses the pillow so it's cool against her face. The trailer is like an oven. The generators are incessant. Perhaps if she calls Frank, and he comes in to lie beside her just for a while, she can catch her forty winks after all.

6.

The record department at Fein's Furniture is in the deepest corner of the store, farthest from the entrance on Main Street, a tiny island of music surrounded by a tuneless clutter of overstuffed couches and easy chairs, kitchenette sets, china cabinets, and a scattering of bedroom suites. The only concession to an organizing principle is an aisle down the center of the store wide enough for two people. To look at particular pieces of furniture, you have to leave the aisle, left or right, and thread your way to them.

The phonograph records are stored on a bank of shelves eight feet or so high, crammed together vertically, side by side in their brown-paper jackets and looking from a distance like the push-pull exercises of Palmer Method penmanship. In front of the shelves is a low counter—a cashbox at one end of it, pencils and a pad for keeping track of sales beside it. Raymond Sevigny, a couple of years older than David, is leaning on the counter, waiting for business.

"How's it going?" Raymond says. He straightens up and pushes the fingers of one hand through his hair. He's tall and red-headed and seems to be growing a mustache.

"Okay," David says. "Did you get in the new Woody Herman?"

"'Northwest Passage,'" Raymond says. "Came in yesterday." He searches through the sleeves behind him and pulls out a red-labeled record. "It's pretty good," he says. "I bought it myself."

David digs into his pants pocket for the change he has held out from his weekly allowance. He is counting out the coins when Warren Fein, the store's owner, emerges from his office behind the carpeting display.

"Hey," Fein says, "Reverend Willard. How they hangin'?"

"Hi, Mr. Fein." He can never think how to respond to Fein's jokes—if that's what they are. Fein is too glib, and David isn't quick enough on the uptake.

"What're you buying?"

"The new Woody Herman."

"Good choice. I heard him play out at the Pier a couple of years ago."

That was another thing. Fein had been everywhere and done everything, just to make you feel left out.

"I saw you at the coffee shop with your girlfriend," Fein is saying now. "That's some hot little number. She put out for you?"

How is anybody supposed to answer that? "Put out" means *fuck*, and of course the truth is that Kate would never put out for David or anyone else, but this is loudmouth Mr. Fein. You don't want to admit that it's all you can do to screw up your courage to hold a girl's hand, but if you lie and try to pretend—like if David said "what a nice piece of ass" Kate is—then Fein might ask for details and David would be stuck.

"That's no business of yours," is what he finally says.

Fein smirks. "Not getting it yet?" he says. "Too bad. But maybe it's just as well. You've got that look about you. Once you get your first taste of it, you won't know when to stop."

"I doubt it," David says. He wishes Fein would go back to his office and leave him alone.

"I don't. You look to me like a born muff diver." Fein chuckles as he turns back toward his office. "Remember," he says. "You heard it here first."

Raymond breaks in. "That's fifty-three cents, Dave."

Fein stops and turns back to them. "Say there, Reverend. What do you think of our friend Ray's new mustache?"

"Aw, Mr. Fein," Raymond says.

"I say to him: Why do you cultivate that weed under your nose when it grows wild around your asshole?" And Fein—the hateful Mr. Fein both David and Raymond despise—leaves them in what almost amounts to peace.

"What a prick," Raymond says.

"Yeah."

David pushes the money toward him. Raymond counts it, puts it in the cashbox, gives David the yellow copy from the pad where he has recorded the sale. He slides the record into a noisy paper bag.

"You seen the new *Esquire*?" he says.

"No. You buy it?"

"Yeah." Raymond draws it from under the counter and shows it to David. "I could let you borrow it."

He opens the magazine to the Petty girl spread.

"My gosh," David says, "you can see right through."

"You can practically see her snatch," Raymond says. "Makes you wonder how they can print stuff like that."

"Can I take it?" If he slips the magazine in with the record, his father won't be any the wiser. "I'll be careful with it."

"I need it back."

"I promise," David says.

As he slips the magazine into the bag and turns away, Raymond stops him by catching his sleeve.

"That new Lash LaRue movie is on at the State tomorrow night. You want to go?"

David hesitates. It's not a question of whether or not his father will let him go to the movies, school not starting until next Tuesday. It's just the idea of going to the movies with another guy, while his friends would probably be taking girls. Still, they'll see him taking Kate to the carnival, and walking her home from school all year.

"Sure," he tells Raymond. "Let's go to the early show."

"You can bring the magazine with you then," Raymond says.

*   *   *

At the curb in front of his house, David dismounts and wheels the bike up the driveway. The garage door is open, the Chevrolet parked inside. He pushes his bike in and leans it against the passenger-side wall, far enough in so the car doors won't hit it. He takes the paper bag that holds the Woody Herman record and the *Esquire* magazine out of the basket and tucks it under one arm. It's unfortunate that his father is home; it means maybe having to explain his purchase, or even risk discovery of the borrowed magazine.

On his way to the kitchen door he notices Brownie, the family mongrel, playing with something in the backyard. He stops to watch, and finally figures out that the dog has got hold of a snake—probably one of those black garter snakes that skitter away from him when he mows the lawn. Sometimes he finds a shed skin in the grass, a couple of feet long, almost transparent, the snake's design still visible—like the pattern of a bike's tire tread on damp pavement.

The dog doesn't see him—or pretends not to.

He calls, "Hey, Brownie. What've you got, huh? What've you got there, boy?" He walks toward the dog, the dry grass whispering under his shoes. His father stopped watering the lawn at the end of August, when the state forest service began putting out fire warnings on the radio. Save water. He drops to one knee. "Can I play too? Huh? C'mere boy."

The dog drops the snake, crouches, jaws open and tongue lolling. The snake doesn't move; it must already be dead. When David reaches out, pretending he wants the snake, the dog snatches it up and runs away. Tossing the snake into the air, letting it fall, snatching it up to run with it again.

"Silly pup," David says, straightening up. "I wasn't going to take it away from you."

In the kitchen his mother is at the sink, doing up the dishes left over from breakfast. She's always alone in the kitchen. His father never helps with the dishes—or the cooking, or the cleaning, or the laundry. When the war was over, the first thing he bought for Mother was an Easy washing machine with something called a Spindrier. That's his father's idea of helping out. His mother acted all excited by the washer, but David thinks that's what it was: acting.

Now she looks at him with one eyebrow raised. "I thought you'd lost your way," she says. "Where have you been all this time?"

All this time is his mother's usual exaggeration, whether he is five minutes later than expected or five hours. She didn't even give him a chance to say, "Hi, Ma."

"Kate and I went for coffee after we watched the carnival set up."

"When did you start drinking coffee?"

"I had cocoa," he says. "Kate's the coffee drinker."

"Coffee isn't healthy at your age," his mother says. "I don't know what her parents can be thinking of."

"They probably don't care."

"Or don't know." His mother brushes a lock of hair away from her forehead with the back of her hand. "What's in the bag?"

"Phonograph record. I stopped by Fein's on the way home."

"That won't please your father," she says.

"I know. He'll tell me I should be saving my money for college." David shrugs. "It's only fifty-three cents."

"Every little bit helps," his mother says.

"Where is he?" David says.

"I think he's in the den, working with his butterflies." She puts the last plate in the drainer and takes a dish towel out from under the sink. She offers it to David. "Will you dry?"

"Sure."

He props the paper bag against the back of a chair and starts with the glasses. His mother isn't the curious type, so there's no danger she'll open the bag to see what record he's bought; that's something his father might do. His mother is looking out the window as she unties her apron. "What's that dog of yours got?"

"Garter snake."

"Ugh." She makes a face. "Why didn't you take it away from him?"

"He was having a good time."

"It's just the idea of it," she says.

"It's already dead," he says.

"Oh, dear."

"Would you rather if it was still alive, all wriggling and slimy?" His mother is easy to tease; she must have a good imagination, because she reacts to the slightest suggestions as if they were really real.

"Stop it, David. You make my skin crawl."

What does that mean? How does skin "crawl" and where does it crawl to? The picture would make Kate laugh; he files it in the back of his mind and puts the last of the breakfast plates on the stack in the cupboard. The dish towel he hangs on its hook under the sink.

"Is Dad in a good mood?" He retrieves the bag and tucks it under his arm. "What do you think?"

"I don't think you should ask for a raise in your allowance," his mother says. "The light bill came in this morning's mail."

"It's not about my allowance," he says. "I want to take Kate to the carnival."

His mother brushes the hair off his forehead—that persistent bad habit of hers. She's not a short woman, but she has to reach up, and when she gives him a peck on the cheek he knows she's on tiptoe. She smells of soap and toothpaste, and for an instant David is embarrassed by the gesture.

"Good luck," she says.

* * *

When his father works with his butterfly collection—David thinks of it as "playing"—he's a different man. Not so much the minister looking down from a pulpit, urging goodness upon the sinners below, and not the stern father imposing time schedules and standards of behavior that David finds unrealistic. Instead, it's as if he has moved into another world, a kind of distant place he doesn't need to share—not with his wife, never with his son. It's oddly scary. The world is notebooks filled with color under cellophane sheets, walls of framed butterflies and moths blue and gold and orange under glass, shelves of books about winged things—and the air heavy with the smells of ether and chloroform that overpower the small room and taint the atmosphere of the whole house, so that coming in the front door seems almost like visiting a hospital. His father's divinity-school diploma is the only framed picture that's unrelated to butterflies.

The door to the den is slightly open. David pauses for a moment before entering. "Dad? You busy?"

"It's all right," his father says. He doesn't turn or look up. "You may interrupt."

"If you're composing a sermon," David says, "I could come back later."

"God has delivered it already." He taps his brow. "It's all in here. I'll write it down later on."

His father is bent over a desk made from a sheet of plywood, its surface a clutter of paraphernalia: jars, glassine envelopes, pins and tweezers, small frames assembled and not, rags and a crumple of wrapping paper. He looks to be in the process of mounting a small yellow butterfly to a cardboard backing. *What does God think about that?* David wonders.

"Don't they feel anything?" he says.

Now Father looks up at him. "Feel?"

"I don't mean when they're displayed. But when they die; when you kill them."

For a few seconds David thinks his father is deciding how to answer the question, but then he says, "What was it you wanted?" He says it coldly, as if he really hadn't wished to be interrupted in the first place.

"I wanted to ask if I could go to the carnival." He has decided that's the best way to deal with desire; just blurt it out and not try to devise some strategy that will make him approve. Strategy is wasted on his father.

So, apparently, is blurting it out. Father looks at him as if the word "carnival" isn't in his vocabulary.

"There's a carnival that came to town this morning," David explains. "Up at The Meadows. Rides and sideshows and concessions. You know."

"And you want to ride the rides and see the sideshows and—" David interrupts.

"See, I've already got permission to go on Saturday, with Tommy and Jack." He breaks off, waiting.

"From whom?" his father says. "From whom do you have permission?"

"From Ma." It's almost the truth—if he assumes that the permission to watch the carnival setting up covers the whole week.

His father says nothing. The way he contemplates David suggests he is trying to see through him, to find him guilty of some kind of transgression.

"But I wanted to go again, on the holiday, with Kate. Kate Meredith."

His father takes up the yellow butterfly, holds it nearer the desk lamp for inspection.

"I've already asked her," David finishes. He feels hopeless.

His father frowns. "Your mother said nothing to me."

"I thought she told you."

"No. Nothing has been said to me about a carnival. At The Meadows, you say? Across the river?"

"Yes."

"And you want to take a girl?"

What is there about his father's manner that makes David feel like a butterfly being pinned to a board? As if a simple action like going to a carnival—or a movie, or a band concert, or a ball game— is a big deal.

"She's counting on me to take her," he says. "Kate is."

His father ponders. "I expect your mother thinks she knows what she's doing. I imagine I'm required to endorse her permission, pro forma."

David waits.

"What about schoolwork?"

"School doesn't even start till next Tuesday. Nobody gives assignments over the summer."

Father clears his throat, as if he is after all the minister sermonizing. "Plenty of temptations at places like that. Gambling. Painted women."

David thinks, *Spare me the lecture.* He shifts from one foot to the other, and the movement rattles the paper bag he's been holding against his chest.

"What do you have there?" his father says.

"Phonograph record."

For a moment David thinks Father is going to reach for the bag, and he wonders how he will explain the magazine—or, worse, how he will be able to replace it. Instead, his father turns back to his collecting.

"I suppose you've got to start learning to resist temptation sometime," he says. "So be it."

David hates it when his father gets smug—when he acts as if he is a generous and liberal man, even though he's only permitting his son to do some dumb thing that any other father wouldn't give a second thought to. "Resisting temptation" isn't the point, but try telling that to the Reverend Harvey Willard, D.D.

"But we'll expect you to be home at a decent hour," his father says, "your mother and I." And then he smiles. "Before you were born, your mother and I sometimes went to a dance or two. But there *are* temptations, I trust you understand."

The way his father smiles is peculiar and unsettling. David never gets used to it, and he thinks probably he never will. The smile is a small one; it comes and goes in an instant, turning up the corners of his father's mouth, then gone solemn again. The smile doesn't show teeth, and it doesn't express itself anywhere else on the face—not at the corners of the eyes or in the lift of an eyebrow. It is a phantom, an accident, as if it is an expression never truly intended for display.

"Thank you, sir," David says. He turns away and is about to go to his own room when his father's voice halts him.

"What's the record?"

As if Father cares. "The new Woody Herman," he says.

His father sighs and shakes his head, posturing as the parent who will never understand his son's tastes. "I know you call that music," he says, "though what you see in that terrible noise is beyond me."

"Yes, sir," David says. It's pointless to defend Woody Herman to his father, who thinks Vaughn Monroe is hot stuff. Now he is ready to escape, but again he's stopped.

"David?" Father says. "Here. Wait. Take a look at this."

He is holding out a new butterfly—not the small yellow one— for David to look at.

"It arrived in this morning's mail."

The butterfly's wings are folded. David bends close, the record bag crackling against his chest. The butterfly is large and blue and iridescent, with a violet fringe to wings at least three inches long.

"How strange," David says. "What a strange-looking butterfly."

"This is a moth," his father says. "Only a moth, from the island of Madagascar. If you saw it on a tree, its wings folded like this, you might think it was only one more uninteresting leaf. But when those wings open..."

He holds the moth between his hands and gently parts the wings to reveal extraordinary yellows and golds and reds in a tangle of design.

"...You see how much secret beauty was hidden away from you."

It's true. The butterfly, the moth, whatever you want to call it, is truly beautiful. David thinks he has never seen anything quite so lovely, quite so delicate—or perhaps it's only that he is focused on the creature, giving it all his concentration. Possibly anything he looked at it with all his attention—like focusing the sun's rays through a magnifying glass to kindle dry grass—would take his breath away.

His father looks up at him, the moth still opened in his hands, and David notices how flushed his face is, how wide the pupils of his eyes have become. It's emotion he sees, isn't it?—something he usually takes for granted is not "appropriate" to his father.

"It's really something," he says.

His father leans back in his chair, the new moth—wings still opened—in his hands. He seems immensely pleased with himself.

"You asked me how I could 'do' such a thing," he says, "how I could kill a helpless butterfly." Now he holds the moth open on the palm of one hand. "For beauty, David. For such amazing beauty, a man might do almost anything."

This must be the sermon, David thinks. This is what he will say at the next church service.

"A creature like this—so gorgeous, so rare—is a reminder of how life is more mysterious and complex than we sometimes think it is." He sets the moth gently aside. "God is moving within such beauty, such rainbows of glory."

"Yes, sir," David agrees.

But his father is not finished. "Imagine Adam in the Garden," he says, "naming the world and its creatures at God's command. 'The Serpent and the Butterfly.' That's the sermon topic. What do you think?"

"I don't know if I believe all that Adam and Eve stuff," David says.

Father points a finger at him. "Metaphor," he says. "The Bible's metaphors are as truthful as any science. Remember that."

"I'll try."

His father turns away. "If you go to this carnival on a school night, plan to be home by ten sharp."

"Yes, sir. I will." He senses that he is about to be released.

"You say it's the Meredith girl? The girl you've promised to take?"

"Yes, sir."

"I believe I've met her father."

"He travels a lot," David says.

"He made—That is, his company made a good deal of money from the war."

"I wouldn't know."

"Aircraft engines, if I'm not mistaken. For warplanes." His father folds the Madagascar moth's wings and slides it into a transparent envelope. "It's an immoral business," he says.

"I don't know what his job is now. Even Kate hardly ever sees him."

"Yes...I don't know what sort of ploughshare is being made from Mister Meredith's particular sword." He looks up at David, as if he is half-surprised his son is still here. "Kate, you say?"

"Kathryn. Kate for short."

Father returns to his hobby. "Indeed," he says, and David is free.

* * *

David's room is plain, with a model destroyer and several model airplanes—a P-51 Mustang, a Hellcat, a gull-winged Corsair—displayed on the dresser and windowsill. A leatherette-covered portable phonograph is on a nightstand. Stuck into a dresser mirror is a black and white snapshot of David and Kate and Brownie, taken earlier this summer by Kate's mother. His father disapproves of the warship displays, just as he seems to disapprove of Kate's father's Air Corps service. Harvey Willard didn't go to war—not because he was a conscientious objector, but because he was "clergy" and had a deferment. David thinks of the models as a private kind of rebellion.

He sails the sack containing the record onto the bed, but then he thinks better of it. He lies across the bedspread and slides the bag between the bed and the wall onto the floor, out of sight. He can play the new record anytime, but what he's really thinking is that he'll get to the *Esquire* as soon as he has a chance. First, he needs to talk with his mother.

He finds her where he left her, standing in the kitchen in front of the stove. She has a dishtowel wound around her left hand, using it to poke at something in the oven.

"Making a pie?"

His mother gives him a look—the kind that tells him he's disturbing her, but not seriously. "It's a sponge cake," she tells him, "and it should have been ready twenty minutes ago." She withdraws the toothpick her right hand has poked into the cake and holds it up to him. "See? Still not done."

He's no cook, but he knows the toothpick is supposed to be clean, no crumbs. "Maybe the oven's out of whack," he says.

"You father had it calibrated last spring. I wonder if the timer is broken."

"Maybe." He takes a bottle of milk out of the refrigerator and pours himself a glass.

"How did you do with your father?"

"Okay. I got to hear his next sermon, I think. About how God gave us such a beautiful world."

"Your father thinks the world is his audience. I hear him talking to his butterflies." She shuts the oven door with elaborate care. "I guess all I can do is let the cake do what it has to do. I hope I haven't wasted all those eggs."

His mother has never gotten over the war, when so many things were either rationed or in short supply. If they needed eggs, they drove out to the country to buy them from some old farmer, and they couldn't even do that unless Father was willing to use the gas. They never had butter; she always made it David's job to mix the little bubble of bright orange powder into the oleo so it wouldn't look like lard. It's her strong memory of shortages and going without that make it difficult for him to ask his next question.

"Do you suppose I could get an advance on my allowance?" He asks as he is replacing the milk bottle in the refrigerator, making his request seem off-hand.

"Did you ask your father?"

"Well…" He has to be honest. "At least he gave me permission to take Kate Meredith to the carnival on a school night."

His mother looks both surprised and amused. "A school night? My goodness."

"So I didn't think I ought to ask him about money, too."

Now his mother turns thoughtful. He knows she will say yes to the advance on the basis of past performance. It isn't so much that he has learned to play Father against Mother; it's more that he long ago realized his mother loves him more than his father does and is therefore manipulable. Of course she will give him money, and it won't be a mere loan.

But she surprises him. Instead of finding her pocketbook and coming up with his "advance", she sits at the kitchen table and indicates that he should sit across from her. He wonders what this is about, but he obeys, moving the milk glass to one side, taking the chair opposite. He leans forward, elbows on the table, determined to look interested in whatever it is she intends to talk about.

"Your father isn't easy with you, is he?" she says.

"What do you mean?"

"He's not easy to talk to. He isn't always very understanding."

"No, I guess not." Where is this leading?

"He has strict ideas about some things," his mother says. "He doesn't always listen to the other side."

"I guess."

She sighs and gives an odd shake to her head. Then she reaches across and lightly brushes the hair off his forehead. "You're very patient with him," she says. "I'm proud of you for that."

David can't think how to respond to her being proud.

She draws back her hands and looks away from him. At first he thinks she's going to get up to look in on the sponge cake again, but she doesn't. "It's funny," she says, "how the man you marry isn't always the man you fell in love with."

He takes his elbows off the table and sits straight. Ma is looking serious, her hands folded, and now her eyes lock onto his.

"When I met your father we were both in college and he was a star athlete. He was on the track team, a sprinter and a high hurdler; I used to clip the news stories about him out of the papers. They'd write him up as far away as Elmira and Buffalo. For years he had the state record in the hundred and the four-hundred hurdles."

"I never knew that."

"He was the hero, and I was the hero's girlfriend. We shone together." She smiles at David. "Can you imagine?"

"Sure I can." Shirley and Tom, he thinks. Just like Shirley and Tom. "But what happened?"

"Then his father was killed in a car crash outside Syracuse, and a week later his mother.... Well, grief just devastated her; she was never the same, turned into one of those recluses who sits at her window and clucks over the neighbors like an old biddy. You remember what she was like, our awkward visits. And your dad was a changed man, losing the father he so much admired. He quit the track squad, quit the school. One night, when I went to the rooming house where he stayed, he'd packed up all his medals and trophies and put them out at the curb. 'I need a new life,' was what he told me.

"Before I knew it, he'd moved across the river and got himself accepted to the divinity school, and of course I followed him. But it was different. He wasn't any longer the hero I'd fallen for—not one whit."

"But he was the same person."

"Maybe." She smiles—an odd, distant expression. "Though I think sometimes that when your father looks at you he sees the young man he used to be, and when he cuffs you or raises his voice he's denying that memory of himself." She reaches across and squeezes David's hands in hers. "So make allowances, and keep on being patient."

"I will," he says. Then: "Speaking of allowances."

For a moment his mother seems not to understand, and when she does, she grins at him.

"Perhaps I could let you have a couple of dollars from the house money," she says. "But you mustn't tell your father. And it's only a loan."

"You bet," David says.

It's always a loan, this under-the-table transaction, but it's always forgiven and forgotten. He waits now while she goes out to the front hall to find the purse she keeps in the drawer of the side table. He pictures her pawing through the purse, finding a few crumpled dollar bills, putting the purse back.

When she puts the money in his hand—three paper dollars— she says, "Remember: you owe me."

He takes the bills and stuffs them into a trouser pocket. "Thanks, Ma."

"And mum's the word."

"My lips are glued shut."

"I hope the Meredith girl is worth the investment," she says.

"What do you mean?" It wouldn't have occurred to him that spending money on Kate ought to lead to some sort of return—that buying her a cup of coffee, for example, should require her to buy something for him. "We're only going to the carnival."

"I didn't necessarily mean the money," she says. "What I think is just that it would be a shame for you to care so much for her—you two really are getting to be thick as thieves—and then have her turn around and give her attentions to somebody else."

"That won't happen," he says. "Kate's not like that." Though how can he be sure?

"Don't let her break your heart," she says.

"Not Kate."

He finishes drinking the milk and sets the glass on the counter. "Should I wait around for a piece of that cake?"

His mother smiles faintly. "I'll call you when it's done."

"Okay."

"But just a minute, young man."

David halts in the doorway.

"Rinse out that glass and put it in the sink," she says. "Don't make my job any harder than it already is."

He runs tap water into his glass. "I'll be in my room," he says. "Listening to music."

"If that's what you call it," his mother says after him.

* * *

Upstairs in his room, David retrieves the paper bag from under the bed, slides the record out and puts it on the turntable of his record player. While the music plays, he takes from the bag the copy of *Esquire* magazine, opens it to the Petty girl calendar page. He caresses the lines of the girl in the picture—the curve of the breasts, the swelling of thigh—his right foot keeping time with the tempo of the Herman band. It is the kind of movement his father frequently refers to as St. Vitus' dance, especially when it happens at the supper table, though at the moment David is scarcely aware of the music that prompts it. The picture transfixes him, and there is only one word—Father would be horrified—that can express his response to it.

"God."

He really can't wait any longer. He hides the magazine inside his shirt and heads out of the room. On the way to the bathroom, he almost collides with his father, who is just coming out, carrying a newspaper.

"What's the big hurry?" his father wants to know.

"Nothing, sir," David says. "Just—you know: when you gotta go, you gotta go."

Father is unamused. "Spare me the vulgarisms," he says. He tucks the newspaper under his arm and disappears into the den.

David closes the bathroom door, slides the bolt as quietly as he knows how. Turning to the toilet, he slides the *Esquire* out from under his shirt and opens it to the page that features the month's Petty girl. The woman is long-legged, breathtakingly pretty, with blond hair under a sun hat. She is talking to someone on a white telephone and all she is wearing is something sheer that might be a nightdress, or a jacket, or even an oversized blouse. Less important than naming whatever it is, is the effect of her wearing it: what it covers, what it reveals—the long legs, the delicate feet in white sandals; the flat belly and the plump vee between her thighs; the pert breasts; the knowledge implied by the arch of eyebrows and twist of lipsticked mouth. It's an amazing picture, as realistic as a photograph, and David is already unbuttoning his fly as he props the magazine on top of the toilet tank—holding the pages open with one hand, fumbling at himself with the other, tasting in his throat the sweetness of his hopeless lust.

His father's voice comes to him from the end of the hall— "Don't tie up the bathroom, please!"—so faint in David's ears that the sound might as well be coming from the moon.

* * *

Afterward, sliding the magazine back into the paper bag, the bag hidden again behind the bed, he tries to imagine his father as the different man Ma described. Harvey Willard is not an active person, sitting for hours writing his sermons, pinning his pretty butterflies, driving to visit his sick parishioners. He doesn't even take out the trash or have anything to do with the lawn except watering it every now and then—and not even that in this dry summer. He walks to and from the car, and exercises his right arm shifting gears, and that's about all he ever does. To imagine him running in a track meet, jumping hurdles, actually winning races against real competition—David can't picture it.

But people change; he knows that. That his father is different, going from top-grade athlete with a shelf full of trophies to dull as dirt old man who disapproves of everything, simply confirms that big changes can happen. He wonders if he will change too. What if the David Willard who likes Kate Meredith turns into a different person? What if that person doesn't have a sense of humor, or doesn't like basketball, or thinks collecting stamps is stupid? Will Kate marry him anyway, and just put up with him the way his mother seems to put up with his father?

He wouldn't like that to happen, and then and there, lying on his bed, his heart still beating a bit faster after his enjoyment of the Petty girl, he vows he will always be the same person to Kate that he is today. Why change what is too good to be changed? And he holds that thought until his mother calls him to lunch.

7.

Her mother is in the kitchen. Kate sits heavily at the kitchen table and for a few moments watches her in silence. Mother is standing at the counter beside the sink, and in front if her is the old mahogany silver chest that was a wedding present from Daddy's parents. She's taking out the silver, one piece at a time, daubing polish on the piece, using a rag made from a torn sheet to rub in the paste, rinsing the piece under the faucet and drying it with a separate cloth. One after another, fork, spoon, knife, her mother polishes cutlery the family hardly ever uses.

It's the kind of repetitive, mindless activity Kate despises, the kind that sums up for her all the things about her mother's life she wishes could be changed.

"Why do you bother?" she says. She watches the polishing routine, chin in her hands. It's almost a hypnotizing activity: repeated motion punctuated by the regular click of the pieces onto themselves as they're returned to the silver chest.

"Why do I bother what?"

"Shining the good silver. We never use that stuff."

"It's tarnished," her mother says. "Imagine how embarrassed I'd be to bring it out in front of company."

"Which we hardly ever have."

"And we do use it," her mother goes on. "We use it at Thanksgiving, and Christmas, and when Grammy visits." She slides a knife silently into its slot in the top of the chest. "And on your birthdays."

"It just seems so pointless," Kate says. "It won't be long before I come home from school again, and here you'll be, getting a backache from polishing the good silver."

Mother gives a small snort of a laugh. "If my back ached," she says, "I'd polish sitting at the table. But I thank you for your concern."

"It makes me wonder what's the point in growing up."

Her mother stops, another polish-smeared knife in one hand, the rag in the other. "Explain that," she says.

"Well look at your life," Kate says. "You never have any fun. You spend all your time doing housework, doing the same dull things day after day, week after week. Laundry. Ironing. Dusting. Cooking. Making the beds." She has to think for a moment to add to the list. "Shopping. Darning socks. Polishing silverware."

Her mother finishes cleaning the last knife, puts it away, closes the lid of the chest. She sits at the table and reaches across to take both Kate's hands in hers.

"Poor child," she says. "You must wonder where I found the time to produce *you*."

Kate grins. "To tell the truth..."

Mother laughs. "What you see is the responsibility of growing up. You're not looking at the pleasures."

"Which are?"

"Which are many, and not always obvious."

Kate waits. Her mother's hands are cool and a little damp on hers, and from them she catches the smell of the silver polish—a sort of metal smell, the way her own hands carry the odor of coins or keys she has handled. What she's waiting for is the list of the *many, and not always obvious* pleasures of being an adult.

But the list doesn't appear. Instead, Mother releases her and leaves the table. She goes back to the counter, screws the lid onto the polish jar, rinses the polishing rag under the kitchen faucet and wrings it out.

"How was the carnival?" she asks. "Did you learn a lot?"

It seems an odd question. "What was I supposed to learn?"

"About the behind-the-scenes? Special things you wouldn't notice if you were just out to have a good time."

"I don't know," Kate says. "What can you learn from a bunch of men with their shirts off, putting up grimy old tents? How to be sweaty?"

Her mother carries the silver chest over to the table and sets it in front of Kate. "Put this on the sideboard in the dining room, would you? That's a good Kate."

Kate obliges. It bothers her that her mother either won't or can't provide her with the joys of growing up, or being married, having children—unless those things in and of themselves are the actual joys. And how can they be? Those men sweating and swearing at The Meadows, are they experiencing the rewards of what school-teachers call "maturity"?

Her mother is pouring coffee, and she sets two cups on the table as Kate returns. "I thought you'd like to share the last of the coffee pot," Mother says.

"Is this one of the grownup pleasures?"

"You needn't be sarcastic."

"I'm sorry." She sits and draws the cream pitcher and sugar bowl to her side of the table. "You would have had to cover your ears at

The Meadows," she says. Her mother has left room for the cream she pours into her cup. "All the swearing."

"That's how men are."

"It's not how Daddy is. He doesn't swear."

"Not around you."

"Of course, he's not around me very much," Kate says.

"Oh, Kate. He's home as much as he can manage. And don't use so much sugar. You'll get diabetes."

"Why does Daddy have to travel? He's always flying off to those crazy places out west."

"It's his job. He has to go where he's sent."

"Can't they send somebody else once in a while?"

"They trust your father," her mother says. "He's very good at what he does."

Kate knows this is true—or believes it's true because her father is so quiet and careful about practically everything. He never seems bothered or impatient. He nearly always has answers for her questions, even when the questions are silly.

"Just the same," she says, "I wish."

"What do you wish?"

"I wish he was home more. The kids at school make fun of me. About him. They say that verse? You know the one? 'As I was going down the stair, I met a man who wasn't there. He wasn't there again today. I wish the man would go away.'"

"That's clever."

"No, it's not clever. It's dumb. It just reminds me that I wish he wasn't away so much." She takes a drink of her coffee and realizes she's put in too much sugar, even for her. "And this coffee is too damned sweet!"

"Kathryn! Language."

"And I wish I *would* get diabetes. Maybe he'd rush home and visit me in the hospital."

It's a dumb statement—as she can tell from the expression on her mother's face. But then that expression changes into a look of genuine sadness.

"Dear Kate," her mother says. "I miss him too. We have to bear up as best we can, and make the most of the times he's here. I know how you feel; don't forget we both went through the war years when he wasn't with us at all."

"That was worse," Kate says.

An unhappy silence lies between them. Her mother sips the coffee. Kate warms her palms around her too-sweet cup.

"Should we invite David for dinner sometime soon?" her mother says, which is a peculiar change of subject. But of course it isn't peculiar at all. Mother wants to put a substitute male in the house.

"We don't have to rush things, do we?"

"He seems such a nice boy. And you like him, don't you?"

"He's nice, but he's no Errol Flynn."

"Thank heavens for that," her mother says.

"But he's taking me to the carnival Monday night," Kate says. "If you approve."

Her mother looks thoughtful. "I'd hoped you and I might go this weekend," she says. "A mother and daughter outing. Wouldn't you like that? We could ride the Ferris wheel. We could eat cotton candy and taffy apples."

"And get sick?" How is she going to deal with this—this collision of her plans and Mother's? "And I watched them putting the rides together. The Ferris wheel looked kind of flimsy."

"You'd rather be with your boyfriend," her mother says. "I guess that's to be expected."

"And he's not my 'boyfriend' in quotation marks and underlined. He's a friend who happens to be a boy."

"You wouldn't consider going in the afternoon, would you? I get uncomfortable when you're out after dark. It's the holiday weekend, a rowdy crowd." Her mother pauses and gives her a helpless look. "They have the same shows in the afternoon. The same rides."

"Are you saying I have to call David and tell him I can't go because we might get in trouble? Talk about *embarrassing.*"

"No, it's all right," her mother says. "Just—Just use your common sense."

* * *

It doesn't surprise Kate that her mother is hesitant about letting her go to the carnival with David, considering what her father once called "your iffy record" with boys, which she thinks of as her precommon sense phase, while Daddy was away in the war. That was wartime, her father stationed in England, and her mother keeping the home fires burning by doing two jobs: substitute teaching at Longfellow School, fourth grade, and working three afternoons a week at the Scoggin Lumber Company as bookkeeper and clerk.

More often than not, when Kate got home from school the house was empty. If her mother had done baking that morning, there would be cookies, or brownies, or a pie cooling on the kitchen table. She would pour herself a glass of milk and eat whatever was available. Then she changed out of her good school clothes into an everyday skirt and blouse, and went downtown. Days Mother was at the lumber yard, she never got home before five-thirty, which left Kate with more freedom than most of her friends enjoyed—as much freedom as boys had. Her mother didn't see it as "freedom," of course, but as "too much time on your hands." But what could she do about it?

In those days Kate's favorite destination was the arcade, on Main Street across from the Scoggin Institution for Savings. A brick storefront with its display windows whitewashed so you couldn't see in, the arcade was filled with pinball machines and electric games, mostly war games. It had originally been an auto parts store, but the owner was a youngish man with no family. When the army drafted him, he sold the building, which stood empty for almost a year, until the new owner made it an arcade like those at Old Orchard Beach. Besides the games, the owner put in a jukebox. Sometimes it seemed to Kate that the only song on the jukebox was "Pistol Packin' Mama," which played non-stop as counterpoint to the rattle and ring of the pinball tables.

What Kate had liked most about the arcade was that she was usually the only girl there. It gave her a feeling of equality that she couldn't find anyplace else. Here were these boys, most of them older, from the town's two high schools, all of them laughing and swearing and smoking cigarettes, pounding on the pinball machines until they went tilt, pretending to be soldiers at the battle games, or champions at the racing games, or great hunters at the game where a bear on a track crossed in front of a woodsy background. When you hit the bear with a light beam from a gun, the bear stopped, gave a roar, then turned back in the opposite direction. It was Kate's favorite; if you hit the target over and over, the bear reversed itself and roared so often it looked as if it was having some kind of mechanical fit.

She spent so much of her time at the arcade, the boys took her for granted. They joked with her and offered her cigarettes—she never took one; her mother already complained about the way her hair smelled of nicotine—and generally treated her as one of them. The exception was that there were always two or three boys who asked her to the movies, or wanted to walk her home, or looked at her as if she was something to cook for dinner. Those boys—the wolves—she learned to deal with, partly by walking away, partly by borrowing their own language and turning it back on them. She supposed that whatever she was learning would be useful to her later, as if the arcade were a classroom outside school.

At school, something about them—boys—disturbed her in a fashion having as much to do with aesthetics as with anything else. What was wrong with them? Their clothes never fit them—they were all bony wrists and strips of ugly socks—and they seemed to have only rough edges. Either they were shaggy because they needed haircuts, or they looked like skinned poodles because they'd just gotten one. Their faces were a mess—blotched and pocked, or showing little sprouts of beard and mustache that might better be chopped away. They had no manners, no sense of what manners were. They moved down the halls like unbridled ponies, lumbering into anyone approaching them, whinnying with coarse laughter, pushing and bucking against one another; they almost frightened her with their self-centered ways. And most of them smelled peculiar. Sweat, was it, from the gym classes they pretended to despise but secretly loved for the liberation of *romping*? Aftershave, to show off with? Or was it some sheer animal odor she couldn't name? One of the differences between girls and boys—she had thought about this quite seriously—was that girls existed within bounds, but boys spilled out all over, as if they didn't know about their limitations.

At the arcade, their behavior made more sense. Away from school—polite society, boys and girls together, the authority of teachers and principals, the demands of books and tests—the restrictions were lifted. They were among their own, no one of them different from any other. They didn't think they acted differently, or smelled differently, or had haircut problems. Watching them in the arcade was like studying animals in the wild.

She had felt out of place, and even afraid, only once, and that was because of Darryl Jenks.

Darryl was a regular at the arcade, and one of the two or three boys who saw her as more girl than tomboy. They had one class together, Beginning Latin; he sat at the desk behind hers. She listened to him clip his fingernails in class, sometimes even felt his breath on the back of her neck. He was forever asking her to go to a movie, a ballgame, a party in neighborhoods where no sensible person would be seen.

On this day he took her aside, actually held her by the arm and pulled her off in a corner of the arcade.

"I wasn't in school today" he said. "What did I miss?"

"Not much," she said. "Just do the written exercises at the end of chapter ten." She tried to walk past him, but he moved to keep her cornered.

"All the exercises at the end of ten?"

"Darryl, if you'd come to class, you wouldn't need to bother people with stupid questions."

"Well boo-hoo on you," he said. "I feel for you."

"It's *all* the exercises."

"You sure?"

"Positive."

"Then why didn't you say so the first time." He had taken her arm again—the fingers just above her left elbow, holding her perhaps harder than he realized—and drawn her toward the back wall. In the hubbub of the arcade, no one seemed to notice her discomfort. "Look," he said. "I want you to see something."

"I don't want to," she said. She tried harder to pull away from him.

"No, wait," he said. From the breast pocket of his shirt he produced a deck of cards, red-backed, their edges velvety gray with wear. "These'll interest you."

She clenched her teeth and resigned herself to seeing whatever it was he wanted her to see.

"Hurry up, Darryl."

Abruptly—as if he were suddenly tongue-tied and only an action could express himself—he had pushed the cards into her hand.

"Here," he said. "Give them back tomorrow." Then he let her go. Kate watched him until he had gone out to the street.

For the moment she was alone, and she turned her back on the arcade to see what it was that Darryl Jenks had given her. She saw at once that they were not ordinary playing cards, for on their faces they carried black and white photographs that left scarcely enough room for the numbers and the suits. Each card carried a different picture, but each was of a man and a woman, nude (except that Kate would always remember, vividly, that the man wore socks, black against his stark skin, with garters holding them up), photographed in a variety of sexual poses. Her first moment's response was revulsion, a catch in her throat that was like choking, and a foolish panic that someone was watching her, studying over her shoulder the ugliness, "the filth" as her mother would say, that she held in her hands.

She hid the cards in a pocket of her skirt, and on the way home she dropped them down through a sewer grate. Darryl would have to find something else to threaten girls with.

* * *

That had been one of her last afternoons at the arcade. In May, the war in Europe ended, and three months later her father was on his way home.

"I hope he can forgive me," her mother said when she heard the good news.

"Forgive you for what?" Kate said.

"For letting his little girl run wild," Mother said.

Kate still thinks that was funny; everybody knew she'd "reformed herself," and it's a foregone conclusion, Kate has known all along, that she will go to the carnival with David. The discussion will not be about the kind of boys she "runs with." It will be about curfew, and how much of her allowance she is to spend. That sort of negotiation is fine with her; she thinks as she has grown into her later teens, her mother is beginning to treat her more and more like an equal.

She has no idea what her future with David will be. From the middle of freshman year she has been aware of him—at football and basketball games, for instance, where he always managed to sit in the bleacher section that was her cheerleading responsibility—and she held him in the back of her mind, in reserve, against some day when his niceness might be useful to her. In those days she was dating Jack Morrison—not going steady, but accepting movie invitations and Coke dates when she felt like it. Jack was really an unlikely choice for her, a throwback to her arcade phase, but he had a brashness that made him stand out from the crowd at school, and so she let her name be associated with his for perhaps longer than she should have. After she quit the cheerleading squad, Jack seemed to lose interest, and so that was all to the good.

David is an entirely different matter, as retiring as Jack is bold. At first she didn't think she was attracted to him, though there had been times when she sought him out in preference to some one of her girl friends—for his calmness, usually, his reluctance to talk or, when he did talk, to raise his voice above the barely audible. Now, with Jack in her past among the rest of what she thinks of as her "temporaries," David seems to have taken center stage.

Being in Thespis with him has persuaded her that David is one of those boys who likes to worship from afar, to be a secret admirer; she rather thinks he likes suffering—or the *idea* of suffering. When he is not "afar," as when they are backstage at a play rehearsal, he is flustered but friendly, and she likes him for liking her. She doesn't think she is influenced by his father's religious calling, or by his being a senior and older than she is. Always her mind turns back to his steadiness, his reliability, his splendid unwillingness to upset the world around him.

He is tall for his age, or at least taller than most of the boys in his class, and awkward-looking, thin and long-boned. As if he is self-conscious about his height he walks with a slouch; when he stands still he has a habit of supporting himself on one leg, the other seeming to be wrapped around its mate. *Stork.* David is, all in all, unthreatening.

"Is David a good driver?" her mother is asking. "Can he be trusted to be careful at the wheel?"

"He's not driving. He's going to ride his bike over here, and then we're going to walk."

"That's a relief," her mother says. She says it a lot lately, especially with Daddy out of town.

8.

Movies at the State Theater are "continuous," so on Friday David and Raymond stay beyond the end of "Law of the Lash" to watch the Daffy Duck cartoon a second time. It's not something David would have done if he'd come to the movies alone—or with Kate—but Ray is a fan, not just of Bugs, but of Daffy and Elmer Fudd and all the rest of the Merrie Melodies characters, and so he sits through it a second time. What can you do?

The house lights don't come up between shows, but as the two of them finally leave, with the Movietone News playing behind them, David sees Jack Morrison by the popcorn machine in the lobby, talking with a couple of Scoggin High football players whose names he doesn't know. Jack looks up and gives him a small salute of greeting. Bad news; Jack will rib him the next time he sees him—probably call him "homo."

"We should've waited," Raymond says. "It's a double feature tomorrow."

"I'm busy," David says. "Chores. And then there's the carnival."

Outside the theater the night air is balmy, humid with a weak breeze. The town's one traffic light is already blinking yellow on Main, red facing Nason.

"I notice you didn't bring my *Esquire*."

"I forgot. I'll drop it off at the store on Monday."

"You can't bring it by in the morning? Monday's Labor Day."

"Then Tuesday," David says. "Tuesday for sure."

There's not much Ray can say to that. "Don't wear it out," is what he does say.

They cross the street toward David's dad's church, which has a signboard out front.

Sunday's Sermon Topic
"The Serpent & the Butterfly"
Service: 11 a.m.
Rev. Harvey Willard

White letters against a black background, protected by glass. Sometimes David gets to change the lettering for future sermons, but not this one.

"We could go to your club," Raymond says. "Play some Ping-Pong."

"You want to?"

"The night's young. Why not?"

True, it's only a little after nine and they're practically there already. The Trojan Club is in the church annex, a favorite project of his father's, who founded the club as an "outlet" for boys in their teen years, the outlet consisting of cards, chess and checkers, and the Ping-Pong table that occupies one end of a large basement room. Twice a year the club sponsors a dance in the gymnasium above, and on those occasions girls are allowed in the clubroom. David isn't much of a dancer, although at Christmas two years ago he and Mary Louise Nickerson won a box of Whitman's Sampler chocolates in a spot dance.

The joke about the Trojan Club is that its members borrowed the name from a brand of prophylactics, and the product's trademark, the kind of armored helmet worn by knights in the Age of Chivalry, is painted on the door of the clubroom. It's the sort of thing that's wasted on David's father, who seems not to have any idea what's going on in the world outside his job and his hobby. People who don't belong to the club think it's rowdy, but it isn't. During the war, when the Navy base was open in South Scoggin, some sailors bribed their way in one weekend and had a drinking party, which scandalized the congregation and handed a laugh to the Unitarians down Nason Street. David's dad pronounced the club's reputation "besmirched" and shut it down for a month.

* * *

The outside door that leads to the club is at the end of a narrow alley between the church and the annex, and as the two boys approach it David notices a dim light is showing from inside. When he reaches the door and looks in through the square of glass he can see the light is coming from the hallway at the foot of the stairs.

"Somebody's left the light on," he says. "Or else somebody's here."

He pushes the button to the left of the door—there's a buzzer in the downstairs hall—and pounds on the door for good measure.

"Haven't you got a key?" Raymond says.

"Of course I do. I'm just making sure." What he's thinking is that one of the club members has maybe brought a girl here, looking for privacy, a safe place to make out. He doesn't want to embarrass anybody, even though he'd really like to know who's here and what they're doing.

"I think we should just fucking go in," Raymond says.

"Hold your water," David tells him.

Just then the light framed by the downstairs door is broken by the shadow of somebody climbing the stairs. It's Tom Gowen, who opens the door a few inches—not to let David and Raymond in, it seems, but to keep them out.

"Hey, Tommy," David says. "We're going to play some Pong. You can take on the winner."

"Listen," Tom says, "give me a few minutes." His voice is barely more than a whisper. "You guys go away—go get a Coke or something—and come back later."

"How much later?" As soon as he says it, David realizes how dumb that sounds.

"I don't know. Just later. When you see the light's off."

"Okay," David says. "Let's go, Ray."

The door closes and latches.

"What the fuck," Raymond says.

The two of them retrace their steps down the alley to the street and stand uncertainly on the sidewalk in front of the church.

"There's a Coke machine at the arcade," David says.

"What," Raymond says, "are you hypnotized? A guy tells you go get a Coke, and you go get a Coke?"

"We have to kill time. What do you want to do?"

"If I go to the arcade, I'll stay and play the games. That's a good time-killer."

"I don't want to spend money on that stuff."

"Suit yourself." Raymond gives him a soft punch on the shoulder and steps off the curb. "I'll see you Tuesday."

"Tuesday," David says.

Raymond stops halfway across the street. "The magazine. Remember?"

"I'll remember."

He watches Ray turn the corner on Main and start to trot in the direction of the arcade. Why didn't he go along? He might not have wasted his nickels on pinball or a shooting gallery, but he could have drunk that Coke. Probably he and Ray would have decided to forget about coming back to the club, and that would have been the end of it; they'd both have gone on home.

Anyway, Ray isn't that much of a friend, and he isn't a very good Ping-Pong player. What they have in common is Ray knowing David's interest in pictures of girls, and David knowing that when Ray pays for one record for himself he slips two or three other records into the bag he takes out of the store. This is what "partners in crime" means.

Alone now, David crosses the street, but he doesn't go home. On this side of Nason is a small park, named after Alfred Leach, one of the town's founders. A bronze statue of Leach stands in the center of the park, and a half-dozen benches are arranged around its perimeter. David chooses a bench that is partly screened by hydrangeas—he knows the name of the bush because his grandmother has a pair of them at the end of her front walk in Brunswick—and there, half-hidden, he watches the church and waits for Tom Gowen and the girl to leave.

He's fairly certain the girl will be Shirley Kostas. He can't imagine Tommy being interested in any other girl, Shirley is so pretty. And she seems to have eyes for nobody but Tom. He tries to imagine what they're doing in that room downstairs, where the most likely makeout place is an old green couch, a bit broken down, that sits against the wall opposite the door. He pictures Tom and Shirl necking at one end of the couch, his hand on her breast—first through her clothes, and then unbuttoning her blouse and working his hands under her bra, maybe pushing the whole bra upward so the nipples are exposed, so Tommy can brush them with his fingertips and bow down to put his mouth over first one and then the other, touch them with his tongue. Shirley will by then be making funny little noises; he's not sure what they sound like, but they're pleasure sounds—moans, sighs, something soft and musical that will excite Tommy even more.

And then. Then his hand leaves her breasts—but he's still kissing them—and slides down to her skirt, her knee, under the skirt and up her bare thigh. Now his hand is between her legs, up against her panties—white; they have to be white—rubbing her crotch through the fabric, making her open her knees wider, making her sounds different, deeper, longer. Then he's in front of her, both hands under the skirt, drawing the panties down, over her knees, down to her ankles, over her shoes—though maybe the shoes are already off, kicked aside an hour ago. And she's naked from the waist down, sprawled in front of him, and he pulls out the cushion she's sitting on, pulls it like some kind of magical carpet she's riding, until she slides to the floor under him, knees wide, her bare thighs open to him, her head lolled back onto the floor...

And they're doing it!

"God," David says out loud. The stickiness against his belly is hot, then cools as his excitement subsides. To hell with Raymond And his stupid *Esquire*. Who needs it?

* * *

Shirley—he knew it would be her—is first to leave, which surprises David. He'd have expected them to come upstairs together, maybe kiss goodnight at the alley's entrance, then go their separate ways.

But here is Shirley. She comes to the end of the alley, stands for a moment or two to look up and down the street—does she suspect David has waited, watching?—then goes out to Main and turns away from downtown. She looks frail, innocent even, in a dark skirt, white blouse, over her shoulders a cardigan whose color he can't quite determine—blue perhaps. Meeting her now, David thinks, you'd never know the wonderful filthy thing she'd just finished doing on the rough couch of the Trojan Club.

He shifts uncomfortably on the hard bench. His underwear is cold, sticking to him; he hopes nothing shows on his trousers, or how can he conceal what happened to him? And it simply happened, didn't it?—it wasn't anything he consciously did. His mother always tells him what a wonderful imagination he has, and now he can agree.

He waits. What Tom is doing is probably straightening the place up, replacing cushions, cleaning off anything spilled. He won't want to leave traces, his or hers, where one of the guys in the club can find them, figure out what's been going on after dark. David's gaze is centered on the square glass of the door, on the light still dimly visible in the deep of the alleyway, and as he's watching, the light vanishes. Tom has switched off the hall light, is climbing the stairway in darkness. David hears the outside door open—a creaking hinge—and slap closed.

Tom appears at the curb, a solitary figure pale in the light cast by the corner streetlamp. David stands, sharing that light, and walks forward.

"David?" Tom says. "That you?"

"I saw," David says. "I didn't mean to spy, but I was still here when she came out. I'm sorry."

For the moment the two of them stand face to face in the center of Nason Street.

"It's all right," Tom says. "It's no big secret."

What a relief that Tom isn't angry. In fact, he puts one arm around David's shoulder and they walk together to the bench David has only just left.

"She's something, you know," Tom says. "Nobody really knows how lucky I am."

"Maybe some people do," David says, thinking of himself. "Are you going to marry her someday?"

"Could be." Tom sits at one end of the bench and takes a cigarette pack from his shirt pocket. "I think I will. I know she wants to."

David settles onto the other end of the bench and watches Tom take a cigarette from the pack, tapping the package—Camels—against the first knuckle of his left hand, lighting the cigarette by flicking the wheel of a fancy gold-colored lighter that David guesses was a gift from Shirley.

"I know how lucky you are," he says. "I wish Kate and I were as close as you and Shirley."

"Almost four years. That's how long we've been going steady."

"That long," David says. How long has he been going out with Kate officially? A month? Two? Maybe it was the first time they rode their bikes up to Mousam Lake for a picnic, and that was barely three weeks ago.

"We started in junior high." Tom takes a long, thoughtful drag on the Camel and lets the smoke eddy from his nostrils. "When I think about it," he says, "it was kind of funny how I first decided to take her out."

"Funny how?"

Tom laughs to himself. "It's kind of stupid."

"But tell me."

"I was dancing with her at the Y—you know when they used to have those Saturday night dances for the little kids?—and it was the first time I'd held a girl real close." He takes a drag from the cigarette. "That was in eighth grade."

"Yeah?" David has moved closer to Tom, as if he's afraid he'll miss something. It might be that he'll hear something that will help him with Kate, make him seem experienced and wise about girls. The images he conjured while Tom and Shirley were downstairs at the club keep flickering at the back of his mind like the moving pictures at the State.

"Anyway, she was really close, right up against me, and all at once I realized she had breasts. I mean, I could actually feel them—her tits—against my chest. It was a weird sensation."

David says nothing. He tries to think of what Shirley Kostas's breasts would feel like against his chest.

"It was the first time I'd ever noticed," Tom says. "I'd never thought about when girls started getting breasts that showed, especially Shirl. It was a weird sensation."

"Did you say anything?"

"To her? Are you kidding? What would I say? 'Hey, Shirley, I notice you've got tits'?"

David feels his face get hot. He feels himself shrinking into a smaller person who's all ignorance and embarrassment. "I don't know," he says.

Tommy Gowen takes a short furious pull at the cigarette and flicks the butt in the direction of the street. "Jesus Christ, Willard," he says.

"I'm sorry."

Now Tom seems to relax—David hopes that's a sort of forgiveness—and leans forward, elbows on knees. "Anyway," he says, "I walked her home after the dance and we sat on her porch steps and made out. And one thing's led to another ever since."

"I envy you," David says. It's true, but he doesn't know where the words came from. Envy isn't something you want to admit—his father would make a sermon out of it—but he just said it.

"Hey, Kate's a damned nice girl. You don't have to envy anybody."

"But we've never made out. I don't even know how to start."

Tom laughs. "It comes naturally," he says. "Believe me."

"I can't even get up the nerve to go into a drugstore and buy safeties. Can you imagine that?"

"You've never?"

"Never. I carry this thing in my wallet that *looks* like a prophylactic—it leaves that funny circle in the leather. But it's just a round metal thing that holds dental floss."

"Cute idea," Tom says, "but it doesn't have to matter. I've never used a rubber."

David lets this information sink in before he says, "Aren't you afraid she'll get pregnant?"

Tom shakes his head. "It's not something you think about at the time. When things are going hot and heavy, you don't stop in the middle and say to the girl, 'Wait a minute; let's discuss this before we go any further.'"

"No, I guess you can't do that." Here are the images again, dancing on the screen of his mind, teasing.

"But I don't come inside her," Tom says. "She wouldn't let me anyway, but I'm not dumb enough to get her knocked up. You just have to wait till the last second, and then pull out. It's messy some-times. Sometimes if she's really horny she'll let me come in her mouth."

David closes his eyes. He's never heard of such a thing. What kind of girl would let a boy do that?

He wonders does she swallow it.

9.

Saturday night is David's first visit to the carnival, a kind of trial run for Monday, Labor Day, when Kate will be with him. Tom and Jack are roaming from sideshow to concession to gambling games, and David tags along. Wherever they go, David thinks the painted picture of Sharita and the serpent is following him, dominating everything, and he finds himself looking back at it—sometimes a surreptitious glance, sometimes a bold, face-on study—as if he is memorizing the canvas scene: Sharita, her bared breasts, her navel with a gemstone mounted in it, her flimsy, see-through costume; the snake, its skin patterned with diamonds of gold, its beady, bulging eyes, its forked tongue poised over Sharita's twisted mouth like the invitation to a forbidden kiss. It's a picture that's wasted on the others. They don't have David's imagination, or maybe they don't have his appetites, his desires, his secrets.

"You want to get some cotton candy? That fluffy pink shit?"

Jack has appointed himself leader of the group. Tom, who ought to lead—because he's smarter, wiser—is letting Jack run the show. David isn't sure why, but if Tom is letting it happen, it must be all right.

"Too sweet," Tom says. "It gets up your nose."

"All Jack wants to do is eat," David says.

"Up yours. What do you want to do, smart guy?"

David isn't going to mention Sharita. "I want to see stuff," he says.

"What kind of stuff?" Tom looks at him as if he cares what David wants.

"I don't know. Whatever they've got."

"How much dough you bring with you?" Jack says.

David tries to think. "Maybe five dollars."

Jack nudges Tom. "You?"

"Who wants to know?" Tom seems annoyed by the question.

"Come on," Jack says. "How much?"

Tom hesitates. "Sixteen," he says. "Maybe seventeen."

"Huh," Jack says. "How'd you get so rich?"

Tom ignores him. Now the three of them have arrived in front of an open-sided tent; in it is a piece of plywood laid flat, maybe six by six feet, with two-inch holes in the middle of colored squares. Each hole is numbered. A live mouse, surprisingly small, more brown than gray, scrambles across the board, disappearing randomly into the holes. What's under there? Cheese? Peanut butter? A couple of people, young guys with handfuls of dollar bills, are standing around, betting numbers. It's like a roulette game.

"What say, boys?" The barker seems to have singled them out. "Play Mouserino? Put your money down, only a buck. Which hole's the little fellow going into? Bet your number."

"That's cruel," Tom says.

They move on. Over his shoulder David catches a glimpse of the dancer, the painted snake, the bright colors of the Paradise sideshow. He stumbles, bumps against Jack.

"What the fuck, Dave?" Jack pushes him away. "Watch where you're going."

"Hey, look," David says. "I can do this."

They're in front of a ring-toss game, square wooden posts of different heights with prizes tacked to their bases. There are watches, wallets, kewpie dolls, and a lot of other stuff. It occurs to David that maybe he can win something for Kate.

The man behind the counter eyes him. "Everybody wins, son. Throw the rings, quarter a toss. Everybody a winner."

"Kid stuff," Jack says. He turns away. "Come on, you guys."

"No," David says. "Wait up."

He fishes a quarter out of his pocket and lays it on the narrow counter. The barker takes it and passes him three rings. The rings are made of coarse rope, yellowish in color and thick as his thumb. With Tom and Jack watching, he throws them. One by one they hit the posts, all of them close but falling away.

"You jerk," Jack says. "The posts are bigger than the rings."

"No they're not." David turns to the barker. "Are they?"

"It's an honest game, son," the man says. "See for yourself." He slides the rings, one at a time, over the posts. "A perfect fit. Am I right?"

"I can beat this," David says.

He puts down another quarter, takes the rings, slowly and deliberately tosses them. Again he has no luck.

Tom puts his hand on David's shoulder. "Come on, Dave. It's a racket. You can't win."

"That last one was really close." He lets Tom steer him away. "I think I was just getting the hang of it."

When he looks back, the ring-toss man is lighting a cigarette, scowling after them. He pokes the cigarette in the air. "Wisenheimers," he says, loud enough for them to hear.

Jack gets the last word. "Up yours, buddy."

* * *

Outside Sharita's tent a crowd has begun to gather. David wants to join them, but he's not sure about the others. He feels he shouldn't be the one to suggest they stop, as if the suggestion would give him away, as if they would find out how preoccupied he is with his private self, as if they would mock him. It's Tom who rescues him.

"What about this?" Tom says.

"Waste of money," Jack says.

"What's wrong with it?" David wants to know. He isn't sure he really intends to see Sharita dance—what happens when you finally do the thing you most desire?—but he doesn't want to leave the temptation behind. Not just yet.

"My brother told me about it," Jack says. "Some old bag with an appendix scar does the hootchy-kootchy with a snake."

"True?" says Tom. "A live snake?"

Jack steps away and does a little dance. "'Oh they don't wear pants in the southern part of France'," he sings.

While he is doing his song and dance, Sharita emerges. She wears an exotic harem costume—fancy vest and gauzy pantaloons—and undulates, hips gyrating and hands swaying, while the barker begins his spiel to draw a larger crowd. David is fascinated, but tries not to let on. Sharita doesn't look to him like an old bag.

Jack goes on with his description. "Rubs it all over herself—her boobs, her belly, her crotch. At the end of her act she does it with the snake."

"I don't believe that," David says.

"Sticks it right inside her snatch," Jack says. "You calling my brother a liar? He saw the show in Bangor last week."

"Jesus," Tom says. "That's sick."

Jack punches him on the arm. "Yeah," he says. "Isn't it?"

David wants to stay, to see what Sharita will do for free, but Jack and Tom are already moving on, and he has to decide if he is with them or on his own. For now, he follows them, where they're standing in front of a makeshift table, presided over by a gaunt old man in a stained fedora. On the table are three walnut shells and a dried-up pea. Two or three town guys, the kind that loiter on the corner outside Thompson's Drugstore, are watching as the man hides the pea and manipulates the shells. One of the guys is playing, putting down dollar bills to guess which shell the pea is under.

"It's under the middle one," says one of his friends. He points, and the gaunt man lifts the middle shell to reveal—nothing.

Jack leans toward Tom. "It was on the left."

Tom shakes his head and walks away, the others following. "You don't know anything," he says.

"I thought it was under the one on the right," David says. He knows; he watched the shells like a hawk, and he didn't miss a move.

"Up yours," Jack says. "It was on the left."

Tom is still shaking his head, as if he is walking with idiots. "It wasn't under any of them," he says. "The guy palmed it."

That settles it. You can tell from the way Tom says it that the shell game is beneath his intelligence. Jack changes the subject. "You guys want popcorn? I'm hungry," he says. "I'll catch you in front of the snake dance."

While Jack goes off to feed his face, David is relieved that watching Sharita do her dance is still a possibility. He asks Tom: "Are you going to that kootch show?"

Tom shrugs. "When I get around to it. You?"

"Yeah," David says. "When I'm good and ready. There's other stuff I want to see first."

"Like what?"

"They've got a whale exhibit I wanted to see."

"A whale? Is it alive?"

"I don't think so. I think it's stuffed."

Tom isn't impressed. "Big deal," he says.

"I've never seen a real whale," David says.

"What's it stuffed with?"

"How would I know?"

They walk on. Ahead of them is a shooting gallery, and they stop to watch a few of the shooters. Some of them win kewpie dolls or teddy bears; some don't win anything.

David thinks this is one of the things he and Kate can do when he brings her here tomorrow. And maybe the ring-toss. She won't go for the Mouserino game because, like Tom, she'll think it's cruelty to animals, and she's too smart to care about the shell game. The merry-go-round—that's good—and the Ferris wheel. The dancer, Sharita, is out of the question.

"You know what I think?" Tom says.

"What?"

"I think you're afraid of the kootch show. That's why you're giving me all this talk about whales. I think you're scared your old man'll find out if you watched a bare-assed lady. Maybe you think you'll go to hell."

David can't respond. It's true that he read somewhere about the whale exhibit, but he doesn't have any real interest in seeing it. He might have wondered why he made such a big thing out of a stuffed whale, except now Tom has figured it out, and even though the tent is behind them, a huge black whale pictured with its tail arched and a water spout gushing over its head, David knows he doesn't have to go on pretending.

"The truth is," he tells Tom, "I thought I should save my money for Monday."

"What's happening Monday?"

"I'm bringing Kate Meredith to the carnival."

"Oh, yeah," Tom says. "You were with her at the coffee shop. I sort of know her. Jack used to date her."

"He did? When was that?"

"Back in her wild days." He cocks his head at David. "That bothers you?"

"A little."

"But that was in junior high. Besides, just because Jack took her out, that doesn't make her damaged goods."

"Who's damaged goods? Anybody I ought to know?"

So, just to make matters worse, here's Jack, red and white box in one hand, fistful of popcorn in the other, the yellow butter dribbling down to his wrist.

"I was telling Dave how once upon a time you dated Kate Meredith. Now he's not sure he likes her."

David protests. "I didn't say that."

"Sure he likes her," Jack says. "She's a dish. It's just she's not as much fun as she used to be."

"True," Tom says. "She's calmed down a lot."

"Hell, now she's too good for us common folk," Jack says. "A couple of years ago you could joke around with her. Now she's so stuck-up, her shit doesn't stink."

"Let's drop it," David says. "Okay?"

What's frustrating is that David doesn't know either of the Kates that Tom and Jack are talking about. Not the Kate of the stories he's heard, about how she'd spend all her spare time at the Arcade on Main Street, watching guys play pinball, and feeding nickels into the jukebox, and doing who knows what else until all hours. And not the Kate who's stuck-up and looking down her nose at the kids who aren't as smart as she is. Both versions of this girl he's bringing to the carnival seem unrecognizable to him. Anyway, where's the evidence? It's true that when she was at Emerson, her dad was off in England, so probably she didn't have as much supervision as she ought to have had. And it's true that she doesn't have a lot of friends at school now—quit cheerleading and doesn't belong to any of the packs of girls who congregate at their lockers and giggle about football players and clothes and who's-taking-you-to-the-dance. But just because she isn't shallow, why does that make her snooty?

Tom says, "Be loose, Bruce," and rests his hand on David's shoulder.

David shakes it off. But why can't Jack ever leave anything alone?

* * *

They stroll on. There are plenty of things to do and see. Watching the carnival take shape, sitting with Kate, getting his hands sugary from the doughnuts she'd brought, he hadn't kept track of all the games, the concessions, the rides. The carnival is bigger than it looked from across the road. You could throw a baseball at a stack of painted milk bottles, or darts at an array of blown-up balloons. Besides the ring-toss he'd been such a failure at, here was a coin-toss and across the way a basketball shoot and, on the other side of a hotdog stand, an old guy under a sign that promised he could guess your weight "within 10 pounds."

"How about a whirl on the merry-go-round," Jack says. "That's more your speed, Dave."

"Ha ha," David says.

The merry-go-round is in motion, pairs of white horses with red and green bridles and leather reins, all of them sliding up and down, up and down on their silver poles. The tinny music comes from a contraption at the center of the ride, and the songs change every so often. He recognizes "My Merry Oldsmobile" and then "You're the Cream in My Coffee" that his mother hums sometimes when she's busy in the kitchen.

They move on. For a few minutes they stand watching a couple of grade school kids trying to pound a nail into a concessionaire's wooden board. Every time one of them tries, the nail bends and they lose their money.

"What's the trick?" David wonders.

"Not sure," Tom says. "Maybe it's just nerves."

Just beyond is a tent with no sign to identify what's inside it—only a hand-lettered sheet of paper on a small table that reads 25c. A small Asian man wearing a shiny black robe stands at the entrance. He bows toward them.

"What's this?" Tom says.

"I think I saw this guy in a war movie," Jack says. "He was a Jap colonel."

"I'm going to go in," David says. He gives the man a quarter and goes inside the tent.

The tent has the sharp smell of meadow grass crushed underfoot, and the air is damp and cool. In the dim interior light, he sees that he's standing between two long tables. On each table is a row of jars, like the Ball jars Ma uses when she cans tomatoes, only these vary in size. He bends to examine the smallest of the jars, which is filled with a liquid that has something floating in it. The *something* is pale and shaped like a sort of vegetable with stubs growing out of it. The thing in the second jar is similar but slightly larger; David can make out what look like the eye spots on the wings of some of his father's butterflies.

"Is wonderful mystery of life's progress."

David realizes now that he has come in alone, and the voice he hears belongs to the Asian man from outside the tent.

"Before you born," the man says, "this what you look like. This how you grow. Be born."

He feels the man's hand at his left elbow and lets himself be steered along the first row of jars, where the objects that must be human float in the preserving liquid and grow older in time, and then back along the facing row, which ends with a sealed jar whose exhibit is nearly as large as a real baby. David doesn't know what to think of what he is seeing. He feels a little queasy, and he wonders if this is really the way we all begin our lives.

"Where do you get them?" he asks the man.

"Ah," says the man. "Secret. Cannot tell."

David has seen enough. "Thank you," he says. "This was very educational."

The Asian proprietor walks out with him. "Tell friends. They come see too."

***

Tom is dismissive. "I've read about these shows. They use pig fetuses. Those weren't humans."

"They looked human to me," David says. "You ought to have gone in."

"Waste of money," Tom says.

They've come full circle now, and here they are again in front of the dancer and the snake and the yellow and orange jungle that represents Paradise. They stand like three guys waiting to cross a street, only the traffic is intimidating and they have to pick a safe moment.

It's Jack who finally says, "Hey, are we really gonna pay good money to watch this hag fuck a snake?"

Tom laughs. He looks at David. "What do you think?"

David shrugs. "I don't know." The truth is that he knows and he doesn't. If he stays outside while the others go in, then Tom will really believe David is afraid of his father's condemnation. If he goes in with them, he has to admit to himself that he hopes his father won't find out. *Damned if you do,* his father would say, *and damned if you don't.*

"Come on, Dave," Tom says.

"No," David decides. "I'm going to save my money."

"More hair than a teddy bear," Jack says. "Last chance."

"I guess not."

"Then up yours." Jack drags Tom toward the entrance. "Let's get a good spot."

David watches them go up to buy their tickets. He is standing well back from the crowd of men listening to the barker. Sharita is moving provocatively—not exactly dancing, but probably trying to entice a larger audience inside. Somehow a live snake has appeared, and the woman is maneuvering it behind her neck and letting it wrap itself around her bare arms. That's scary—but of course the snake isn't poisonous; it couldn't be.

David couldn't have said why he pretended not to be interested in this show. If he'd let on how much he really wants to see it—to hell with his father—perhaps he's afraid the others would have made even worse fun of him, especially Jack. Now that they're inside the tent, the time has come for him to make his real decision, never mind saving his money for Kate.

All this time the ticket seller is raking in money and talking a blue streak.

"The lady does it all, gentlemen, and it only takes one half of an American dollar, four bits, fifty cents or two quarters. Lovely and sensuous Sharita. She's got moves the Mayflower van folks never heard of."

The crowd of men is surging now, hands holding out coins and currency, the barker making change, fingers fast and deft, never dropping so much as a quarter.

"She has more steps than the Empire State Building." He rattles on. "She's hornier than the whole Moose Lodge of Scoggin, Maine."

David keeps his gaze fastened on Sharita, the snake worn like a scarf, her hips swaying. And then, just there! she winks at David and gives him a smile. Did she do that? Anyway he thinks she did. He feels a little thrill down his spine, and now he promises himself never to take his eyes off her—to be certain not to miss any attention from her.

"She'll make you hot," the barker says. "She'll make you hungry for you-know-what." He nods in the dancer's direction, not for an instant stopping his ticket selling. "Show the gentlemen that trick Little Egypt taught you. Watch these hips, gentlemen."

Sharita does a sinuous grind, pushes her belly in David's direction. He feels how hot his face has gotten.

"She does it all," the seller says. "More than any of you can handle. Inside, for one half an American dollar."

Sharita does a couple of slow pelvic movements—he doesn't know what to call them—in David's direction.

"She'll make a man out of anybody here."

David turns away. He's a little embarrassed for what's happening to him—his excitement, the changed taste of his saliva, the beginning of an erection.

Sharita seems to be watching David as he moves into the darkness, and he wonders if she can somehow read what's happening to him. She moves in her same suggestive way, doing it for all the men in front of her, but isn't she really intending her dance for David?

"Line up, gents. Fifty cents, fifty cents. Sharita thrills you, one at a time. Fifty cents."

David watches the men crowding into the tent. He begins to follow them as Sharita makes a last bow and slides the snake from her neck until it's looped around her arms; then she's gone. When most of the men are inside, David reaches for his wallet, counts the few bills and takes out a dollar. As he hands up his money, from somewhere in the tent he hears a phonograph playing a scratchy record. The music is familiar, but he can't think of its name.

* * *

When he gets home, it's late enough that his parents have gone to bed. It's a miracle his father hasn't waited up, to lecture him about his responsibilities.

In his room, getting ready for bed—hanging up his trousers so they'll keep their crease, tossing his shirt and underwear into the corner nearest the door so his mother will know they need to be washed, putting on his pajamas—he is thinking about Sharita, her dance, the way she seemed to single him out and what that attention made him feel. What he feels now is a need to go to the bathroom— but only to brush his teeth, he tells himself.

On his way, David notices that the door to his father's den is open a few inches. He pauses, then pushes the door open wider and goes in. This is not quite "forbidden" territory, though he imagines his father would wonder why he's interested in something that's certainly none of his business.

He enters the empty and dark room, turns on the desk lamp and rummages through the materials on the desk, nudging things aside as if he's looking for something in particular. He finds the envelope his father showed him earlier, opens it, shakes out the Madagascar moth inside.

He holds the moth close to the light to study it, holds it in one hand, opens its wings with the forefinger of the other hand, parting them by stroking the place where they join. The softness of the wings—his fingers are stroking both of them—is velvety and smooth at the same time, perhaps the way skin feels, perhaps the way Sharita's skin would feel if he dared reach out to touch her the way a couple of the men at her performance did, perhaps a sexual sensation.

* * *

In fact, David's discovery of sex—his first realization that the world held a certain pleasure he could enjoy by himself—happened years ago in this very room.

He was not quite thirteen. His parents were out, and he was bored. He could read; he had *Boys' Life* and the latest *Air Trails Pictorial*, but he had already read them both. He was stuck with the job of amusing himself without any noticeable tools of amusement—except the books in his father's den. It was among those books that he found—unbelievable!—a book about sex, tucked away among solemn-looking volumes on religion and the spiritual life, the collecting of butterflies and moths, and how-to books on plumbing and electricity. Now, whenever his parents were away from the house, he trespassed, letting himself into the den to read about the world of grownup sex. Sometimes he thought he could never know enough about it.

If this sex book was any measure, then the whole world couldn't have enough of it. The great revelation for David was that girls too craved the secret joy of masturbation. The book was full of the ways women pleased themselves. They chafed their thighs together. They rubbed themselves against bicycle seats. They sat in front of sewing machines and used operating the treadle for sexual friction. The examples in the book reminded him of Vernon Wiley, who worked in the produce section of the IGA and told stories about women who came in to buy a single cucumber, and then trotted out of the store like a dog going to bury a bone. Girls had a big advantage over boys, there were so many objects they could put inside themselves. Boys had to improvise, and it wasn't always easy.

The message of the book was that nothing was wrong with giving yourself pleasure. It didn't make you crazy or blind. David considered himself licensed. These days, if he felt guilty as he came out of bathroom with *Esquire* or a lingerie page from the Sears, Roebuck catalogue hidden inside his shirt, it was simply that the pleasure—intense as it was—died so quickly, not because he felt he had sinned. And that was a guilt easy to dispose of: he could do the deed again. As, apparently, did everybody else.

One terrible day, the book was gone. David was in a panic. Had he not returned it to the exact place where his father kept it? Had he been found out? Carefully, so as not to disturb anything on his father's desk or bookshelves, he searched every square inch of the room, wall to wall, floor to ceiling. It was gone. *My sex book*, the foundation of his knowledge of the connections between men and women, was truly gone.

But if his father had found him out, wouldn't he have said something to David—given him a lecture, a whipping, something to make clear the enormity of his transgression? No preacher could have passed up such an opportunity to sermonize; certainly not the Reverend Harvey Willard. And why did his father own such a book in the first place? Had he bought it to help him do what David was doing, and had he finally, as old as he was, felt what David sometimes felt after jerking off, and decided once and for all to destroy the temptation of the book?

It was a puzzle, but the book was never mentioned, and the puzzle was never solved.

* * *

Finally, he puts the moth in its envelope and replaces it where he found it. He has to use the bathroom more than ever.

David wonders if there is something wrong with him, that he thinks about sex all the time, that everything reminds him of it, that sometimes if he thinks about it hard enough—like waiting outside the club and picturing Tom and Shirley downstairs on the floor—he creams his jeans. It's lucky he doesn't have many opportunities to see pretty women, especially pretty women not wearing very many clothes. Vic Peterson, who runs the Jenny station where David stops when his bike tires need air or when he puts fifty cents worth of gas in his dad's car, has calendars—some of them years and years old—on the walls of the garage where he does oil changes and lube jobs and minor repairs, and they're about the best pictures David has seen in public. They advertise companies that sell spark plugs and tires and motor oil, and all of them show beautiful girls in short skirts or shorts and tight sweaters that outline their breasts. The girls have expressions on their faces as if they've just been surprised—caught doing something they shouldn't have been doing, though David can never figure out exactly what that *something* is.

Anyway, these calendars are in Vic's garage and in other garages and repair shops around town; the car-parts companies don't mail them to ordinary people, and even if they did, they certainly wouldn't send them to the minister of a church. But it doesn't matter. You can't really see anything, but the hints are there and you can go on to use your dirtiest imagination.

David remembers a *Life* magazine that came to the house when he was younger, and in it was a full-page picture of a blond woman wearing a polka-dot two-piece bathing suit. The caption said she was a favorite pin-up of "our boys in the service." Her name was Chili Williams. A few days after the magazine arrived he'd looked for it to take to the bathroom with him. His father kept magazines and newspapers next to the rocking chair in his den, stacked up until he got around to reading them, but there was no sign of the *Life* with Chili Williams inside. His father must have already thrown it out. David had to settle for the Sears, Roebuck catalogue.

This time he doesn't need any such pictures to look at. Sharita's dancing is still fresh in his mind; all he has to do is close his eyes and he can see her all over again, her nipples the color of pennies and the hair between her legs like cornsilk and the thin slit opening into moist pink when she slid to her knees at the front of the stage, the knees apart and her hands holding herself so the pink opened wider. When she did that, the man beside David had reached out and touched her, *there*, that private place. Jack had nudged David in the side with an elbow. "You see that?" he said. "He stuck his finger in her pussy."

What's strange is that while this was happening, Sharita was looking at *him*, at David. This man had his finger—maybe more than one—inside the naked dancer, but she was looking at David, smiling at David, until her eyes rolled back in her head and she lay back, dragging herself away from the hand, scrambling to her feet while the men in the tent whistled and shouted.

"David? Are you going to be in there all night?"

Wouldn't you know it? His mother is at the bathroom door, calling his name exactly at the instant of his climax, the intense mix of pain and pleasure welling-up from some depth in him that contains nothing else. Straddling the toilet, he holds on to himself, spilling into the water the milky threads of his unraveling excitement.

"No, Ma." The words are more gasp than ordinary speech.

"Are you all right?"

"Yes, Ma."

"Well, don't stay in there too long. Your bowels will drop."

And then she's gone, her footsteps fading down the front stairs. His father would have hammered on the door with his fist. "Get out here now!" he'd have shouted, as if he knew what David was doing. You could be sure he wouldn't care if David's bowels dropped all the way to China.

10.

When David wakes up the next morning—Sunday—and reaches to turn the face of his alarm to a readable angle, he sees that it's already nine-thirty and it won't be long before his mother will rap on his door and tell him he's going to be late for church. Never mind that he hates church. Why is it his obligation to attend just because Harvey Willard is the one giving the sermon—especially this week when he's already heard his father rehearsing out loud, pacing back and forth in the upstairs hallway? He's practically memorized the whole thing, for God's sake, about butterflies and beauty and all the sorry temptations of life.

The thought has barely occurred to him when he hears the knock at the bedroom door.

"David? Time to get dressed for church."

Message delivered, his mother leaves. He hears her steps on the back stairs, knows she is starting breakfast, knows his father is already in the bathroom shaving.

The question is: how shall he avoid church? His mother was awake when he got home last night—a shame she's such a light sleeper—which makes it impossible for him to claim lack of sleep. But lack of sleep isn't the same thing as lack of rest. What if he ate something at the carnival that disagreed with him? Popcorn, candy, taffy apple—almost anything, taken in excess, might upset his stomach, give him a headache, keep him awake, restless. Why else spend so much time in the bathroom? Trying to throw up. Looking for aspirin. Mother is his witness.

He draws the covers up to his chin and rolls onto his side, facing the wall. When his mother calls a second time, he doesn't answer. When he hears his father's voice, he concedes an incoherent moan as answer. Finally his bedroom door opens and his mother comes in.

"David?"

She stands by the bed, waiting for a response. When none comes, she sits on the bed and puts her hand out to touch his forehead. He hopes the forehead is hot.

"What is it, sweetheart?"

"Don't feel good," he says, the words muffled by the bedclothes.

"Where don't you feel good?" The hand leaves his brow and arranges the covers so she can see his face.

"My stomach. My head."

His mother is quiet. David is conscious of her presence, hears her sigh, waits.

"Did you eat too much junk at that carnival?" she says. "Is that the problem?"

"Maybe," he admits. "Probably."

She stands up. "I'll fix you an Alka-Seltzer," she says.

"I'll take some later."

Outside his door a conversation begins. Mother. Father.

"What the deuce is the matter with him now?" As if David's entire life is a succession of digestive mishaps contrived to keep him home from church.

"Too much cotton candy is my guess," his mother says.

"He has no common sense," his father replies. And then: "I haven't the time to deal with this. I'll see you in church."

His father is gone, and a few minutes later his mother pauses long enough to poke her head into his room.

"Try eating some cereal," she says. "The Wheaties is on the kitchen table, milk in the fridge."

"I'll try," he says.

"If you need it," his mother adds, "the Alka-Seltzer is in the medicine chest."

"Thanks, Ma."

Then she's gone, the front door closes behind her, and David is alone in the house.

For a while he stays in bed, the covers up to his chin, pondering the play of light on the ceiling of the bedroom, which changes and dances when a car passes in front of the house. He's rescued himself from a boring church service, but he has no plan to replace it, and so by default he leans over the side of the bed and slides his hands under the mattress until he can retrieve the *Esquire* he has promised to return to Raymond day after tomorrow. The magazine opens to the Petty girl page as if by magic.

* * *

Afterward, as soon as he has bolted down his cereal and drunk a glass of milk, David wheels his bike out of the garage and heads toward The Meadows. He makes one small concession to family and God: he detours to his father's church and stands for a few minutes in the vestry behind the church proper, being careful that he is seen by several other stragglers. The vestry doors are open—for overflow, though today is not really an overflow day—and the butterfly sermon is clear and solemn, even heard from this far away. He listens only long enough to confirm that yes, he already knows the thrust of his father's argument, and then he turns away and leaves this place of worship for his other, stronger religion.

He doesn't know what the carnival schedule is for Sundays, whether there is or isn't an afternoon show, but in his head the magazine image and the memory of Sharita's nude dancing are blurred together into a single picture that overrides the vestry of the Congregational Church. It is an enticement irresistible, and it draws him up the long hill to the showgrounds like a magnet, a beacon, like any force that shows the way to perfect relief. He scarcely thinks of his parents—of what they will think when they come home from church to an empty house—but concentrates instead on how he can manage to meet Sharita face-to-face, what he will say to her, how he can speak without stumbling and seeming foolish in her eyes.

The grounds are nearly deserted as he rides his bike through the main entrance and pedals past the games and concessions he and Jack and Tom took in the night before. A couple of men in work clothes are roaming the beaten-down grass, carrying burlap sacks, cleaning up the debris—wrappers, popcorn boxes, crumpled cigarette packs—left by yesterday's patrons. The shooting-gallery proprietor is rearranging the stuffed animal and doll prizes behind his counter; the Mouserino manager sits in a folding chair beside his game, drinking from a bottle of beer. There is an air of expectancy, but no action.

David threads his way through the displays toward the trailers housing the workers and performers. He leaves his bike lying on the ground behind one of the generators that noisily powers the World of Pleasure's lights and sound, and walks in the direction of an Airstream glistening in the noon sun. He knows the trailer is Sharita's; he followed her after her dance, he saw her go inside.

A man is lounging outside the trailer in a canvas beach chair, his legs crossed, cigarette in one hand and coffee cup in the other. It's the barker, the ticket taker, the man who let all three of them into last night's show without challenging their ages. His eyes are half-closed, but as David approaches the man sits up.

"Hey," he says. "Where the h-hell do you think you're g-going?"

The question startles David. The tone is so harsh, he can't think what answer he ought to give.

"Wh-what are you hanging around here f-for? This is off l-limits for the l-likes of you."

Maybe David is wrong. This looks like the same man who sold him his ticket last night, but the man last night was a smooth, quick talker—none of this stammering. What if this isn't the right trailer?

"I wanted to talk with Miss Sharita," David says.

"T-talk?" Coggio takes a swallow of coffee, drags on his cigarette and exhales a cloud of gray-blue smoke in David's direction. "Wh-what the fuck about?"

"I want to interview her."

Coggio drops the cigarette and grinds it out under his shoes. He swings himself off the beach chair and stands up.

"Interview?" he says. "What's that m-mean?"

"I told you. I'm a reporter." Stretching it, he knows, but if he stays with the paper, who knows where it might lead? "I'm with the *Tribune*. The town paper. We want to do a story on Miss Sharita."

The man gives him a long, sardonic look. "Wh-what horse sh-shit."

"It wouldn't take a lot of time. If she's busy, I could come some other time."

"Sure you c-could." Coggio studies him. "Where's your p-p-pencil? Where's s-something to write with?"

"I've got a good memory." How stupid could he be, not to bring the tools of the reporter's trade?

Coggio grins. "I never h-heard such a p-pile of horse shit in my l-life. You don't w-want to talk. You w-want something else. Adm-mit it."

"I really do work for the *Tribune*. You can call—"

Coggio interrupts. "You were here last n-night."

"Yes, I was." No point in lying.

"Christ, you c-can't be more than fourteen, f-fifteen years old."

"Almost seventeen."

"You trying to g-get me in bad with the t-town coppers? Get m-me arrested for letting m-minors sneak in to the b-blow-off?"

"No." He has to protest, for Sharita's sake, even though he doesn't understand what the barker could be arrested for. "I wouldn't do that."

Coggio comes toward him, threatening, it seems to David, and he backs away. "P-piss off, kid. We d-don't want you hanging around h-here. The l-lady don't give interviews."

He reaches for David, grabs him by the collar.

"Anyway," he says, "you ain't b-big enough for the lady." He shoves David. "Get the f-fuck out of here."

"It's good publicity," David says.

"Take your p-publicity and sh-shove it," Coggio says, and he pushes David hard enough to knock him off his feet onto the bare ground.

* * *

Sherrie has just finished washing up when she hears the commotion outside the trailer, Frank's voice rising and falling around bits and pieces of profanity. She finds her robe and belts it tightly at her waist. She realizes there are two voices out there, the second one smaller than Frank's—and cleaner. A woman? Why would a woman be hanging around the grounds in the middle of the afternoon?

She unlatches the trailer door and swings it open.

"What's going on, Frank?"

It's like a tableau, a carnival set-piece or a blackout: two men about the same size, one holding on to the other's shoulder, the other cowering. She realizes it's a boy, teenaged, Frank is trying to drag away from the trailer, shouting and swearing.

"F-fucking kid. You're the s-size Sherrie'd throw back in the pond."

She takes one step out of the trailer. Something about the boy takes her interest—something familiar. Outside the show, yesterday, while Frank was talking up the crowd?

"Frank," she says. "Let him go."

"He was n-nosing around," Frank says.

"I didn't mean any harm," the boy says.

"Sure you didn't." She waves a hand at Frank. "Let him loose."

"You know wh-what he's after."

"I'm not." The boy manages to pull free.

"Stop it, Frank." She holds a hand out to David. "Don't mind him. He's not my keeper. Just thinks he is."

"I just wanted to talk," David says. "Honestly."

"Sure you did. You come inside. We'll talk." Now she takes the boy's hand and leads him up the step.

Frank is furious. "For Chrissakes, Sh-Sherrie. The kid's trying to hustle a p-piece of tail."

"I'm not."

"You come on in," Sherrie says. "I'll see if I can hustle us something cold to drink." She winks at Coggio. "Scram, Frank."

Coggio raises his middle finger, but turns and walks away.

Inside the trailer, Sherrie motions for David to sit at the breakfast table. "Don't you mind Frank," she says. "He's one of those men thinks he owns a body."

She rummages in the icebox and brings out two squat bottles of Narragansett ale. She half-turns toward David, who despite her invitation is still standing just inside the door of the trailer.

"Well, come on in then. Take a load off." The boy is so shy, it's beginning to make her feel downright maternal. "We don't have any Coca-Colas. You like Narragansett?"

Finally he sits down. The cat seems to have his tongue and he sits quietly, his hands folded on the table in front of him. While she finds a bottle opener and pries up the caps on the two ale bottles, he watches as if he's never before seen such an activity.

"Frank's not a bad sort," Sherrie says. "We go way, way back. He just likes to bark, like a good watchdog. Anyway, you're my visitor, and he can like it or lump it."

She sets the bottles on the table, pushes one toward David, then sits across from him.

"Like I said. He's not my keeper." She takes a long drink from the bottle. "Hits the spot, don't it?"

She looks at David as he reaches for his bottle and takes a wary sip, not for a moment looking away from her. In response to the intensity of his gaze, she lifts her hand to the collar of her robe.

"Frank's from Southie," she says. "South Boston. Lots of Italian families, and Frank's from one of them. Thinks he's real tough. . . . And I guess maybe he is." She drinks from the bottle, sets it down. Why is this boy so silent?

"Baby?" she says. "You haven't said one word since you came in. And you haven't touched your drink."

"I've never had beer," he tells her. "Ale. This."

"Never?" This is a delicate flower, Sherrie tells herself. This is not a man of the world, and therefore not to be treated the way she treats other men. Frank is dead wrong in his judgment; that's clear. This boy is no more looking for a lay than the man in the moon.

"If I'd known you were coming," she says—and she draws the ale bottle away from him across the table—"I'd have gone to the store, got a Coca-Cola or something."

"I saw you dance," the boy says.

"There. I knew you were a fan." She studies him as he sits uneasily, his hands one minute on top of the table, the next minute in his lap. Yes, she remembers him: the boy hanging back from the crowd outside the tent, the boy who couldn't take his eyes off her.

"With the snake under the curtain. And with the cigarette. With no clothes on."

"Oh, Lord." She puts her hands to her face, ashamed for him, then can't help but smile. "Oh, baby. They weren't supposed to let you in to see that part of the show." She leans close and covers David's hand with hers. "You're supposed to be eighteen to go behind the curtain."

"You're a swell dancer."

"Thank you, honey," she says. It is a praise that makes her want to weep, coming from a child whose knowledge of the world—and of her life, her actions—probably amounts to next to nothing. "Thank you very much."

"It must be pretty dangerous—that live snake. I'd be afraid all the time."

"That old snake? It isn't poisonous. Besides, it's just for show. I only really danced with it a couple of times—and I didn't like it."

"But it could still have bit you. Or squeezed."

Sherries laughs. "Honey," she says, "We keep that snake on ice. It's so cold it can hardly move."

"Just the same." He leans toward her. She can see him mustering an odd kind of intensity, and behind that intensity is something tentative, a little fearful. Is Frank right after all?

"Most people wouldn't dare to dance that way," the boy says. "I sure wouldn't. It would make a really neat story."

"A story?"

"I work for the Scoggin *Tribune*—the local newspaper."

It's an announcement followed by nothing; the silence suggests that the fact of his job explains what is left unsaid. Sherrie has to interrupt the silence.

"Is that so?" she says.

"And I really would like to write a feature story about you. For the paper."

Sherrie gazes at him, amazed and sad at his eagerness. Poor foul-minded Frank. How wrong he can be.

"That's truly all you want from me," she says, confirming what she's just heard. "A story."

Now his eagerness brims over. "It would be good publicity," he says. It's an excitement of the kind she hardly ever sees, intentioned and innocent at the same time. "It would bring people to see you dance. You could carry the clipping with you and show it to people. People who'd hire you."

Sherrie is already shaking her head, slowly, in disbelief as well as refusal. The boy doesn't seem to notice.

"My name would be on the story," he says. "My first byline. 'By David Willard.'"

He stops, as if all at once he realizes she is going to deny him.

"It would be a way for you to remember how much I like you," he says. But the words fall hopelessly, a forlorn last try.

She wants to put her arms around him. "Oh, baby," she says. "Oh, David—is that it? David?"

"Yes."

She squeezes his hands. "David, honey, I just can't. I can't let you write a story about me."

"I know I don't look like a newspaper reporter." His voice rises. "I know you think I'm too young and that I'm probably fibbing—But I *am* a reporter. Truly, I am."

"It isn't that. Of course I believe you." Good Lord, who wouldn't trust a child like this? Who could help but believe him? She lifts her hand to touch his face—brow, cheek, the sweet mouth. "I don't think these lips could tell a lie if you wanted them to."

She takes her hand away. "But if I said I'd give you something to put in the papers, I'd be the one would have to lie."

"Why would you lie?"

"Because a lot of people who join the carnival, or who run off with the circus—they do it because maybe they're running away from something that gave them misery, or because they got something to hide, or they had a close call with the law. All sorts of reasons.

"You take Frank there, he joined the carny to help me out of a bad situation, and he stayed on because being a talker was the only thing he could do that took away his stammer."

"Are you running away from the law?"

She has to laugh. "Oh, David, honey—No, I'm not on the lam. But I got my secret, just like everybody else has their secret. Even you—you've probably got a secret you wouldn't want to let out for the world to see." She sets her beer aside. "Here. Let me show you something."

She's almost forgotten the story that dumb woman in Rochester wrote about her, and she's pushed to the back of her mind all the trouble it caused her—how she started to get letters from some guy who claimed to be a friend of Joe's and who kept wanting her to meet him in one place or another: a hotel, a motor court. *Or else*; that's what the letters threatened—or so she read them at the time. *Meet me and fuck me or I'll tell Joe Connors how to find you.* Oh, she lost plenty of sleep over shooting her mouth off that time. Still, when the piece appeared in the Rochester paper, it flattered her, made her out to be both arty and religious.

She rummages under her underclothes in the top dresser drawer. She's not exactly sure why, but in a funny way she wants to impress this shy young man who thinks she's such a star, such hot stuff.

"Here," she says, finding the clipping at the back of the drawer. "This was my first and last newspaper story."

> *EXOTIC DANCER*
> *"BARES ALL"*
> *FOR THE LORD*
> *By Dana van Herk*

God moves in mysterious ways to perform his wonders. If you think an exotic dancer can't appear half-naked in front of an audience of men and still spread the word of the Lord, then you've never met voluptuous Sharita D'Arvonne—that's her stage name—who can cast a spell that's both physical and spiritual.

For the last three years this sincere, shapely performer has been combining her talents as a dancer with her beliefs as a Christian, and she estimates that in that time she has reached out to as many as 50 thousand persons, "Mostly men, of course," with God's word.

"I started out as just another dancer," Sharita admits, "but that left me somehow unsatisfied. One day it finally dawned on me that the human body was God's creation too." As soon as she brought together her stage act and her faith, says Sharita, she began to experience a new "inner happiness."

"That happiness has never left me," she announces with a sunny smile.

The young dancer—she's only in her thirties—is with Bell-Nilsson Amusements, Inc., of Ft. Lauderdale, Fla., whose Midwest-area tent show, World of Pleasures, is at the fairgrounds, north of town. She dances in a flimsy costume made of satin, chiffon, and other sheer fabrics which sometimes reveal "a little more than a nice girl is supposed to show," according to Sharita, and she admits she has been known to perform in "even less."

How does this square with her evangelistic work on behalf of Jesus Christ? "It's no problem," she says. "The men in my audiences know it's just an act. They know I'm only out there *making a living, and that I'm not an evil and lustful woman in my real life."*

After each show, the lovely missionary reports, the men "flock" to the stage to accept the Christian literature she carries with her. "I know I can't prove if I've ever saved anyone for the Lord," she confesses, "but I certainly can get their attention."

Sharita says she is "just a devout Christian," and not "one of those born-again kooks."

The showgrounds are open from noon until midnight through next Wednesday.

She can see that David is impressed. "That's a pretty name— D'Arvonne," he says. "It's like music."

"Sweet boy," she says, "I made everything up, just for the occasion. At least I was smart enough not to tell that woman my real name."

"Then are you not really religious? Is that made up too?" He sounds disappointed. "Because my dad is a minister. If you *are* what the story says, maybe you could come to church with me."

This time she stifles the laugh. "I guess I'm not much of a church-goer. It's Sunday, and here I sit, getting ready for the show." She reaches to touch the boy's cheek. "I'm awful sorry to let you down," she says.

"It's all right," he says. "You can have faith, even if you don't go to Sunday services." He grins at her. "I skipped church myself, to come here."

"We're a couple of bad eggs," she says. "But God loves us all."

She turns to look at a clock on the counter. "Jesus, look at the time," she says. Turning to face David, she realizes he's staring at the front of her robe, which has gapped open. She draws the robe closed. "I've got to get ready."

Looking flustered, David gets to his feet. "I better go."

"Two matinees every afternoon, sometimes more; four shows every night," Sherrie says. "It's not much of a life, is it?"

"I think it's pretty great," David says.

She faces him, nearly toe to toe. He is barely an inch or two taller than she is. "You come back and see me again," she says.

"I will."

She cradles his face in her hands. "I don't mean see the show," she tells him. "I don't want you to do that again. I mean come see me here. Come talk to me. I'll lay in some sodas."

"I'll come. I promise."

"You're a sweet boy." She raises herself and kisses him gently on the mouth. His eyes show his surprise and his pleasure.

"You're—You're very beautiful."

He sounds dazed. Leaving the trailer, he stumbles and half falls. Then the door closes and he is gone, leaving her with her feelings of—what? Amusement. Fondness. Regret. All of them together.

Sherrie turns back to the business of getting ready for the next show. She is half out of her robe when the light from the doorway touches her again and she turns her nakedness toward it. Frank, a smirk on his face, is silhouetted in the doorway.

"You gonna f-f-fuck him?"

Sherrie picks up David's full Narragansett bottle and gestures with it toward Frank—but she doesn't throw it.

"You son of a bitch—Here," she says. "Drink this so it don't go to waste."

But when he has given her one more sneering look, the bottle already on its way to his mouth, and when he is down the steps with the door slapped shut after him, she thinks there are worse ideas than taking that boy to bed. And not a one-time thing, either, but the beginning—this is the daydream as she undresses for the next performance—the lovely start of an endless teaching and learning. All she knows of making love—and how much she does know!—she can share with this boy, and all he doesn't know: the artless desire, the unpracticed attentiveness, the never-known thrill of the body's pleasures—all that she'll re-learn. She will create a perfect lover; he'll make her young again and worthy of such perfection.

Or, at worst, it will be like playing with dolls. She'll dress him in stylish suits for taking her to dinners in fancy hotels, polo shirts and shorts for drinks at the country club, silk pajamas loose enough that her hands and mouth can slide under to young flesh, kissing and tonguing, caressing and teasing. All the coarse, rough men Sherrie Adams has ever suffered will vanish in the warm breath of this sweet boy.

God, she thinks, *what the hell is wrong with me?*

11.

Monday morning, the last holiday before school starts, Kate is hungry, just as he knew she would be, for the whole story of his visiting Sharita, his talking with her, drinking beer with her. Sitting across from Kate in a booth at the coffee shop, coffee regular in front of her, nickel Coke in front of him, he can feel her excitement—how she's excited to hear everything, but at the same time excited for him, wanting him to relive his yesterday pleasure. He leaves out the very beginning of his interview, the run-in with Coggio, the humiliation of being treated like a child or, far worse, like some kind of ignoramus only interested in sex. (*But what if?* whispers a voice at the back of his mind.) Instead, he tells Kate how Sharita happened to look out her door, saw him and invited him in.

"But why would she do that? Why would she let a perfect stranger inside the place where she lives?"

"I don't know," David says. "I suppose she noticed me while she was dancing, so she sort of felt as if she knew me." That's plausible, and it's true that the dancer admitted she'd seen him before the show.

"You saw her dance?"

"Sure. We all did."

"Who's 'all'?"

"Tom, Jack."

Kate wrinkles her nose. "Oh, Jack. That awful person."

"He says he—he has a history with you."

"Not a history exactly. More like a footnote at the bottom of the page. We danced at the Y a couple of times. I think we went to a movie." She takes a sip of coffee from the mug between her hands. "Are you jealous?"

David is perplexed. The conversation has taken this wrong turn, so that now, instead of impressing Kate with his closeness to a carnival dancer, he's being teased about his feelings for Kate—which are real enough to make him doubly annoyed.

"Do you want to hear about Sharita or not?" he says. He can't help but let the annoyance come out.

"Of course I do. Go on from where she invited you in. What's the inside of one of those trailers look like? Is it like a room in an ordinary house?"

"There's stuff built in. A stove, an icebox. A table, like in a breakfast nook." The truth, he realizes, is that he didn't look around him much because he was focused on Sharita in that pink robe she was wearing. "I didn't pay much attention to the trailer," he admits. "I was there to get a story for the *Tribune*."

"So after you told her you wanted to do a story, then what did she say?"

"She said I couldn't."

"No. I mean what were the actual words? You said, then she said, and then you said."

He ransacks his recollection of the day before, even though his memory keeps tripping over the Saturday images of Sharita naked, of hands reaching for her, of the secret place open between her legs and of his mother worried outside the bathroom door.

"Well," he says, "I said I'd like to write a story about her. I said how it would be good publicity, and that she could show it off wherever she went, to attract people to see her dance."

"And what did she say? Her exact words."

"She said—" Then: "Wait." He stops and holds up his hand, meaning he's trying hard to remember *exactly*. "She said, 'David, honey, I can't let you.'"

Kate frowns. "Honey? She called you *honey?*"

"She called me honey, and later on she called me *baby*."

Kate slumps against the back of her seat. "Honey and baby," she says. "That's so neat. That's really nice."

It's a little embarrassing to hear those words coming from Kate; it flusters him. "Well," he mumbles, "That's what she said."

"And then what? What did she say next?"

"That was about all." Never mind that in fact there was more, but Kate is being relentless and that makes him uncomfortable.

"She didn't tell you why she was with the carnival, doing what she does? She didn't tell you her dark secret, or what she was running away from"—Kate leans forward—"in her other life?"

"She offered me a bottle of beer," David says. "Or ale. I'm not sure what the difference is."

"Did you drink it?"

"I tasted it. I didn't like it. It was too bitter."

"That's good," Kate says.

Then David coughs and tells the important thing. "And she kissed me."

He can see the amazement on Kate's face, but it isn't a sign of jealousy—though that's what he would have liked. Instead, it's an expression of disbelief.

"She *kissed* you?"

"Right on the mouth." He has tried to say the words calmly—tried to be what his mother would call *blasé*—but he is aware that he's being smug.

Kate seems not to notice the smugness, and now there does seem to be a touch of jealousy in the way she looks at him, the way she half holds her breath before she says, "Are you going to take me to see her dance?"

This hasn't occurred to him. He's clear in his own mind about what is suitable for Kate's eyes and ears at the World of Pleasures. Merry-go-round, Ferris wheel, shooting gallery. Cotton candy. Popcorn. That dumb whale. "Take you to that?" he says. "No, thanks. Not me."

"You won't take me?"

"It's not a show for girls."

"Why not?"

He wants to say, *If you don't know, I can't tell you*, but that won't satisfy Kate. In the same way she wants his interview with Sharita spelled out word by word, she'll want a serious explanation of why he can't let her see Sharita dance.

"Because it's not," he says. "It's men only."

"Who says?"

"I don't know. It's just a rule."

"How can it be men only if it's a woman dancing?"

"Don't be dense," David says, then immediately regrets it. "You know what I mean."

"No. I *don't* know."

How frustrating she's being. "Look," he says. "That's just the way it is."

Kate looks down at her glass, turns it in her palms, scowls at it. "I hate that," she says.

"Hate what?"

"That. People dividing the world in two halves. One side shutting out the other. Men only. Women only."

"It's not *my* rule," he says.

"And anyway, what kind of man are you? You're just seventeen. You're a *boy*."

"All right," David says. "*Males*. The show is for males only."

Kate leans back and folds her arms across her chest. "If you care about me, you'll take me."

"Aw, Kat, come on." Is he whining? Yes, he is, because he can see that she isn't going to listen to reason, no matter what.

"It's simple as that," she says.

And she means it; he knows she does. "Okay," he says. "I'll try. But I can tell you right now that they won't let you in."

"Don't worry. They will."

He recognizes the set of her jaw, and the way her lips turn thin and pale. She looks the way she does at play tryouts, just before she takes a part away from snooty Edris Bedford.

"And even if you get into the first half of the show, you'll never get past them into the second half."

"Is that where she dances all naked? That's the part I want to see most of all." She slides out of the booth and reaches for his hand. "Come on," she says. "I have to go get ready."

He lets himself be pulled to his feet. "They won't let you," he insists.

"It's all right," she says. It's as if she's telling him that, whatever happens, she knows it's not his fault. "Maybe I'll dress up like a *male*."

* * *

Walking home, she keeps David's hand in hers. She's never seen him get so touchy about something that doesn't even have anything to do with him, and she supposes that if she holds his hand, she can exercise a kind of control over him.

"Is the show dirty?" she asks. "Does the woman do something obscene?"

"No. Never mind."

"Then why this cuteness, David?" She stops walking, obliging him to stop beside her. "Are you trying to protect me? From what?"

"Listen," David says. "She just dances."

"She must do more than that."

"No," he says—and why is she so certain he's lying? "I should never have brought it up."

"But you did. Tell me."

"It's nothing. You already know. Just, she dances with no clothes on."

"Is she a strip-teaser? I mean, does she take her clothes off while you watch her?"

"No, she just comes out nude and starts to dance."

That peculiar word—the sound of it, the novel taste of it when you say it. Her mother used to avoid the words "nude" or "naked"— as if they were dirty. "Kathryn, stop running around in your birthday suit," when Kate was eight or nine. "Ladies do not parade around in the altogether," when she reached junior high school.

"Then why not take me?"

"I told you, Kate, they won't let girls in."

"I'll bet they would if I insisted," for what was the objection to having a female in the audience? "Who would stop me?"

"The police, that's who."

"Seriously?"

"They put a policeman inside the tent with the crowd."

There seems nothing further to be said, and yet to be prevented from going where David has gone, seeing what David has seen, undercuts the evening for her and makes any more fun impossible. The carnival, which has at first promised to be her great end-of-summer adventure, now appears in its true disguise—one more kind of world divided into *yes and no*, into *men* and *women*.

She sees that one difference between male and female, boy and girl, man and woman, has not much to do with obvious biology, nor with subtleties of psychology, nor with science at all. Instead, it has to do with possessions and secrets—what did a boy know that a girl should not? And what was the special business of being female that no male ought to care about? The sexes are not so much *different* as they are *separate*. And the separateness can be insisted, by custom, or tradition, or silent agreement between the sexes. Women say: "That's a man for you"—perhaps scornfully, but making it clear that one has to expect men to behave in certain ways. And men say: "Women"—with a tone of voice so deprecating it makes you shiver; yet at the same time they act pleased to have located some predictability in a woman's behavior.

And what makes going *together*—men and women sharing their spaces—even more difficult is the insistence that there can be no crossing back and forth. Maleness and femaleness apparently rub off on things—subjects, interests, aptitudes, occupations, tastes, sensibilities. Men who interest themselves in matters female are supposed to be "funny" or "queer"—and so you have jokes about hairdressers and decorators. Women who interest themselves in matters male are tomboys when they're young—and that's all right—but are made fun of when they're older. Even men and women who travel for whatever reasons in the society of the opposite sex are looked down on. Kate's mother doesn't want her to ride in a car with more boys than girls; she would be disturbed by Sharita, who dances naked before an audience of men.

And what if Kate really did manage to brazen herself into that company? She doesn't know, but neither does David, who thinks he is being protective, but is really shutting her out of a private gender world. It's all right for a girl to be sexually savaged by a boy, like Shirley Kostas being savaged by Tom Gowen in the back seat of his father's car, but it's not all right for her to watch sex in the distance of a carnival show.

"Policeman or not," she says, "if you care about me at all, you'll get me in." It's her final, only argument.

* * *

That afternoon Kate comes into her mother's room, not for any special reason, but because in a little while she has to get ready to go with David to the carnival, and perhaps she can reassure Mother that all will be well—though what her mother will think about her get-up for the evening, *that* she can't imagine. Anyway, she loves her mother's room, the *austerity* of it, which suggests to Kate that her mother can survive quite nicely without a husband. Or any man, for that matter.

Mother has her writing desk in one corner of the room, where she sits sometimes when she's reading, and where she pays the bills as they arrive in the mail because Daddy is rarely home long enough to keep up with them. A framed photograph of Kate and Daddy sits at the back of the desk. Along the wall under the two side-by-side bedroom windows is a bookcase—two shelves, the bottom one high enough to hold the *Life* magazine nature series books, and the top one just the right size to hold the Literary Guild novels that come every month in their dust jackets with the colorful abstract shapes. Beside the double bed—mahogany, the bedposts in the shape of a minaret out of the Arabian Nights—is a nightstand with a lamp and an alarm clock; in it is a drawer that Kate knows holds a small, pearl-handled revolver, always loaded. Daddy bought the gun for her before his squadron was shipped overseas, even though she protested. "What makes you think I could ever shoot anybody?" Mother said. "If the worst happens, you'll find it's the easiest thing in the world," was what Daddy had told her.

Her mother is at the writing desk, a book opened in front of her, and for a moment or two Kate stands in the doorway, watching. She knows it isn't necessary to speak—that the mere pressure of her gaze will touch the woman and make her turn her head. That is exactly what happens.

"Do you need something?"

Kate sees now that her mother is holding a yellow pencil—making marks in a book!—and she taps the eraser end against her jaw, idly, as if she doesn't know she's doing it. "No," Kate says. "I just wondered where you were."

"Where I usually am. Inside a book."

"Pleasure or school?"

"My evening class. Where have you been?"

"I had coffee with David," she says. "Making a plan for tonight."

Her mother lays the pencil down. "Is tonight carnival night?"

"So they say."

"And tomorrow's the first day of school?"

Kate smiles. "You know it is."

"I ought to have my head examined, letting you be out late on a school night." She closes the book. "Your father wouldn't have stood for it, and you know it."

"Daddy's not here. Besides, you forget how I can always get around him." It's true; her father is stern, but it's a brittle sternness and shatters easily. "And it's not as if I had homework, is it?"

Her mother sighs and pushes her book to the back of the desktop. Kate sees now that the book hid a small notepad, and the pencil marks are after all not in a precious book.

"Daddy didn't call?" Kate says.

"He never calls before seven. You know that."

"You're missing him."

"Of course," her mother says. "What do you think?"

"And you're upset."

Her mother heaves an exasperated sigh. "Katie, please. I have my class tonight and I've got to get through this chapter."

Kate stands for a solemn moment, trying to decide how she wants to put her next question. Does she want to add to Mother's loneliness by raising the matter of what Father does while he's away from her? Is it any of her business? Then she blurts it out:

"Do you think he's with other women?"

The question seems startling. "Do I think *what?*"

"Do you think Daddy sees other women when he's away from home?"

"That's an awful suggestion," he mother says. "How could you even imagine such a thing?"

That hasn't occurred to Kate. She has never *imagined* her father with another woman; that would mean creating a picture in her mind of Daddy and the woman—having drinks in a barroom, holding hands in a movie theater, even sharing a bed—and it would mean *creating* the woman. Would she be cheap-looking or sophisticated? Blond-haired or brunette or even redhead? Where would she and Daddy have met? In a real estate office? A factory office? And should she invent only one woman, or a different woman in each of the places where Daddy's job takes him?

"I don't imagine anything," she says. "I just wondered if you worry about what he does when he's away."

"Well I don't worry about *that*. Your father does his work for GE, and when it's done he comes home. He hates being away as much as I do. He tells me how much he misses us, you and me. He talks about the dismal hotels and the greasy food and the bumpy flights in those tiny planes. But it's what he does; it's his job, and he owes it to the company to do it well."

She gets up from the desk and comes to her daughter, putting her hands at Kate's shoulders, holding her tightly.

"You should be ashamed of yourself, Kathryn Meredith," she says. "You don't know how honest your father can be."

Kate feels terrible for that, she would have to admit—though the vehemence of her mother's defense, the passion of it, make her wonder. But never mind that. She didn't mean to hurt her mother, demean her father.

"I'm sorry," she says. "Forgive me."

"You're forgiven." Mother raises a hand to push the hair back from Kate's forehead, then touches Kate's cheek. "You should take a little nap before you go out with David. You've got dark circles under your eyes."

"Maybe I will," though she thinks she won't.

"With school starting, you're going to have to adjust your schedule. You mustn't get overtired."

"Don't worry, Mom."

"I do worry," her mother says. "And put some of that Pond's cream on your face and arms, to keep your skin from drying out in this weather."

That might have been the end of it, until Kate asks as inno-cently as she can, "Will Daddy be home tonight?"

"Katie..." Now she seems flustered. "I told you about his maybe going to Tulsa. Probably not tonight."

"Don't you even feel neglected?"

"Sweetie, you're being annoying." She goes back to sit at her desk. "Now go. Take your nap. Get some beauty sleep for David. I really do have to get this chapter read."

"But when he's home—even then, don't you wish he paid more attention to you? You and Daddy hardly ever do anything together. I don't just mean that he's away so much of the time that you can't possibly do things, but when he's home you don't go anywhere, like a picture show or dinner out."

Her mother smiles—not looking at Kate, but keeping her eyes lowered to the book open before her. "It's sweet of you to be con-cerned for our social life," she says. "I don't believe your father and I feel a lack, but perhaps he and I should discuss it."

"It just seems to me sometimes that the two of you don't have much in common. Daddy has his job and you have your schoolwork, and you both chug along on your separate tracks. At home he reads his newspaper and listens to his radio, and you read your books and keep up with the housework. The only time you talk with each other is over the supper table."

Now Mother looks at her. "You mustn't be so hard on us," she says. "You make us sound like a couple of sticks. We do socialize, we do get out and about—though we're not social butterflies and gadabouts, I'll give you that. But we see movies that we think will interest us, and we play cards with Pat and Pat, and your father takes me to dinner on special occasions—and sometimes on no occasion at all."

"But none of that happens very often," Kate says.

Mother sets aside her work. "Things don't stay the same," she says. "Your father and I used to be thick as thieves with the Emerys and the Greenwoods, but then the Emery boy was killed and Hope Emery went into the hospital. The important thing is that your father and I like each other's company; it doesn't matter what we do or don't do in public."

"David thinks..." Kate leaves unfinished what she had intended to say, which provokes her mother.

"David thinks *what?*"

"Nothing." Further provocation. "I'm going to take that nap." Leaving Mother on the verge of being angry.

* * *

But the important thing to Kate is that her parents live unexciting, circumscribed lives, and if growing up and getting married means cooking and doing the dishes and washing and ironing, with monthly canasta thrown in at Patrick and Patricia Conroy's house, then what's the point?

David is philosophical about the whole business—but that's David.

"I've given up trying to figure out my parents," is the sort of thing he says. "My father has a fit if he thinks I'm being exposed to temptation—and that's how he says it: 'exposed to temptation,' as if we're all in the Garden of Eden and there's a snake behind every bush—but then he and I go down to Fred's barbershop and we sit in a cloud of cigar smoke with these old guys reading *Esquire* magazine and telling jokes about traveling salesmen and farmers' daughters."

"I don't see what that has to do with anything," is what Kate says.

* * *

For the rest of the afternoon she practices walking. No nap, and certainly no Pond's skin softener if she's giving up her femaleness for the evening. Walking, she feels, will be the most difficult of the temporary manly arts she has to carry off if she wants to get in to see the dancer, and she goes about the house and yard in an exaggerated swagger, flat-footed and as graceless as she can manage, keeping her toes out, letting her upper body and head sway from side to side, tucking her closed fingers into the back pockets of her slacks. She has determined that she needs to do very little to herself; she is small-breasted, and she has inherited her mother's slim hips. She puts on tennis shoes and white socks, blue jeans, and a blue work shirt borrowed from her father; as a precaution, she wears under the shirt a summer tube top that is uncomfortably tight. She sees to it that the tennis shoes are scruffy and soiled, that the socks droop. She scrubs her face hard and puts on no makeup. All she needs now is something to hide her long hair; the pink softball cap won't do.

She is posturing in front of the bathroom mirror, trying on faces that will make her ugly, when her mother looks in.

"You certainly don't look very dressed up," her mother says.

"It's a carnival, mother," she says. "Not the prom." Kate wonders what happened to her mother's studying.

"What in the world? Is that your father's gardening shirt?"

"Yes."

"No one would ever guess you were a young lady getting ready to go out with a boy. Is it some kind of costume?"

"Sort of. David and I have a bet." She leans into the mirror to push the hair away from her ears. "Do you think I'd look good with really short hair?"

"Oh, Kate. You have lovely hair," her mother says.

Kate sighs. "I know."

"It's a good thing your father's *not* here. He'd have a fit at the very idea of you cutting your hair."

"Probably. Do you suppose he'd mind if I borrowed that black cap he wears when he works in the yard?"

"What is this 'bet' anyway?" Mother says. "Is it some kind of hobo party?"

"Could I use your full-length mirror for a second?" She knows she's frustrating her mother by pretending to ignore her questions, but it's the only way she can think of not to be annoyed—by making a game of the conversation, teasing her mother. It may be that she's not sure Mother would approve of her plans for the evening, though she knows in the end she'll be found out. Finding out is what parents do.

"I suppose. What *is* going on?"

"Nothing." Then, as if she's giving up, "I'm trying to be a boy. That's why I need the cap. Mine's pink."

Her mother gives her a look of disbelief—though Kate has to admit: what other kind of look could she possibly give? "Dare a mother ask why?"

"Because of the way the world is."

"And what way is that?"

"Fenced," Kate says. "We stay on our side; the men stay on theirs."

Her mother settles herself on the closed toilet seat—the seat Daddy refers to as "the throne"—and it's hard for Kate to decide if she is genuinely perplexed, as she appears to be, or if she is simply amused.

"Oh," she says. "I see." One eyebrow lifted, a funny curl at a corner of her mouth.

"You're not taking me seriously," Kate says. "Do you *like* that?"

Her mother shrugs. "As you say: It's the way the world is."

"So we have to let boys—men—follow different rules?"

"I agree that we shouldn't," her mother says, "but—"

Kate interrupts. "Well, that's why I'm dressing this way; so I don't have to go by different rules."

"Which means?"

"Which means that there's a woman at the carnival who dances naked, and only men are allowed to see." She takes Mother's arm and steers her out to the hall. "Come on," she says. "I need your mirror."

In her mother's bedroom, Kate postures in front of the full-length glass on the back of the door. She remembers helping Daddy install it, drawing the horizontal pencil lines to mark where the screws were supposed to go. The mirror is just ever so slightly askew; probably she let the level skip when she drew the lines. She tries on Daddy's cap, takes it off to rearrange her hair on top of her head, puts the cap back on. She still looks like Kate Meredith; maybe it has something to do with her skin—how smooth and pale it is, almost translucent in the fluorescence of the medicine-cabinet light. Boys are coarser.

"I wonder if this is a wise thing for you to do," her mother is saying. "In the first place, does David's father know what David is up to? I'm sure he'd disapprove."

"That's not 'in the first place,'" Kate says. "That's 'in the second place.'" She holds the bill of the cap between her teeth while she does her hair over again, piling it on top of her head and resetting the bobby pins. "And of course his father would disapprove. He'd hit the ceiling."

"And your own father..."

Kate feels as if she'll explode. "Isn't here!" she says. It would be different if he were. She can manage her father's criticisms, but not if they're going to be delivered secondhand.

Her mother won't let up. "But he has expectations for you. He wouldn't want you to put us through another awful arcade phase, if that's what this is going to lead to."

"Give me more credit," Kate says. "And what about Daddy's expectations for you? And your expectations for him?"

"I suppose everybody expects something from everybody else." She reaches out to tuck a last wisp of hair under Kate's cap.

Kate opens the bedroom door, putting the mirror out of sight. "And is that why you take those night school classes?" she says. "Do you expect to go back to teaching full-time?" Just in case. Because that's what wives are supposed to do, so if the husband dies. . . . Or if he walks out on them.

"Stop it," her mother says. "I feel guilty enough about school, as it is."

That takes Kate by surprise, because it's a curious thing for her mother to say. "Guilty why?"

"I'm not working toward a teaching certificate. I'm not working toward any particular degree."

"What *are* you doing?"

"I just don't want to be a dull housewife, and I certainly don't want to go back to being a dreary schoolteacher, day in and day out in front of a bunch of bratty kids. I want to *know* something, be excited by things. I'm just taking courses that interest me."

Kate hugs her mother. The revelation pleases her, and at the same time it reassures her a little—as if, by not planning to teach, her mother has made Daddy's faithfulness more real. "Good for you, Mom," she says.

"You're right that women have as much claim on the world as men do.... Not that I'm crazy about you standing with a crowd of men to watch some woman dancing in her birthday suit."

"But you won't stop me."

"But don't you ever tell your father," her mother says. "And please don't make a habit of pretending to be a boy."

12.

Even when he has finished with the trash, emptying the waste-baskets in the kitchen and laundry room into the galvanized can outside the back door, half rolling and half dragging the can to the curb, David's anger at his father is still simmering. What's the point of having a driver's license if he's never allowed to drive?

In the kitchen, his mother is about to begin baking—a mixing bowl, sugar and flour, a pint bottle of milk are arrayed on the counter—and she sees his mood.

"What is it?" she says.

"He won't let me have the car. Kate and I have to walk."

"Why on earth would you need a car to go The Meadows? It can't be more than a mile."

"It's just the idea of it," David says.

"Ah." His mother smiles. "You wanted to impress your girlfriend."

"But he doesn't understand that. You'd think he never took a girl out." He realizes what he's just said. "You know what I mean."

"I do," she says. "But you know by now: your father is not an emotional man. He's not the sort who expresses himself with great shows of pleasure or pain. It's what makes him a fine preacher, I think. He has a deliberate and measured way of dealing with life."

"He's a cold fish," David says. "It's as if he's shut himself inside a closet, and nobody can get at him."

"Unless he permits it," his mother says. "He's not unreachable. He simply needs to be able to choose who he lets inside his world, and when. Remember what you and I talked about, the other day." She goes to the Frigidaire and takes out the oleo dish. "Your father's mind is always busy. Sometimes I'll ask him a question, and I'll get no response at all. And then, maybe five or ten minutes later, he'll answer. It's as though what I asked him had to stand in line—like people in his church waiting to take communion. Your father always gets to them, every one of them. And he always gets to you and me."

"But we're his family. We *should* come first."

"I know." His mother leans on the counter, the oleo between her hands. "Sometimes I think that if I didn't have the Auxiliary and the bake sales and rummage sales to occupy me, I'd be a very bored woman. As far as your father is concerned," she says, "it's always God who comes first."

"Or his damned butterflies."

"David! Language."

"I'm sorry. It's just that he's so—so remote. What's so complicated about letting me use the car this one time?"

"Oh, David," his mother says. "Can't you just make allowances the way I do? It's only a noisy, smelly machine anyway. What does it matter?"

And that ends the discussion.

* * *

Walking from Kate's house to The Meadows, David feels obliged to apologize, even though he never promised that the two of them could drive to the carnival. "I'm sorry I couldn't borrow the car," he says. "My dad is using it tonight." There isn't any way he can say, "Dad told me not to be so lazy, and don't forget to feed Brownie and take out the garbage before you leave."

He's immediately sorry for bringing it up at all. What will Kate think? That he's showing off. Maybe she'll even think he's lying, hoping she'll be impressed. But it's true. He has his license; he's driven the car twice—no, three times. Twice to church, with his father beside him and his mother in the back seat, and once by himself to buy gas at the Jenny station, to save his father a trip.

"It doesn't matter," Kate says. "I can practice my new walk."

David decides that what she means is a sort of swagger that makes her resemble one of those round-bottomed dolls that pops back up, no matter how many time you push it over.

"What do you think?" she asks him at the end of the second block.

"About what?"

"The way I'm walking. Do I look like a boy?"

"Kate, I can't tell." It's a perplexing question. "I know who you are; I can't pretend you're something else."

"I know. Wait."

She piles her shoulder-length hair on top of her head and freezes it there with two amber combs. Then she puts on her father's cap, pushing stray wisps up under the sweatband. She fusses with the cap bill. "How's this?"

"All right, I guess. You could pull the hat a little more forward— a little down over your eyes."

"Like so?"

"That's better."

She nudges him with an elbow. "Let's go dig that Sharita broad." Her voice sounds funny—lower and hoarser than her real one.

David gives her a pained look. "Cute," he says.

But saying is not meaning, and what David really feels is an apprehension not quite like any he remembers having felt before. It's bothersome that Kate's curiosity about sex is healthier than his, that probably she doesn't sit alone in her bedroom daydreaming about naked bodies and losing control of herself when she gets close to the real thing. Probably she isn't at herself the way he is, crouched over pictures with a door locked behind her. The books say girls masturbate too, that when a girl sits jiggling her feet she's really rubbing her thighs together, exciting herself, but he can't imagine Kate doing such a thing; she's too calm, too in control of herself. Like pretending to be a boy; that's how coolly she plans, and it's not "cute" at all.

If the two of them actually do get into Sharita's performances together—and he isn't as sure as he makes out to be that Kate will be prevented—then what? He knows the dancing will excite him, just as it did the first time, when he hung back from his friends so as not to betray himself. This time, standing close beside her, will his body let him down, embarrass him, show Kate what's really on his mind and how he can't do anything about it?

When he thinks how much he's been looking forward to taking Kate to the carnival, David can't believe how miserable he feels as he trudges up Hospital Hill. He is a guy who has to try not to be male, walking beside a girl who is trying not to be female. It's crazy.

* * *

When he'd first come to the carnival, tagging along with Tom and Jack, the three of them joking and jostling as they came onto the grounds—Jack bragging about how much money he'd made the day before by helping old Doc Bragg put snow tires on his fancy Cadillac—David hadn't especially noticed the music of the merry-go-round. Everything on Saturday had been visual: colored lights, scraps of paper windblown underfoot, the gestures of the concessionaires, the faces of people out for a good time. He had found it all exciting—a kind of promise that here was a different place, a different experience, something to wake him and refresh him after a long dull summer, and an escape from the oppression of home and chores and a remote father. Perhaps an adventure, before the humdrum renewal of school, where the best thing that could happen would be if he and Kate ended up in a play together. True, he was a senior and this was his last year before going to a college of his father's choice, but considering the classes he was signed up for, and the teachers who taught them, he saw no promise of adventure there. That being true, the dazzle of The Meadows was tonic and exhilaration.

But this second visit—Kate in tow, wearing her "disguise" that wouldn't fool anyone but a blind man or an idiot—is more threat than promise. Perhaps because he's looking at the ground, seeing only his own feet moving relentlessly toward Sharita and doom, it's the music of the merry-go-round that fills his head like the threatening organ background of a State Theater horror film. What good can possibly come of this obligation he has reluctantly accepted: to smuggle a fifteen-year-old girl into a tent where a painted dancer shows off her tits and pussy? And how will he deal with that, Kate Meredith standing beside him, pressed against him by the push of the crowd? What if he soils his trousers the way he did the first time? What if the stain shows? He'll have to carry a Coca-Cola in a cardboard cup, so if the worst happens, he can pretend a spill.

"How about riding the merry-go-round?" A postponement. A reprieve.

"Too childish," Kate says. "I got a kick out of that when I was ten, but I think we've outgrown that, don't you?"

"I guess so." He can't not agree.

They have just arrived, but night has already fallen. The carnival lights are vivid from the fronts of sideshows and concessions, brilliant from bare bulbs suspended overhead on wires strung in all directions. The beaten grasses underfoot glow yellow in the artificial light, the ground already littered with candy wrappers, part-eaten ice cream cones, discarded popcorn boxes, and cardboard cups spilling their dregs. Above them the lights of the Ferris wheel turn like a merry-go-round tipped on its side.

"What did you and your pals do?" Kate says. "You and Jack and Tom and all that crowd? I bet you boys didn't ride the merry-go-round."

"That's true," he says. "Mostly we watched people trying to beat the games—trying to outguess the men who ran them. They hardly ever won."

"Did you win? Did you beat them?"

"I lost fifty cents on the ring toss."

He doesn't tell her about spending a quarter to visit the dark tent with the unborn babies—how upsetting it was, and how when he tried to tell the others about it, Tom made fun of him by saying that what was in the Mason jars were pigs, not babies. She would disapprove of the exhibit, and at the same time she would disapprove of Tom because she thinks David wants to be like him and wishes she was as easy as Shirley Kostas.

Yet the thought of her disapproval doesn't stop that wishing. Would Kate ever let him persuade her to descend the stairs to the seclusion of the Trojan Club? He knows she likes Ping-Pong; maybe that could be the lure. Once the two of them were inside the club-room, surrounded by the broken-down furniture and the atmosphere of making out, what might happen? They might hold hands, sitting on the couch where he'd imagined Tom and Shirley. They might kiss. He might touch her—breast, knee, thigh—but he would have to be persistent. Certainly she would push his hand away the first time, maybe the second, but eventually she would give in. That's how it happened; everybody said so. A girl had to give the appearance of being offended, even when she liked—or wanted—to be touched.

"Is that the dancer?"

Kate breaks into his reverie with the question. He realizes that the Paradise tent with its garish mural is in front of them, and that it must be almost time for the next performance to begin. The barker, the man who took his ticket on Saturday and threatened to beat him up on Sunday, is already into his script, drawing as much crowd as he can. Sharita herself is on the platform, wearing a different harem costume: see-through trousers, red slippers, a red vest that opens not quite far enough to show her nipples. She has her eyes closed, isn't dancing but swaying in place, her hips making a slow rotation to the scratchy music from a portable record player that's probably the same one they use inside. No sign of the snake.

"Yes, that's her," David says. "But let's walk around first. There's a shooting gallery. There's this whale exhibit I didn't get see before."

Kate takes his arm and steers him toward the show. "Come on," she says. "I want to hear what he's saying."

David has to push her hand away, slowly, not making a big deal out of it. "Remember. You're supposed to be a guy."

Kate drops her hand. "I forgot," she says.

"Better not."

* * *

The man doing all the talking is simply trying to persuade anyone who'll listen that the dancer on the platform, dressed in that silly costume that's supposed to make her look like a harem princess, is the best dancer "this side of the Mississippi and south of the Canadian border."

Kate is amused. The idea that this ordinary-looking woman wearing too much makeup is better than Ginger Rogers—and if she were, what would she be doing in Scoggin, working for a sleazy carnival—is not even slightly believable. Would anyone be taken in by it?

"Last chance to change your mind," David says.

"No," she says. "You promised."

The words are bolder than she feels at this moment, surrounded by men—their heat, their smells, their interest in words that seem to her clearly to be lies. No one is this talented, this exciting. Will she regret this? Looking back will she be angry because she wasted her time? She glances at David, to see if he has misgivings of his own, but his eyes are straight ahead and his jaw is set.

"Is this smart?" she says.

David looks at her. She can tell by his expression that he really doesn't want her to go through with this. "It isn't too late to change your mind."

She has to show him; she has to show herself. It's like spending time at the arcade when she was younger. She doesn't have to be intimidated by men's worlds.

"I don't think anybody will say anything," she says.

And nobody does. David buys the tickets from the barker, and he and Kate are carried along the short canvas corridor into the tent's dim interior by a tide of men—most of them old: thirties, forties, she thinks. She feels very small, very much like a child among grownups, but she's determined to be grown up herself.

"We've got to get somewhere near the front," she whispers to David, "or I'm not going to be able to see."

"Just shove your way through," David says.

She manages to elbow a path to the front of the crowd and finds herself against the stage, a three-foot-high platform lighted from the back of the tent by a floodlight. A gray curtain—perhaps it's white but soiled—hangs from a line at the back of the stage and extends almost all the way to the canvas sides of the tent. To the left, at the edge of the stage, is a portable phonograph, its power cord trailing over the rim of the platform—probably, she thinks, to connect with a longer wire leading outside to the generator she can hear drumming through the soiled canvas walls.

When she looks about her, Kate can't see much; men tower over her and press her against the stage. It's like being a stranger, a foreigner, pushed inside yourself because you have no language to connect with others.

"How big do you suppose the crowd is?" she says.

David stands on tiptoe and looks back. "Sixty or seventy."

"That's thirty or thirty-five dollars. How many times does she do this?"

"I don't know. It only lasts about twenty minutes."

"Say they do two shows an hour," she said. "That's a ton of money."

Then someone starts a scratchy record on the phonograph and the show begins. At first Kate is disappointed, for when Sharita appears through a slit in the back curtain—though she has a pretty face, and Kate feels an unexpected and instant attraction to the woman—she is dressed almost respectably. She wears the harem costume, and now Kate has the chance to see it up close. The top is made of a gauzy material with sleeves slit to expose the skin, the pantaloons of a glossy, satiny fabric that reaches below her knees. A silver vest covers her bosom; she wears several bracelets on each wrist and a single gold-colored bangle on her left ankle. When Sharita dances, she jingles. *What is it?* Kate thinks. *What attracts men to her?*

When the woman moves into the dance the dark coins of her nipples show through the sheer blouse, and when the bending of Sharita's knees open the sides of the pantaloons, Kate can see she has nothing on underneath. When Sharita turns away from the men and slowly lies back, her arms outward for balance, the full breasts are white against the darker skin of her upper chest. Her eyes are closed. She is so supple that her hair brushes the stage floor before she lifts her arms and raises herself again. The men murmur among themselves; a few of them applaud; one man reaches out as if he intends to touch the woman, but she dances—eyes opened now—lightly away from him.

"I don't call this very sexy," Kate whispers.

David doesn't respond. There are occasional comments from the audience—a whistle, a hoot, "Let's see something, baby." The record comes to an end, the needle continuing to ride the final grooves, around and around, scratching and hissing like static on a radio until Sherrie lifts up the arm and sets it aside.

Now she retreats to the back of the stage. The curtain behind her parts slightly and something slender and dark slides into the light. It's the snake Coggio bought in Worcester, but its appearance takes Kate by surprise. She clutches David's arm.

"David! What is it?"

As if to answer her, the snake begins to talk. "Sharita," it says. "Shareeeeta. C-come behind the curtains with m-meeeeee."

The snake weaves and bobs as Sherrie kneels before it, her back to the audience. Coggio's hand, steering the snake's head, side to side, up and down, is barely visible, and Kate understands that the dancer is supposed to be hypnotized by the movement. The snake gradually sinks to floor level, while Sherrie, on the lighted side of the curtains, sinks downward to follow it. Her audience is almost silent—no noise but a cough, a murmured comment, the scratch of a cigarette lighter.

"C-come to meeee, Shareeeeta. Come c-crawl with meeeeee."

The voice is thin and high-pitched, as if the speech is taking the shape of the snake, the sentences elongated and languid.

"You could really believe it," David whispers. "You could really believe the snake is talking."

"I never heard of a stammering snake," Kate says and David shushes her.

"D-don't you want to beeee with m-meeee?" the snake says. "Yesss, Sh-Sharita. Yessssssssssss."

Sharita is lying on the floor, arms outstretched, her face close to the snake's. "Yes," she tells the snake dramatically, "oh, yessssss," and crawls into the curtain.

The snake is withdrawn. All lights go out. In the sudden darkness there is laughter, a scatter of applause, a good deal of talking. Kate nudges David.

"What's that about, do you suppose?" She is thinking how maybe this is the literal Bible story, an acted-out version of the way it's depicted on the mural in front of the tent, the way it's told in Genesis. She wonders what went through David's mind as he watched. His dad is a minister, uses Bible stories in his sermons—wasn't the Serpent, the devil tempter, in his service yesterday?—and this is the second time he has seen it played out. Is the tent Eden? Is Sharita Eve? And who is Adam?

"Wait and see," David says.

"But is that all? I thought you said she danced naked."

"I said to *wait*." David seems angry, for no reason she can think of.

So she waits. Something else is supposed to happen, and it frustrates her to realize that she is the only person here not to know what. She doesn't dare ask David again; he certainly doesn't seem interested in discussing Bible stories. Around her she hears lighters clicking and matches struck, smells tobacco smoke, feels a gradual rising in the level of talk, in the instances of coarse laughter, in the weight of anticipation. She glances shyly at David; the muscles in his jaw are working nervously; he looks straight ahead.

Then the barker appears on stage from behind the curtain. A sharp rattle of applause greets him, and he waves familiarly at the men in the crowd. "Gentlemen," he says, as if he were beginning a speech. The crowd hoots at the word; the barker lifts his palms for silence. "I call you gentlemen," he says, "because the law is on hand tonight." He gestures in the direction of a uniformed policeman standing at the rear of the tent. "I don't have to tell you why the tariff for this second show is one American dollar—and please, men, no one under the age of eighteen years." The barker moves to the side of the stage and jumps to the ground; the men surge toward him.

"Another dollar!" she says into David's ear.

"Don't you have enough?"

"Could you lend it to me?"

He reached into his shirt pocket and unfolds the thin packet of ones. "Here."

"Thank you," she says. "But now I think you're right that he won't let us in."

"Why not?"

"Under age. Both of us."

David grins at her. "They *have* to say that."

Still, Kate knows how young she looks, and sure enough, when she draws almost even with the barker and holds out the dollar bill she sees the hesitation in the way his hand reaches for the money. When she peers at him from under the short bill of her cap she sees his eyes—they are cold and gray—narrowing to read the details of her face. Then he takes the money.

"Got to start sometime, right, son?" And already his attention is on the next customer.

She nudges David's elbow. "I did it," she says.

* * *

When Sharita appears the second time, she seems to Kate incredibly pale—so white as to seem bloodless—and for the first few moments her movements are like a ghost's. It is this apparition of Sharita she will remember, and not only the excitement of an alien world with its sweet, mildewed smell of damp canvas and the rotted grasses under foot, the good-natured jostling, the odor—as real on these men as on the boys at school—of something especially and mysteriously male, of beer and sweat and stale gray smoke. If you watch something too brilliant, and then close your eyes: that is how Kate will remember the woman on the stage—an image burned onto the screen of sight, imposed over the commonplace objects of the real and present world. Though it might be the lights. When she looks up she sees the two black-metal floodlights aimed toward the stage, and over each of them a pale violet filter; the lights make the woman's lips, fingernails and toenails so red they seem black.

Sharita is naked, as David has promised her. Only the bangle at her left ankle—a small golden disc on a thin chain—has survived from the earlier costume.

"Do you think the man at the door knew I was a girl?" Kate whispers.

David snorted. "Probably."

"Why did he let me in?"

"For God's sake, Kate." His voice is like a hiss. "Watch the show, would you?"

"No, really. Why do you think?"

"For the money."

"Is that all?"

"Kate!"

Sharita has walked to the front of the small stage, her arms outspread—in her face, so far as Kate can see, no expression at all. The dancer's gaze is straight ahead; mouth set, chin high and a little pushed forward.

"She really is old," Kate whispers.

And so she thinks. Perhaps late thirties, even forties, as old as her mother. Only a touch of shadow under the eyes, sardonic lines at the corners of her mouth. An appendicitis scar accented by the light. Breasts full; under the belly—

Kate is surprised. Shocked?

Sharita has shaved the pubic hair; the outer vaginal lips are a fleshy pink between her thighs, looking like something ugly, looking—like a dried apricot.

"She shaves between her legs," Kate whispers. She touches David's arm; his muscles are tense.

"I guess she does."

Kate wonders why. Does she think it makes her look young? Like a child, a girl young enough to be a daughter of some of the men in this tent? How old was Kate when the first fluff appeared down there? Long before her first period; eleven? twelve? What's the sense of shaving it off in your forties? Do men like that?

But Sharita is beginning her dance—though this is less like a real dance than her performance in the first part of her show. Then the dance was consistent with her costume—exotic, a bit "Egyptian," like a movie belly dancer—but this new act seems uncontrolled, a slow milling and reaching of the arms, a sinuous display of the body. She's only trying to show off her breasts—is that a tiny rash alongside the nipples?—and her naked sex. The men clap hands, they talk to her, some of them whistle. Finally she brings all motion to a halt by coming to a kneeling position at the front of the stage, her thighs slightly apart, her hands on the stage floor, her head bowed and the dark hair flowing down to the stage between her knees. The men applaud and murmur approvingly among themselves. Kate tugs at David's arm.

"Is that all she does?" she says into his ear. "What happened to the snake?"

David shakes free. "Kate? Did anybody ever tell you that you talk too much?" He refuses to look at her; she can tell his teeth are gritted.

Perhaps she does talk too much, but it's mostly because she is so close to Sharita—right in front—that she wishes for the performance to go on and on. She has never been so intimate with an entertainer; when Sharita lifts her head Kate can see the beads of sweat on her forehead, between her breasts, on her belly and thighs. She knows Sharita's effort by the way she is breathing, the way she holds her mouth. She can see that Sharita is clenching and unclenching her fists, even as the men applaud her. She can even read what is engraved on the gold disc at Sharita's ankle: *Love*—all the letters capitalized, with a tiny decorative serif on the *L*. Kate wants to nudge David again, to tell him what the anklet says, but she thinks better of it. *Love*. The word disturbs her in this place.

Still on her knees, Sharita begins a new part of her dance, stroking herself, sliding her hands along the backs of her legs to the bend of the knee, caressing the insides of her thighs and letting the hands meet over her belly, rubbing her breasts—the fingers lingering at the dark nipples—traveling her hands over her shoulders, behind her head; now she bows and lets the hands pull her black hair forward before they drop again to the floor beside her.

The men are hooting and shouting, and Sharita throws her head back to toss the long hair into place; she looks to be smiling, but Kate is near enough to see—from the way she shows her teeth, from the curl of the lips—how the smile is like an animal's snarl.

David leans toward Kate.

"What do you think now?"

"I don't know," Kate says.

"I think she's sexy," David says. Sharita is repeating the caresses of herself, and he is watching her intently—eyes wide, mouth partly opened. "She really makes a guy hot," he says.

Kate thinks this is probably true; it interests her that the reflected light from Sharita's white body plays on David's face and makes shadows, the image of Sharita seeming like a tiny candle flame twinned at the center of his eyes.

"She's wonderful," David says softly.

She supposes that what excites David is the idea that the hands playing over Sharita's body are *his* hands—that is what her gestures intend, what her audience is expected to imagine—but nothing about her movements is either subtle or clever. This is not like the mime scene Kate once watched on a stage in Boston, in which a woman turned her back to the audience and then touched her shoulders, her neck, her hair with hands that looked as if they might have been someone else's. That had been a funny illusion. This is real; this is ugly. Now Sharita is fondling herself at the crotch, her thighs open, her dark-nailed fingers rubbing the slit of her sex. The men like that; Kate can feel the weight of them—the heat of them crushing her against the face of the stage. She feels queasy: layers of smoke, the confinement, sights she wishes she could turn away from. How could you believe in love and do such things?

"How's about a smoke, Sharita?" The man's voice is off to the left of Kate; she can't see who has spoken.

"Yeah, Babe, time for a cigarette?" A different man.

David pokes her. "Watch this trick. It's amazing."

"What?" she says. "What's happening?"

"Watch and see."

"Here you go, Sharita." A man behind David reaches over him toward the stage; he holds out a lighted cigarette. The dancer takes it, holds it above her head so all can see it, then does a graceful pirouette to the center of the stage.

The two floodlights are suddenly out. In their place the beam of an unfiltered spotlight cuts through the tent's smokiness from above the heads of the crowd. Sharita takes a puff on the cigarette; its tip glows bright orange and—as if that small point of color were a signal—the men are hushed.

"Watch," David says.

Kate watches. There is no music to soften the sharp edges of this performance, no pink filters to highlight it, no applause or whistles or cheers for accent. An uneasy silence—a cough, the clearing of a throat, nervous whispers, the sound close by her of men breathing as if they have been climbing or running—settles in the darkened tent; the path of light is a cylinder Sharita stands at the center of, her hips moving suggestively, her head back, the hand holding the cigarette falling slowly until it stops below her belly. As her hand drops, the circle of light grows smaller; now it is scarcely a foot in diameter, glowing on her thighs, her shaved mound, the burning cigarette in her right hand. Kate *knows* what is going to happen.

Sharita brings the cigarette between her legs—her knees parted and bent, so that the intimacy, the near relationship of her body with its admirers, is closer still—and separating the petals of her sex with the fingers of her left hand she inserts the unlit end of the cigarette with her right. She takes her hands away; the cigarette remains. Then, even though Sharita seems to do nothing, Kate sees the tip of the cigarette glow orange. In the tent no one is talking, no one moving. This is horrid, Kate thinks.

But there is no way she can move, hemmed in as she is by men on every side, in front and in back of her. In this crowded space she can feel a collective intake of breath, a collective tensing of muscles that carry her along in spite of her will. She claws at the cap that holds her hair out of sight and pulls it over her face. The cap smells like her father, but it is darkness and a mask of protection from the garish performance on stage. Her hair spills down to her shoulders.

"Hello, sweetheart," says a voice behind her. "Wish you was up there, do you?"

Kate pushes the cap back into place and presses her face against David's shoulder. "Please," she says. "Please."

By now Sharita has removed the cigarette and holds it at arm's length.

"Who wants it?" she says. Her voice is hoarse, flat.

A half-dozen hands reach out; she gives the cigarette into one of them. Meanwhile, the spotlight is unwavering, fixed between her thighs. With an abrupt forward thrust of her pelvis—it happens together with a sound she makes—a puff of gray smoke expels itself from her sex and drifts over her audience in the shape of an imperfect circle.

Sharita sinks to her knees and sits back on her heels, the spotlight enlarging to bathe all of her. She spreads her arms and bows her head into the hoots and laughter and clapping of the men. *Hiding her face.* Kate pushes at David, pummels his arm. She wants to run away, but she is afraid if she opens her mouth to tell him so, she will be sick in front of all of them. So she pushes dumbly at David, trying to steer him through the crowd and out through the flap of the tent.

"What's the matter with you?" David pushes back to maintain his balance. "Wasn't that something?"

She shakes her head and shoves harder. The men are still crowded against the stage, Sharita is still on her knees, thighs opened; they're wild animals, Kate thinks, watching them ravenous between the woman's legs. The barker has resumed the stage and is taking more money; she can see fives, tens, from raised hands, smiling, talking—my God, Kate thinks, is there another curtain, another horror?—but she can't force her mind to take it in.

At last David understands and begins to work his way out, opening a path for her. Outdoors in the cool dusk she runs to the side of the tent furthest from the lighted midway and takes her hand away from her mouth; she doesn't vomit, but her stomach is churning as if she ought to and her throat holds a harsh, sour taste. She can feel cold sweat on her forehead and under her false clothing.

* * *

David stands beside her, looking at her. She takes off the black cap and gives it to him. She feels a little better, though if she closes her eyes she can see vividly that ugly apricot pouting open to discharge its dirty smoke ring, the laughing men eager to inhale the smoke that has come from the angry woman with her tight fists outspread.

"I'm all right," she says.

David shoves her cap into his pocket. "Really, wasn't that something?"

"It made me sick," she says. "Where was that policeman? Why didn't he stop it?"

"Well, it's a little weird," he says, "but I thought it was neat stuff, all the same."

"What were they doing to her—those men down front—after she gave back the cigarette?"

"I don't know," David says. "Some kind of sex."

"It was awful. It's the worst thing I've ever seen in my whole life."

"I think you're exaggerating," he says.

Kate realizes they are walking not toward the carnival entrance, but behind the tent where Sharita has danced—David with his hands in his pockets, looking not at Kate but at the ground ahead of him. "Maybe that small space got to you a little is all. Maybe you're claustrophobic."

"It was horrible, David. How can you like it?" Now his hand is on her arm, her shoulder, steering her. "Where are we going?"

"I couldn't help liking it."

Now he's stopped her. They are out of sight of everybody, in a corner of The Meadows where no lights shine, behind a trailer that looms over her. She can't believe what he thinks he's doing, but she knows she should keep talking.

"God, David, I didn't think my disguise was so perfect you'd forget I'm not a boy."

"No—I only, I thought—" How unlike him to stammer. "Didn't you just put yourself in her place when she was doing—those things?"

"You mean imagine I was her?" He's facing her, one hand holding her left shoulder, the other hand around her right wrist.

"Yes." Pulling her hand.

"Poking things inside myself? Showing myself?" What is the matter with him?

"You could imagine this. Couldn't you?"

Kate feels a chill.

"Imagine what?"

"Touching me." He holds her hand between his legs—somehow he has exposed himself, has made her touch the curious flesh she has only seen that once in Darryl's pictures—and she wonders, like a bird trapped inside a room, what she should do. "Please," David says.

They are in a blank world—no houses she can run to, no people to cry out to. A million miles away, the merry-go-round is playing "Tea for Two." "David, don't," she says. "Don't make me do this."

"Kate? Come on. Please." He has both hands on her shoulders, trying to drag her down, wanting her—she realizes this—on her knees. "Do it to me. You know how."

"No." She tries to push him, tries to break the pressure of his hands and arms. She wants to hide. She wants to run away, to go home and be alone. Who would have imagined this nice boy saying and doing such things. "David, please don't make me."

"God, Kate, I'm so crazy for you." His voice breaks, changes registers. "Please. I'm begging you."

"I won't." She screams it: "I won't!" He's gotten her to kneel on the cold ground, forcing himself against her face. *He ought to be naked; he ought to be wearing black socks.* She feels the heat of him, smells the smell of him, like sweat, like mildew. Then from a distance between his legs she sees a flicker of light—a man carrying a flashlight.

"Hey, you two," the man says. "What the f-fuck is this?"

The man breaks into a run and pulls David away from her, turns him so he can shine the flashlight in his face. Kate crawls away in the direction of the trailer. She manages to stand, then leans against the cold metal.

"She's my girlfriend," David says.

"No!" Kate screams. The word has come unbidden—a reflex denying whatever it is David imagines he is to her. "I'm nothing."

"What's wrong with you, k-kid?" Coggio says. "You're the s-same one was hanging around here yesterday. You got s-sex on the brain or s-something? Why'n't you just go home and j-jack off?"

"This is none of your business." David breaks loose and stands uncertainly between Kate and the stranger, hands crossed in front of himself. "I wasn't doing anything."

Coggio flicks the light in Kate's direction, then back onto David. "You b-better get out of here," he says. "Or this t-time I'll call the c-cops on you."

David hesitates for another moment, looking at Kate as if he expects her to say something that will change the world for him, but she is mute. She realizes she is shaking, not from cold but from anger, from disappointment. The whole adventure of the carnival and the dancer and the disguise that, if nothing else, was to test her as an actress—all of it is ruined. To think she brought this on herself.

"Kate?" David says.

"Go home," Kate says. "Just go home and don't talk to me."

And finally he leaves—slowly at first, a boy walking away in no special direction, and then he begins to run. In no time he has turned a corner behind the Sharita tent and vanished.

Kate watches, hugs herself. Now what? The man—she recognizes him as the ticket taker inside the tent—comes toward her and plays the light—briefly, politely—across her face.

"That's more like it," he tells her. "You're p-prettier with your hair d-down."

"I wondered if you knew," Kate says. "When you let me pass."

"I'm slow," Coggio says, "but I ain't b-blind."

"I wish you'd stopped me."

"Because of your b-boyfriend? I thought it was some k-kind of g-game." He switches the flashlight off; the only light now is from the concessions at the center of the carnival. "You okay?"

She straightens her clothes and runs her fingers through her hair. "Guess what," she says. "His father's a minister."

13.

Coggio helps Kate into the trailer. She lets herself be led without giving it any particular thought, except that if she leaves The Meadows now, David might be waiting, might renew his pressure on her to do what he so badly seems to want. She stands unsteadily in the middle of a small kitchen—a stove, an icebox, a narrow table beside her like the one in her parents' breakfast nook.

The dancer, Sharita herself, comes into the trailer. Her costume, what there is of it, she flings across a low bed at the far end of the trailer. She looks tired, carries herself like a woman who aches in her bones. If she notices Kate, she doesn't acknowledge her, but instead goes to a narrow closet by the bed and puts on a pink robe she ties together with a frayed pink belt. Chenille, it looks like.

"I didn't know where you'd got to," Sherrie says to Coggio. "It's a good thing matters didn't get any worse for me. One of these days those apes are going to climb up onto the stage and murder me."

Now she looks at Kate. "What's this?" she says.

"Your boyfriend's g-ginch," Coggio says. "He's got s-sex on the brain. This one n-needed rescuing." He steers Kate toward the breakfast table. "She was at the after."

Sherrie gives Kate the once-over. "You couldn't see she was a lady—and just a kid at that?"

"She had her hair p-pushed under a cap. I don't qu-quiz the customers like your D-Doctor I.Q."

"I'm sorry," Kate says. "I shouldn't have gone behind the curtain."

"And miss my dancing?" Sherrie touches her elbow. "Here. Sit."

"May I?"

Sherrie presses. "This isn't 'Simon says.' Sit down and take a load off."

Kate sits at the table and rests on her elbows. "Thank you."

Sherrie goes to the icebox beside the small kitchen sink and takes out two green bottles. She opens both and sets one in front of Kate.

"I don't know if you drink," she says.

Kate shakes her head. "I don't."

"Then this is for Frank." Sherrie passes the bottle to Coggio, who takes a long swallow and leans against the kitchen counter.

Sherrie sits across from Kate. "Why don't you take that outside," she tells Coggio. "Sit on the steps and drink it in the cool of the evening while us girls get acquainted."

Frank shrugs. "Why not?" he says, as much to himself as to Sherrie, and slips out into the darkness.

* * *

First stepping inside the trailer, Kate had been in a kind of daze. Then as Sherrie moved about the place, opening the icebox, offering the drink, crossing the floor to sit at the table, her reflection in the polished metal of the curved ceiling was a dazzle of color and light. It was like being able to walk inside a child's kaleidoscope— Kate had such a toy when she was in kindergarten—or entering some medieval palace carved out of brilliant ice. Watching Coggio leave, she has kept one eye on the ceiling, seeing herself mirrored there—the pale balloon of her face shimmering, the gray jacket like a disturbance of water, her bare hands slender fishes swimming to the table with its flowered settees likewise reflected overhead—and Coggio leaving the trailer like a shark gliding away.

"It's a fairyland," she tells Sherrie. "I'd never have guessed the inside looked like this."

"You love it, then you hate it, then finally you get used to it," Sherrie says. "When the lights are on, it's too damned much. I'd like to paint the ceiling black, or some flat color, but Frank doesn't want to take the trouble."

"I can see how it might keep you awake."

Sherrie shifts in her seat, leans on the table. "Come to think of it," she says. "I do believe there's Orange Crush in the icebox. Have a look-see."

It's a welcome suggestion. Kate is surprised at how thirsty she is, how dry her mouth, and she thinks it must have something to do with shock, or fear, or both.

The contents of the icebox are meager: more ale bottles, a half-loaf of white bread, jars of mayonnaise and jam, and a couple of small items wrapped in butcher paper.

"When you go to college," Sherrie is saying, "then you'll have to learn to be a beer drinker."

"So I'm told," Kate says. She pushes the mayonnaise jar aside. "I can't find any tonic."

"Look in the ice compartment."

Kate opens the smaller door. A block of ice, blue-gray and glistening, takes up much of the space, but here are two bottles of

Orange Crush, leaned against the ice into melted cradles of their own shape. Reaching for the nearest one, her hand encounters something that is neither glass nor ice.

She pulls her hand away. "My gosh," she says. "Is that the snake?"

Sherrie stands beside her and reaches into the darkness of the ice compartment. Kate steps back as the snake emerges.

"It's really real," Kate says.

"What did you think?" Sherrie slides the snake's head around the back of her neck and closes the icebox door. The snake seems docile—like a sleeping pet, Kate thinks, but as Sherrie jostles it, its eyes open and it flicks its tongue in Kate's direction. "Don't be scared. He can't hardly move, he's so cooled down."

"I was surprised. That's all."

"He takes some getting used to." She lets the snake curl around her right arm and across her chest to her left shoulder. "Imagine me dancing with a real live serpent?"

"I'm not sure," Kate says. But then, she would never have imagined what Sharita really did do.

"I kind of have to be in the mood," Sherrie says. "When Frank first got the idea of putting a snake in the act, I said huh-uh, not on your tintype; I'm not going in for any of that geeky stuff. But you know, he wanted the act to look like the billboard out front. So far I've used it a couple of times. Not here, but a month ago in Worcester, last week in Bangor. It's not dangerous—and it sure does give 'em a charge."

"I can see that." Though from the looks of tonight's crowd, Kate imagines it's Sharita—and nudity, and the awful cigarette—that provides the charge.

"It's a kind of iffy thing," Sherrie says. She pats her belly. "They look for holes they can hide in."

The picture crosses Kate's mind only for a repulsive instant. "That's awful."

"Oh, Sweetie," Sherrie says. "I forget myself." She holds the snake out to Kate. "You can pet him. He won't hurt you."

Kate touches the snake behind its head, strokes it tentatively. The skin is smooth and dry, not what she expected. "What's its name?"

"We've never named him. He's just 'snake.' Ain't he cool to the touch? A good hot-weather pet, I'd say."

"What's he eat?"

"Mice, mostly. He don't eat a lot. Once a week or so Frank has to find a pet store and buy a couple of live ones. I don't watch the dinner service." She slides the head of the snake behind Kate's back and steers it over her shoulder. "Here. Get acquainted."

Now Kate has the full weight of the snake across her back, its head lying along her right arm. It barely moves, but it's like someone stroking her, petting her—as if she were an animal owned. She wonders if in a way this is what Sherrie is doing: capturing her, owning her, making her a temporary possession.

"It makes me uncomfortable," Kate says. The tonic bottle is in her right hand and she uses her left to nudge the snake's head away from it. "It feels—eerie."

"But ain't it nice?" Sherrie says.

"In a way. It's okay."

Sherrie rescues her, lifting the snake away and carrying it to the icebox. Kate watches her feed the length of snake into the ice compartment, where it lets itself be pushed against the block of ice that will make it lethargic again. This is nothing like Eden.

"But I don't like dancing with it. Frank sticks it under the curtain and pretends it's talking, then it's back on ice. I want no part of the snake if I can help it."

Kate sits at the table. Sherrie opens the Orange Crush for her, settles across from her and takes a long swallow of ale.

"Now," she says. "Tell me what the boy did to you."

* * *

"I don't think David intended to hurt me," Kate says. "He just wanted me to do—to do something to him." She knows the name, both the slang and the Latin, and she knows how it's done—can see still it happening in her mind's eye—because of Darryl's pictures. She isn't sure why she can't say either of the words in front of this woman who is so worldly.

"To him or *for* him?"

"I guess both." She hesitates. "I can't say what. You got him excited. Your dancing." How to explain the way he behaved—the expression of his eyes when they reflected the small light of the carnival? "That sex thing."

"And you weren't ready for that," Sherrie says. "But that's men." She takes a swallow from the bottle, points the neck of it toward the door of the trailer. "Now Frank," she says, "he's never been like that. He doesn't so much think of himself as he thinks of what's right and proper. You wouldn't know it to look at him, but Frank is in favor of order."

"I think David is too—but it's an order that puts him in the center of it. He takes after his father."

"Frank is selfish sometimes," Sherrie says, "but usually he's selfish on behalf of me."

"That's neat," Kate says. "That's caring."

"He was my rescuer, you know."

Sherrie smiles at the thought, and Kate looks forward to the story. She's feeling better now—calm, almost relaxed in this bright, shimmering Airstream castle. She'll have her own stories to tell: about David's lust, about the snake and what it feels like to the touch, about getting to be friends with a carnival dancer.

"I'd been with Joe Connors almost five years. I hadn't seen the man forever, but he'd showed up and talked me into marrying him and settling down in Connecticut. He worked for Pratt & Whitney and I was supposed to be the homemaker. Cook his meals, do his wash, spread for him every time he opened his fly. And all this while—the five years going on six—he'd got rougher on me and more abusive.

"Don't get me wrong. Rough sex is okay by me, within reason. I don't mind hard push and shove, so long as it's pleasure for both parties. Sometimes, if you don't know you're being loved, maybe you ain't—like the feller says.

"But Joe—"

Sherrie pauses. Kate wonders if her fascination, which already borders on horror, is showing, and if Sharita will stop—not finish the story. Kate doesn't want the story interrupted, doesn't want to miss its ending. When they talk about drama in Thespis, Miss Samways talks about *catharsis*. Kate wants catharsis.

"Joe was all about Joe," Sherrie is saying. "The way your David is all about David. We've got to ask ourselves, we women, how on God's green earth do we get hooked up with these men who want us on our knees in front of them, even if they have to knock us down to put us there? That was Joe. All for him, none for me. Once, he held me down and burned his initial on me with his cigarette. 'Just so you know who owns you,' he told me. 'J for Joseph.'"

"That's so evil," Kate says. David would never grow up to do such a thing—would he?

"It healed," Sherrie says. "You can see it if you're looking for it, just below the nipple."

She parts the robe to show her left breast. The letter is a faint pink outline, slightly bigger than an inch.

"If anybody asks," Sherrie says, "I tell them it's J for Jesus. That's what I tell myself."

Kate wants to ask about Sharita's anklet, but this is not the right time. The path to catharsis is what's more important.

"How did you get away from him?"

"All those years, I hadn't really kept track of my old friend Frank Coggio, but after the cigarette business—never mind all the times Joe'd slapped me around—Frank started to seem like the only hope I had. I didn't have a car of my own. I didn't have any money of my own saved up. I didn't know a soul. When you're a stay-home wife, what do you have to fall back on?

"You can't work, except vacuuming and cleaning the toilet. You don't get out of the house except maybe to go to the grocery. Most of the time you stay home to keep company with the radio set—'Ma Perkins' and 'Vic and Sade'; those are your friends. And what good are they?

"So then I started looking for Frank. While Joe was at work, I was on the telephone. I didn't know if Frank was still with Railway Express, but I hoped he was. I called the company office in Syracuse, which was the last place I knew he'd been a driver, and they said he'd been transferred to Boston. But when I called Boston, they said he'd quit. They thought he'd taken a defense job somewhere—this was right at the start of the war—so he could make more money.

"Then I got lucky. There was a guy in the Boston office who'd known Frank. He said he thought Frank had gone down to Maine to take a job at the Bath Iron Works, building destroyers for the Navy. I thought, 'Frank building ships? That's some change.'"

"Is that where you found him?"

"Sure enough." Sherrie drains the Narragansett bottle. "Then all I had to do was persuade him to come and get me—but that was the easiest part."

"Frank loves you," Kate says.

"I don't believe you'd get him to admit that," Sherrie says.

"But don't you worry that your husband will find you?"

"All the time, Sweetie. All the time." She hugs the robe tighter around her shoulders. "And you can bet on it: he will. It's just a matter of *when*."

Both women are silent now. Kate can't know what Sharita is thinking—what buried fear she must feel—but what Kate thinks is that it was nervy of her to announce "Frank loves you" so abruptly. Yet she's certain it's true—intuits it—in the same way her mother is able to read her own emotions.

"Tell me about your anklet," she says, abrupt again. "I noticed it first thing."

"My anklet? My gold chain?"

"It says *Love*." She wonders if she's saying that David put the two together—love and sex—and that explains what he tried to do.

"It's not a dirty word."

"I know."

"But you think about it?"

"Sometimes."

Sherrie gets up from the table as if she's restless. "Everybody needs it," she says.

"So they say."

"Don't let the boy put you off it, just because boys aren't as smart about it. They have to catch up."

"I don't know if boys ever catch up, even when they're men. My mother..." She hesitates, thinking of her parents, their odd connections.

Sherrie stops behind Kate's chair. "Your mother what?"

"Nothing." If she speaks for her mother, is that a betrayal? A disloyalty?

She feels Sherrie's hands caressing the long hair over her neck and shoulders.

"Gorgeous hair," Sherrie says.

"My mother doesn't seem to miss love." There; she's said it, to change the subject. "She doesn't mind being alone."

"Your daddy left her?" She takes her hands away from Kate and comes back to the table.

"No. No, not that. He travels."

"Ah."

"It's all right when he's home. If he stays long enough, we forget he was ever gone."

"No, baby, no." Sherrie says it sadly. "Maybe we forgive them being gone, but we never forget the loneliness."

* * *

"We could be sisters," Sherrie is saying. "When I was a girl, I had beautiful long hair like yours, down over my shoulders like a great silky hood. Men love hair like that."

"I know," Kate says.

"And you know it's not always a good thing when men admire your hair. It touches something in them. Something base." Sherrie lights a cigarette. "I could tell you stories," she says.

"Boys say my name in the streets," Kate says. "If they don't know my name, some of them call me Rapunzel." The first time that happened, she'd been amazed. How did this kind of boy know that kind of fairy tale?

"They can't wait to get their hands on you, I bet," Sherrie says.

"I guess."

"What does your father think? When he's home from his travels."

The question perplexes her. "What does he think about what?"

"Your long, pretty hair."

"Oh. He likes it. He says it will be a shame if I ever decide to wear it shorter."

Sherrie takes a long drag on the cigarette. "Men," she says.

The word hangs in the air between them like an accusation, like the blue smoke that in this confined space irritates Kate's nostrils, that makes her want to sneeze.

"My daddy liked long hair too," Sherrie says. "He never lived to see the bad of it."

"What happened to him?"

"Killed in the war. Not this last war, but the one before it. He was a doughboy—that's what they used to call soldiers—and he died in France." She puffs on the cigarette, exhales the smoke toward Kate. "He's buried there. The army sent my mother a medal."

"It must have been terrible not to have a father," Kate says.

"His brother Calvin was in the same regiment, and he survived. Along with the medal, we got Calvin. He moved in with us, shared the bedroom with my mother. He was my make-believe daddy. I was twelve."

"My father was in the Army Air Corps," Kate says. "In this war. He was lucky."

"And you were lucky too," Sherrie says, "to get him back in one piece."

"At least you got a make-believe father."

"'At least' is right. Calvin was no prize. He'd been gassed—mustard gas, he told us—and he wheezed when he talked. He couldn't work, so he was always around the house." She crushed the half-smoked cigarette butt into the saucer in front of her. "He was the first of the bothering men in my life."

How did he bother you? Kate wants to ask, but she thinks it would be rude, and so she keeps still. She tries to see, in the woman across from her, the Sharita of twelve, thirteen—the school girl with long reddish-brown hair, a whole generation before Kate—but it isn't easy. The woman in her forties uses some kind of rinse that leaves her hair a harsh shade of orange; the hair is shoulder-short. Her skin is pale, though the eyes and mouth are heavy with makeup, and where the lapels of her pink robe lie open, the V of skin is darker and coarser. Kate sees no innocence, no trace of little-girlness. Will this happen to Kate? Will the girl she is today disappear into a woman so different, she cannot even imagine her?

Her eyes follow the robe downward to where it falls open to show the woman's bare legs. Sherrie has dancer's legs, shapely but with prominent muscle behind the calves; looking at them now, and remembering the tent performance, Kate decides the legs are the youngest thing about her. One of the virtues of exercise, she supposes.

And the anklet: *Love*.

"Do you ever take it off?" Kate asks.

Sherrie wrinkles her forehead. "Take what off?"

"The anklet."

Her brow clears. "Oh, that." She stubs out the cigarette in the saucer she uses as an ashtray. "I hardly think about it. Frank gave it to me after my rescue. And it's true: I've never had it off."

"It must mean a lot to you." *It's a gift from Frank. I was right about him.*

"It's never turned my ankle green," Sherrie says. "That means something to a girl—to know it's the real thing."

Kate smiles. In eighth grade a boy gave her a necklace that used to leave a thin green mark on her neck in hot weather; all the more reason she didn't care when eventually it was stolen. "I meant that love must really mean a lot to you," she says.

"It's important." She pulls the robe together and holds the lapels closed. "Too bad it's so rare in the world."

"That's what my mother says."

Sherrie looks over at the clock on the stove. "Look at the time," she says. "It's nearly midnight. I'll get Frank to drive you home."

14.

As soon as Kate comes into the front hall, her mother is standing at the head of the stairs. She's in her blue nightgown, but she doesn't look as if she's been asleep. She holds a book in her left hand; her right is resting on the newel post.

"Where in the world," are the first words out of her mouth. "Where in the world have you been," not angry but relieved, "and why on earth are you being brought home in an old truck?"

"You knew where I was," Kate says. "I was at the carnival."

"Until a quarter to midnight? What was David thinking?"

"I don't know what he was thinking." This is sadly true. She wonders if she'll be able to bring herself to tell what's happened to her—or what might have happened, if not for Frank Coggio.

Mother takes a step downward, but stops. "Are you all right?" A first note of concern has colored her words.

"I'm fine." And now that she's home, she believes she is. Terrible David is far behind her, way on the other side of a performer who calls herself Sharita and whose bruises are worse than Kate's will ever be. "I have lots to tell you."

"Turn out the lights," her mother says, "and come up."

Kate turns off the porch light and climbs the stairs, switches off the upstairs light and goes to her room. She flings the windbreaker onto the bed, slips out of the work shirt, and bends toward the dresser mirror to assess the damage on her bare skin. David held her shoulders so hard, his fingers have left faint bruises high on her back and one more visible bruise on the front of each arm. They don't hurt, but she knows with a little time they'll turn yellowish-purple before they fade away. Damn David, she thinks.

"Well, did they think you were male?" Her mother is in the doorway, still looking anxious.

Kate hugs herself, hiding the bruises. "Some did," she says. "Some didn't."

"Are you glad you went?"

"Up to a point." She pulls the tube top over her head and tosses it to the bed, slides her pajamas out from under the pillow and puts on the jacket. Buttoning it, she is turned away from her mother, waiting. How much of the night she can tell, she isn't sure. Mother would want to shut David out of her life, but Kate isn't ready for that. Doesn't David need a chance to explain himself?

"What happened?" Her mother comes into the room and sits on Kate's bed.

"Nothing." She sits beside her mother, unlaces the shoes and kicks them off. "I guess you could just say it was a hectic night."

Mother leans toward her. "You reek of cigarette smoke. You'll have to wash your hair in the morning."

"I will."

And then, for no reason she can imagine, neither at this moment or when she looks back on it, she begins to cry. She hasn't cried in front of her mother since she was eleven and Daddy went

away to the war, and here she is, like a baby, letting her mother hold
her and stroke her hair while the tears stream down her face.

"God, Mother," says, the words broken between sobs, "it's such
a man's world. It makes me so sick."

"Hush, Katie," her mother says. "Hush."

"Why can't Daddy be here?" Kate doesn't know where *that* came
from, as if the presence of the important man in her life makes the
"man's world" more bearable. Where's the logic of that?

"Tomorrow," Mother says. "He'll be here tomorrow."

"He's never here at the right time. He should be here today."
Still sniffling, and the picture in her mind isn't of her father, but of
David forcing her down to her knees, pulling her face toward him.
And the smell of him—that's what comes back to her now in a rush
of bad memory. "How can he bear to stay away from you?"

Her mother is quiet, holding Kate against her, stroking her hair.
In a peculiar way, Kate realizes she has managed to find a way to begin
to get over what David has done; all she has to do is take control of
herself the way she always has—by focusing on her parents' marriage.

"You deserve better," she says.

"Dear Kate," her mother says. "Why do you fight your father?
You're being so emotional."

"It just makes me mad." Anger at Daddy is slowly pushing out
her anger at David. "He so neglects you."

"When your father is on the road, I don't think about him," her
mother says. If anything, her embrace of Kate tightens; Mother's
voice is gentle, her lips warm against Kate's cheek. "I'd drive myself
crazy at first—when he first started traveling for GE I made him
telephone me every night from wherever he was. I had to hear his
voice. Had to know he was safe."

"What's different? Don't you miss him now?"

"Oh, honey. You were just a baby then. I wasn't used to being alone, and it took some getting, I don't know—*acclimated*. But after a while, I got stronger. And more patient, taking care of you.

"Time went on, and I began to realize that it was a mixed blessing—his calling me every night."

"The phone bills, I bet," Kate says.

She can imagine her mother's smile. "That was the least of it. The most was that it got me really down after I'd talked with him. Yes, I'd be relieved when the phone rang. Hearing his voice would lift me."

"I talked to him too, sometimes."

"That's right. You did. I'd put you on the line and he'd tell you stories that made you giggle."

"Not *real* stories," Kate says. "Mostly he told me what he'd had for supper—but he tried to make the food sound funny. Like he'd say, 'I had macaroni and fleas tonight' or 'I had dinner at the leaning tower of pizza.' Silly stuff like that."

"You see," her mother says, "he isn't an ogre. He doesn't leave us women alone because he wants to."

Kate slips out of her mother's arms and sits straight. She can feel the tears drying on her face, and with the palms of her hands tries to rub them away. "I suppose," she says.

"You hold your father to much too high a standard," her mother says. "You seem to think he's a cog in the General Electric machine and nothing else. I guess I see a side of him that you don't see."

"If you mean the side that goes to the Conroys' and plays canasta, I don't think that counts."

"No, I don't mean anything of the sort. I mean his romantic side."

Kate snorts. "You couldn't prove it by me," she says.

"And don't be disrespectful, just because your father isn't here to speak for himself."

"Tell me one romantic thing Daddy has ever done."

"I could tell you a dozen things," Mother says. "But I'll tell you my favorite." She isn't looking at Kate, but seems to have her gaze fixed on some point in the distance—or perhaps she isn't looking at anything at all. She has a kind of grin on her face, and she has her arms, empty of Kate, crossed to hug herself as she talks.

"Tell," Kate says.

"Once," her mother says, "it was only a year or so ago. Your father was in Chicago, on a business trip with some other GE executives, and one night after he'd had dinner, he and a couple of the men went to the nightclub at the hotel where the company put them up. The club had some kind of Latin entertainment—dancers with castanets and musicians with maracas, and a guitarist who was quite famous."

"What was the hotel?" Kate wants to know.

"I don't know, dear. I think the Ambassador, but it's not important."

"I'm sorry. Go on." As if details—names of people and places—weren't important. She'd never forget the dancer—Sharita—or the man she shared a trailer with, named... She has to think. *Frank.*

"This particular night I'd already gone to bed. It was about one in the morning—and I'd fallen asleep with the book I was reading still open in my lap—when the telephone rang. I thought *What in the world?*"

"And it was Daddy," Kate says.

"And it was your father, sure enough."

"What did he want at that hour? Just to say good night?"

Mother shakes her head. "Eventually he said good night, but the first thing he said was, 'Listen to this.' The next sound I heard was a guitar, playing some kind of flamenco rhythm. Your father had dragged this guitar player all the way from the floor show into a phone booth in the lobby, and made the poor man play for me—all the way from Chicago. Can you imagine?"

"I'm not sure. What was the significance of the music? Did you used to be a flamenco dancer?"

"Oh, your father and I had gone to a Tyrone Power movie once, just before the war started, and I'd raved about the music. It was a film about bullfighting, and the music was the kind that's so passionate it seems to get in your blood. It was thrilling, and your father knew how much I liked it, so he called me up to give me a concert."

"And that's your idea of 'romantic'?"

"Oh, sweetie," her mother says. "You just don't know."

No, Kate tells herself, I guess I don't.

* * *

"Talk to me," Kate says. "Talk to me about when I was young."

"You're still young," Mother says.

And that was parents, wasn't it? They deflected you; they turned aside their children's wishes, questions, wants. It was as if they were afraid they might reveal something that—what? Something that diminished them in the children's eyes? Here she was, home after the worst night of her life, and her mother was teasing her.

"About when I was a baby. You know. The way you did that time we were visiting Grandma and the three of us were sitting in the kitchen after Saturday supper."

It must have been a Saturday, Kate tells herself, because supper was franks and beans. She remembers that evening vividly because both her mother and grandmother had drunk a glass of wine with the meal—red wine—and they were slightly tipsy; Mother's cheeks and forehead were flushed, and Grandma kept giggling over the things Mother was saying. How old was Kate then? She must have been ten or eleven. The war was on; Daddy was in the army. Yes, Grandpa had just died—that was it: the three of them had come home from his funeral and made an easy supper; the wine was like saying their goodbyes.

Her mother sighs. "Really, Kate."

"Come on," she coaxes. "It'll cheer us both up. Especially me."

Because she thinks it will, that it will take her mind off David and Mother's mind off being left alone. That was the way it had been, the day of Grandpa's funeral. Mother and Kate had taken Grandma back into a happier world, made her forget for a little while that she'd just buried the man she'd loved and lived with for her whole grownup life.

"You were a sweet child," her mother says now. "Nothing like the way you've turned out."

"Don't tease. Tell it from the beginning and don't lie."

Her mother slides herself to the head of Kate's bed and pats the space beside her. Kate brings her legs up and props herself against the headboard next to Mother. She likes the gesture—the invitation. It means they are friends and allies, not just mother and daughter.

"Your first appearance was not pleasant," Mother says. "I guess you didn't really want to be born. Finally the doctor had to induce labor, and it was a hard, hard birth. The most painful thing that ever happened to me. I hated you. I hated the doctor—"

"What was his name?"

"Dupré. Harold Dupré. He was fresh out of medical school and he kept saying, 'Give it your best, Mrs. Meredith. Give it your best,'" and I kept pushing and screaming that I couldn't give any more than I was already giving. I think I probably swore at him too. Oh my, how I hated that man."

"And me."

"And you. And especially I hated your father. Even inside the pain I kept hating him, kept thinking *How could he have planted this agony inside me?*" Her mother squeezes Kate's hand. "Oh, it was a peach of a scene—like living in a horror movie."

"But I got born."

"Well of course you did."

"Because here I am," Kate says.

"And once you were out in the world," Mother says, "I really think you tried to make it up to me for all the pain you'd caused me."

"How did I do that?"

"You were just the sweetest child imaginable. You slept through the night almost from the beginning. You hardly ever cried. When it came time to wean you, you took to the bottle like a little drunkard."

"What does that mean: 'wean'?"

"To go from mother's milk to formula," Mother says. "To stop needing something you were dependent on. You knew that."

"I forgot." It isn't as if it was a word that came up very often. "You can't expect me to remember every word I've ever heard."

But she would remember it now. Maybe she could wean herself off David—just in case tonight's was the *real* David.

* * *

Kate wakes up at first light, for a moment thinking she is in her mother's bed, then remembering it's her own bed and Mother must have left when she fell asleep—the smell of her mother's cologne lingering on the pillow.

How lucky she is to have a mother who is patient and doesn't ask questions, who is willing to wait until Kate chooses her own time to tell the whole awful story. They must have been up together until two or three a.m., her mother finally going downstairs to Daddy's study and coming back with the family scrapbook. Snapshots dating back to the nineteen-thirties, when Kate was a baby. Katie in her crib; Katie at the beach in a flowered sun hat; Katie in her wicker baby carriage with her kitten. My cat Carmody. A short-haired female, gray with white socks. Daddy had brought Carmody home when Kate was three months old—there was a date notation under the scrapbook snapshot—and girl and cat, practically the same age, had been almost inseparable until they were both twelve years old, though Mother wouldn't let Carmody sleep with her because "cats take your breath."

When Kate was three, Carmody slipped out the door and stayed away for a week. It wasn't too long after that Carmody gave birth to five impossibly small kittens behind the furnace in the cellar. Mother and Daddy both insisted Kate watch: the emergence of the babies, the slimy afterbirth, Carmody licking away all traces of the time they had spent in the wet dark of the womb. Years later, when Kate was told how babies came into the world, it was the event of Carmody's kittens that first informed her imagining of her own arrival into the world. Now, of course, she had refined the image: it wasn't as easy as cats, and it was a different kind of messiness.

After that, after the kittens had opened their eyes and started eating from saucers and—finally—been given away to an assortment of playmates and neighbors, Daddy took Carmody to a vet to be spayed. Then there was no worry about letting the cat outside, no danger of kittens. "We really wanted her to have one litter," Mother had said. "It seemed the right thing. But more than one..." And Daddy had laughed and remarked how the Meredith family would run out of friends to give kittens to. "Then we'd have to put them in a sack and drown them," he said, "and that wouldn't be pleasant."

Kate has wondered more than once what Mother's reasoning was for wanting Carmody to have "one litter"? Did she think the cat wouldn't be "fulfilled" if it missed motherhood? Was Mother fulfilled by Kate—never mind the apparently awful pain involved? Sometimes, too, she wonders if she ended up as an only child because Daddy didn't want to have to drown her siblings.

But once it was "safe" for Carmody to have the run of the outdoors, her problems were just beginning. First there were fights, and Kate, growing up, supposed it was possible—though how and why could she have arrived at such a possibility?—that Carmody fought with the tom who had sired her single litter of kittens. As the adult world became more complicated—behavior that was cute when she was three, for example, was forbidden when she was five—she began to borrow human motives to account for natural occurrences. In the matter of Carmody's quarrels, her bites and cuts, her torn eartips, her abscesses, it was easy to imagine jealousies and rivalries; it was even possible to ascribe to Carmody's tomcat the sort of rage a human father would feel if his children were put up for adoption without his approval.

Kate's mother seemed partly amused and partly offended by her theories. "Carmody is a cat, a dumb animal," she would say. "What concerns her are eating and sleeping and a safe place to do both. She's not emotional, not complicated. For heaven's sake, Kathryn, she's only a cat."

* * *

Carmody has been gone from her life a long time. It was a loss rarely mentioned in the Meredith home, because it was a loss that probably could have been prevented. Kate thinks now, after returning the scrapbook to its proper place in her father's study, that human indifference had killed Carmody—a simple and unforgivable matter of not noticing the poor cat's difficulties.

Fleas. Nothing as noticeable as a torn ear or an abscess, and nothing to be taken seriously. You see the cat scratching herself, you dust her with flea powder. Problem solved. Except that the powder didn't do the job, the flea problem got out of control, the house— carpets, drapes, bed linens—was infested. Carmody was miserable, Kate's mother and father were at wit's end.

The last day of Carmody's life: Kate can even now close her eyes and see old Doc Jackson pick the cat up, roughly, by the nape of the neck, force her into a burlap potato sack, and tie the top of the sack with twine. Doc Jackson was one of Scoggin's two veterinarians, a stout, stoop-shouldered man with a red face and a bulbous nose. Kate's father called him "W. C. Fields's unfunny cousin" because the man was known to drink. For Kate, watching the vet walk away with the burlap sack dancing against his leg while Carmody struggled inside, Doc Jackson was the ogre of her dreams ever after. She had never cried so much in her life—she was nine—and if her parents from time to time suggested getting another cat, she would scream "No!" and begin sobbing all over again. She persuaded herself that she hates cats—as a way of protection against another such loss. She doesn't dream often of Carmody, but even now she sometimes has nightmares that include a murderous veterinarian, drunk and bloody-handed.

15.

Tuesday is Hell for David. The plans that he has looked forward to all summer, walking to school with Kate, maybe even holding hands so kids passing them on the York Utilities bus that runs back and forth between Scoggin and North Scoggin will see them and start the gossip both he and Kate will pretend to be embarrassed by, but will really be proud of; now and then begging permission to take his father's Chevy so they can drive smugly past their pedestrian classmates—those plans went down the drain last night outside the Paradise tent. In fact, he's walking alone, the whole three-quarters of a mile from his house to the high school, his head bowed because he's looking at the sidewalk, not caring to make a connection with classmates or Thespis friends or other members of the Trojan Club.

He still has the black cap Kate wore to the carnival to hide her long hair. He's carrying it along with a new loose-leaf notebook, the cap partly concealed between the notebook and his hip. No matter how angry Kate may be, David sees the cap as his return ticket into her good graces; it's her father's, she'll have to have it back. He plans to keep it in his locker until the first meeting of Thespis. Whatever she may think of him this morning, she'll have to talk to him, even thank him for returning the cap. After that, sooner or later she'll forgive everything.

Ordinarily, what's fascinating about the first day of school is seeing people he hasn't seen all summer long, the rich kids mostly, the ones whose fathers are executives with Scoggin Textile or Allied Shoe, who spend the summer months on Square Pond and Long Lake in white cottages with screened porches and pine-board docks that float on rusting oil drums. David knows about these places, all of them at the end of a double track of sandy roads, grass and wildflowers growing between the tracks, a canopy of green-leaved birches overhead, the pine trees taller but offering little shade. The cottages—the owners call them "camps"—are one-story, their asphalt-shingled roofs showing a scatter of red pine needles, and if they are built on a downward slope to the water they have a kind of walkout cellar for the winter storage of rowboats and canoes hidden in slatted shade.

He knows them, though from scant experience. Once, a couple of years back, one of his father's parishioners invited the Willards to spend a weekend at his camp on Square Pond. David will never forget that weekend. The parishioner was Mr. Hansen, a vice-president of Scoggin Textile, and his daughter is Priscilla Hansen, the most beautiful girl in all of York County—according to every local boy who has ever seen her—and probably in the entire state of Maine. Priscilla is tall, honey-blond, always tanned even in winter, and when she graduated from Scoggin High, a year ago last May, she went to Smith on a full scholarship. Her high-school teachers still rave about her.

David's images of life at the summer lakes are all derived from his weekend at the Hansens'. Looking back, he sees, too, that it was

the first summer he began to notice girls; not the girls on gas station
calendars or in the Sears, Roebuck catalogues, but real live girls you
could be in the same room with, whose perfume could make you
dizzy, whose good looks occupied your dreams and daydreams until
you almost couldn't stand it. Of course it was Priscilla he dreamed
of, and of course she was unattainable—older, wiser, and already
encumbered with a boyfriend.

Fortunately, that weekend was a full one, so that his clumsy
hunger for Priscilla found enough distraction to keep his hands out
of his pockets. She had an older brother, home from college for the
summer, who taught David to play roof tennis, a game that involved
two teams—David and Jimbo Hansen versus Priscilla and Ward,
her boyfriend from Dartmouth—stationed on opposite sides of the
cottage, lofting a tennis ball over the roof. It was a dumb game, but
it turned out to be a lot of fun; you couldn't be sure what angle the
ball would be following when it appeared above the roof line, and
getting to it to hit it back involved a terrific amount of running and
swearing. The parents stayed out of it; they sat on the screened-in
porch and drank iced tea and talked about things like how the mills
were adding a third shift, business was so good, and how Priscilla
had been torn between Smith and Mount Holyoke, poor baby. It
was David's mother who said that—"poor baby"—when the family
drove home on Sunday. His father didn't respond. Summers were
hard enough for him, what with no church services until September,
without having to pay attention to family envy.

So it's the girls especially David looks forward to today. He
knows they'll come back to school in fashionable new clothes and
shoes with heels and an attitude that says they know how pretty
they are, how smart, showing off the tans they got from all the time

they spend swimming and canoeing and lying on the dock with their bathing-suit tops undone so the strap marks won't show and spoil their caramel shoulders. That was something else about the weekend at the Hansen camp: Priscilla and her white two-piece bathing suit and all the time she spent taking care of her tan. The Hansens had two docks—the one that jutted out from the sandy beach into Long Pond, with the outboard motorboat tied up to it, and the other, maybe ten feet square, that was moored thirty or forty feet offshore. Priscilla—and Ward, wouldn't you know—spent most of her time on the offshore dock.

David always watched the two of them. Priscilla would sit with her knees tucked under her chin while Ward slathered suntan lotion on her shoulders and back, and then she would look over her shoulder and say something, and Ward would untie the straps that held the top of the suit, so it fell away from her breasts, and fill his palm with lotion, applying it to her back where the straps had been. Then he reached around to the front—she always had her back to the shore, so you couldn't see what you weren't supposed to see—and he took an unusually long time rubbing the lotion onto her breasts. It was maddening, this twice-a-day ritual. When his mother sarcastically called Priscilla Hansen "poor baby," David had said, "Thank goodness it was just for the weekend," meaning it and not meaning it at the same time.

* * *

After the weekend at the Hansens' camp, David was haunted all the rest of the summer by the image of Priscilla Hansen, tawny-fleshed, topless, her long hair fanned around her head on the distant dock. He supposes now that it was the hair, its sheen, its length and fullness, that first drew him to Kate Meredith—as if the Priscilla image gradually gave way to the Kate image, the one girl transformed into the other, the magical way such things happened when scenes in the movies overlapped. It was a fortunate change; Priscilla Hansen would never have given him the time of day, he being so young, so inexperienced. But Kate? In his imagination from the beginning he saw the two of them learning together—never mind learning *what?*—their new experiences absorbing them both, so that when he had first noticed Kate at the basketball game with Thornton Academy, Priscilla's long hair was becoming Kate's, her skin already seeming to be Kate's flushed with the game's excitement. For the rest of the metamorphosis, even then David in his mind's eye was seeing Kate in her own white bathing suit, its top straps carelessly undone to accept all the sun's light. Even then he saw Kate attending to him in every way that Priscilla would have denied him.

Well you sure fucked that up—he can hear the words, not in Tom's voice, which would have made him feel sheepish, but in Jack Morrison's, which makes him angry. Standing across the street from the high school, surrounded by guys smoking a last cigarette before going onto the school grounds, he sees Morrison sitting on the curb, talking and laughing with Patrick Levin, the school's only Jewish student, whose claim to fame is that he can belch at will. But David agrees with Morrison's words, he fucked it up, and now he will have to cross Main Street and come face-to-face with Kate—idealized Kate, desired Kate—perhaps in one of the school's narrow and dimly-lit corridors where lockers line the walls, or in the cafeteria balancing a tray of food he won't want to eat, or, certainly, after classes at the year's first meeting of Thespis. What he will say to her, he doesn't know. What she will say to him, he doesn't dare think.

He trudges across the street. The school bus that brings the farmer kids from Shapleigh and Newfield and Acton Corners is just pulling away from the entrance. Its passengers—the girls in dresses made from colorful flour sacks and the boys in blue work shirts and overalls—drift into the building. Shirley Kostas—white blouse, dark blue skirt, pale blue sweater, saddle shoes, white ankle socks—is sitting on one of the concrete outcroppings that frame the front steps. David is about to walk over to her, to say hello even though she'll probably snub him, when Tom appears. Shirley's demeanor changes in an instant, from sullen detachment to new interest in the world. She waves and tosses her hair; Tom goes to her; David watches.

At first the two of them only talk, smiling, attentive to each other—friends like any other boy and girl. Then Tom slides his hand under the dark blue skirt, up between Shirley's bare thighs, patting or stroking—David can only imagine which—her most private place. She leans toward Tom, their foreheads touch, and gradually Tom withdraws his hand. Now their conversation seems to have turned serious. What are they saying? David wonders. What are they planning? Will they meet after school at her house, or at the Trojan Club, or at a hidden place known only to them?

David has a sharp edge of pain somewhere below his stomach. He hitches his new loose-leaf notebook up against his chest, the magazine he has promised to return to Ray after school tucked safely between its covers, and turns away. Some people have all the luck, he thinks, and in that very moment he sees Kate coming up the walk. When she sees him, she makes an obvious change of direction that takes her past him at a distance too great for speech. She doesn't even look as if she knows him.

* * *

All at once Jack Morrison is besides him, singing.

> *Don't know why*
> *there's no buttons on my fly.*
> *Got a zipper . . .*

That's Jack. Always a bad song, always a dirty joke, always something that will make him the center of attention, especially if it's anything that is—his mother's word—"risqué".

"Hey," Jack says now, "did I scare off your sweetheart?"

"Naw," David says. "She's on her way to the office, to sign up."

"Sign up for what?"

"I don't know." He's still focused on Tom and Shirley. "Some club thing."

"How did your date go?"

"Okay," David says—his mind far under Shirley Kostas's skirt.

"Did you see that?"

"See what?"

"Where Tommy put his hand?"

Jack grins and elbows him. "That's their little game," he says. "Tommy pats her pussy and says, 'How is she today?' and Shirley either says, 'She misses you'—which means the two of them will get together after school somewhere—or she says, 'In the bleachers at Fenway'—which means she's got the rag on. Red Sox, red blood—get it?"

"I get it."

"He can't always put his hand up there," Jack says. "Sometimes the wrong people are watching." He nudges David again. "Days she doesn't wear panties—watch out." He pounds David on the back. "That reminds me." He sticks the middle finger of his right hand under David's nose. "Here," he says, "smell my new girlfriend."

Then Jack is gone, plunging through the crowd at the entrance to the school, glad-handing, smiling, everybody's best friend. There are times when David envies him. But Shirley not wearing *panties*—the very word excites him. He's heard that Edris Bedford doesn't wear underpants, and once in Mr. Ambrose's class, where the desks are in a semi-circle, David sat directly across from her, but no matter how far he slouched, he couldn't see anything up there. You never know how much of what guys say is true and how much is wishing.

By now, Kate has vanished, probably already sitting in her home room, storing new notebooks in her desk—one for each subject, because that's how organized she is—memorizing her new locker combination, waiting patiently and quietly for the opening bell that will signal everyone to stand and salute the flag displayed at the front of the room. Without her, David is at loose ends.

* * *

This year Kate is in Mr. Clarke's home room. Mr. Clarke teaches history and coaches baseball; he insists that he be addressed as "Coach"—never as "Mr. Clarke." On the room's bulletin board is the complete 1947-48 schedule of Scoggin High School sports events, and on the wall at the front of the room, on either side of the American flag are pennants: Boston Red Sox on the left, Boston Braves on the right. Mr. Elliot, who has the room across the corridor, coaches football and teaches math. He too wants to be called "Coach." Kate and David sometimes entertain the other Thespians with a comedy routine in which both partners are named "Coach" and get so confused they forget which of them is which. It's like Abbott and Costello, only better, and Kate wonders if she and David will ever again do anything together.

She feels guilty about what happened last night. But why is that? David is the one who overstepped what her mother would call "the bounds of decency," so why should any guilt attach to Kate? Thinking about it, arranging her notebooks in her new desk, she supposes it's because she's done something—or, rather, that she *hasn't* done something other girls would consider ordinary. Edris and Cynthia and Betty Anne, that threesome of Scoggin High taste-makers, will condemn her for resisting David—when they find out, that is, and certainly they will find out. David will tell; he'll complain to Tom Gowen, and Tom will tell Jack Morrison and, once the story eventually gets to Harold Armitage, the whole school will know.

Her only consolation is that David will probably suffer more than she will. David craves society, wants to be accepted, wants to be one of the guys. Being turned down by Kate Meredith is a setback, makes him seem weak. But Kate is pretty much a loner; except for sophomore year, when she was on the cheerleading squad, she's never tried to "belong" to any group. Thespis doesn't count because it's *artistic*. And she only did the cheerleading that one time, as an experiment, to show the rest of the school that Kate Meredith could be just as *normal* as anybody else. When the girls hear about last night they'll shrug it off. "What do you expect from that one? She's always on the outside, looking in." David will get teased; Kate won't.

How she will deal with David as the days go by—that's a difficult problem. She avoided him this morning, but she can't avoid him forever. There's Thespis. There's third-year French. There's cafeteria. And there's always pure chance. Anyway, she needs to get back her cap—Daddy's cap. Let's say David will bring it to her house, pedaling over on his bike. That's best, she decides. She'll be calm, keep quiet, let him make his apology. She's not sure she'll forgive him— she's not sure she *can*—but she'll listen. It's the least she can do.

Now Mr. Clarke is at the front of the room in his blue suit and white shirt, maroon tie, brown loafers; a small pin in the buttonhole of his lapel that tells you he belongs to Rotary.

"Good morning, ladies and gents," he begins. "I'm Coach Clarke. Welcome to the brand new year."

He is all business. He leads his home room in the pledge of allegiance, takes attendance and makes up a seating chart as each of them answers. By the time the principal's voice sounds over the intercom with his own little welcoming speech and the first day's announcements, Kate feels as if she's been in school forever.

16.

David sees Kate three different times during the day, always from a distance. Once is in the cafeteria at second lunch, when she carries her tray to the other end of the room—and when he tries to follow, she leaves her tray and bolts. Once is in the corridor outside the library during fourth-period class change. The third is after school in Miss Samways' room, where Thespis is having its first meeting since last May. Kate is leaving by the back door of the classroom as David is coming in by the front. In each of these instances, he isn't sure she's even seen him, but whether she did or not, he had no opportunity to talk to her.

After Thespis, David drifts past Coach Clarke's room, just in case Kate has gone back there for some reason. Of course she hasn't. At his locker in the school's south wing he hangs her father's cap from one of the hooks and puts the new textbooks he's collected on the bare shelf above it. He makes sure the *Esquire* is mostly concealed inside the loose-leaf notebook before he slams the locker door shut.

By the time he gets to Fein's Furniture, it's nearly three o'clock, and he walks in hoping Mr. Fein won't be there, that maybe he'll have gone across the street to the Maine Diner for a cup of coffee.

He's not in the mood for Fein's kind of humor, which seems always to suggest that David needs to get more sex into his life. If Mr. Fein knew how much this bothers David—and why—perhaps he'd quit it.

"Well look who's here. How they hangin', David old man?"

"Hi, Mr. Fein." What kind of answer can you give to a question like that? And why couldn't David have come just five minutes later? Fein is on his way out; David almost bumped into him. Now he's stuck.

"Sit down, son." Fein gestures toward a couch that's on display, and David sits, the notebook tucked under his chin like a shield. Fein perches on the arm of the couch. "You like airplane stories? Sure you do."

David shrugs. "I guess so."

"So this guy is flying Transcontinental out to California, and this stewardess is going up and down the aisle serving the passengers, and she's a real good-looker too. So she gets to this guy, and she says to him, 'Would you like some of our TWA coffee?' And so this guy says, 'No, thank you, but I sure would like some of your TWA tea.'" He reaches out to give David a playful punch on the arm. "Get it? T-W-A-T?"

"That's a good one," David says. Is that how it's spelled? He's always thought it must be with an "o", the way it's pronounced.

"I knew you'd like it," Fein says. "A muff diver like yourself." He gives David another punch. "I gotta run." But as he is about to leave the store he stops and shouts back, "Ray? Don't forget to play that record I picked out."

"I won't forget."

Ray is shaking his head as David reaches the record counter. "He heard that twat joke over the weekend at the Elks' Club," Ray says. "I bet he's told it twenty times, just today."

"I wish he'd lay off me," David says. He can't imagine that twenty people have come into this store today. The place is always empty.

"Shit, he's harmless. You bring the magazine?"

"Yeah." He lays the *Esquire* on the counter. "It's a pretty good issue."

Ray slides the magazine under the counter. "You ever find out who the girl was at the Trojan Club the other night? Was it Kostas?"

"I can't say."

"I thought so." As if David had named her. "Tommy's not the only one she puts out for, but he's her favorite. I guess he doesn't mind sloppy seconds."

"I never heard she does it with anybody else," David says. "Who told you she does?"

"It's common knowledge," Raymond says. "Which reminds me. How'd your carnival date go?"

"Fine. We had fun."

"You make out?"

"A little," David says. "Nothing serious." The lie makes his cheeks burn.

"You see that naked dancer all the guys are talking about? The one smokes a cigarette with her cunt?"

"Yeah. Not with Kate, but Saturday, with Jack and Tommy."

"She make you hot?"

"Are you kidding? It's only an act."

"I heard she lines 'em up after the show and fucks all comers, two bucks each."

"Jesus, Ray, you believe everything you hear?"

Raymond grins. "Just the good stuff," he says. Then: "Hey, I'm supposed to play this for you." He drops the store's phonograph needle onto a black-label record. "It's Duke Ellington—a thing called 'Caravan.'"

David feels his cheeks redden. It's the music Sharita dances to. How did Mr. Fein know that? Was he in the tent last night, watching?

* * *

When David gets home, the car is gone and the house is empty. Tuesday is the day of his father's hospital and nursing home visits; his mother is at her Canasta club.

He can't say why he decides to ride his bike to The Meadows again, to wander the grounds, to see Sharita—which is what he still thinks of her as, even though she's told him her name is Sherrie. Probably Mr. Fein's dirty joke, or Ray's rumor about Shirley Kostas and using the *c* word to refer to the dancer, or the record Ray played, stirred David up inside. Possibly he's simply lonely. Now that he's on the outs with Kate, second choice is Sharita, though if she knows what happened outside her show last night she may not be so friendly. There's only one way to find out.

He locks the bike and leans it against a lamppost across the road from the carnival. This is the show's last day and there aren't many people on the grounds—a few kids wasting time between school and supper, not many adults, probably because it's a weekday and they're still at work. Hardly anybody is on the Ferris wheel, the merry-go-round isn't even running, and there's not a soul in front of the Sharita billboard.

As he makes his way between the shooting gallery and a popcorn concession, he thinks he feels his heartbeat speed up. Is it because he's looking forward to being with this woman he's seen naked? Or is he afraid he'll run into what's-his-name, Coggio, and be made fun of? But here he is outside her trailer, and Coggio is nowhere to be seen.

On the step David hesitates, then raps—tentatively—at the metal door. Twice, three times; not loud, just with one knuckle. When no one comes to answer his knock, he reaches for the latch, moving it slowly so it makes scarcely any noise. The door opens—something he hasn't expected—and without really thinking about what he's doing he slips inside the trailer. The interior is dim, the only light entering through the narrow windows at the front of the trailer, and for a moment or two he stands unsteadily. By the time his eyes have adjusted to the gloom, he realizes he isn't alone, that someone is lying on the bed at the other end of the trailer.

"Hello?" David says—almost a whisper. "Sharita?"

The figure on the bed stirs, turns toward him, raises itself on one elbow to face him. "Who's that?"

"It's me," he says, "the *Tribune* reporter."

Sherrie sits up and swings her legs to the floor. She's wearing the chenille robe, which is open most of the way to her waist, where the belt holds it together. She draws the lapels close at her throat and draws up one side of the robe so it covers her thighs. David wishes she weren't so modest.

"David, isn't it?" she says.

"Yes'm."

"I heard something at the door," she says, "but I thought it was a part of my dream. Then I heard the door open, and someone come inside, and I thought how this was the realest dream I'd had in a long, long time."

"I'm sorry I waked you."

"What time is it?"

"I don't know. I guess almost four o'clock." He's still standing in the middle of the shadowy space. "Do you have to dance?"

"Only a late matinee on weekdays," she tells him. "I should be getting ready. Three shows tonight, four tomorrow, then teardown. Thursday we're in Manchester."

"I was hoping," David says.

"To watch me dance?" She gets up from the bed, yawns, then goes to the icebox. "I told you," she says. "I didn't want to see you in there again. It's not your sort of dance."

He wishes he could argue with her, to say that her dance is more for him than she thinks it is, that she isn't a calendar on a gas station wall or a page in a men's magazine, or even a picture from a catalogue. She's all of those made real, a moving and breathing woman with no secrets—nothing withheld.

"Your little girlfriend was here. Last night, after the show," Sherrie says.

"I thought that's where he'd take her." He wonders what Kate must have said, what terrible things.

She opens the ale bottle and takes a long swallow from it. "What did you think?" she says. "Did you truly think she'd go on her knees in the dirt and suck you off?"

"I don't know what I thought." But he wants to say, *No, that wasn't it.* He wants to explain that he never expected Kate to do any such thing, that he wanted something less than being *sucked off*—a sort of starting point that might lead further or might not, because how could you know the outcome if you've never been there? "And she isn't my girlfriend anymore," he adds. That's probably the truth.

Sherrie shakes her head as if she's sorry for him, and she goes back to sit on the edge of her bed. She pats a space beside her on the mattress, meaning he should sit there, and so he does. The bed is firm, with not a lot of give, and when he sits his hip is against hers—a warmth and a soft pressure he finds distracting. The woman's presence is like something tangible, a force that encloses him, and her perfume is heavy and sweet. He wonders if this is what his father's butterflies experience, just before they give up their lives to have their beauty fixed in time.

"Listen to me," Sherrie says. "You mustn't ever rush things. Whatever you want from a girl—from a woman—you have to be patient. You have to bide your time. You have to wait for her to come to you, and not the other way around." She lays her hand, cold and moist from the bottle she has been cradling, on one of his. "You're a sweet boy," she says. "You don't have to force yourself."

"I don't know how to make girls *like* me," David says. Sherrie is so close, when she speaks he is aware of the brush of her breath against his cheek, the sweet smell of what she is drinking. He wonders if she would let him kiss her. He leans against her, and his right hand, as if it has a will of its own—God knows he couldn't have planned this—parts the front of the chenille robe and slides inside it until his fingers touch her breast.

Sherrie straightens up and grips his wrist, pushing him away. "Don't," she says.

He drops the hand to his lap. "I'm sorry," he says. "I didn't mean—"

"We both know what you meant." She wraps the robe around her, tight, and holds it closed. "But you didn't have my permission. That's what I was saying: the woman has to come to you."

"I don't know how to make that happen." But she's making him think. She's forcing him to recall times when it actually *has* happened. He thinks of coffee with Kate, how they seem to read each other like open playbooks, what fun it is to make each other laugh—and all because Kate trusts his quickness, his humor. But that's in public. How can he draw Kate to him in private, in settings where intimacy is possible?

Sherrie has moved away from him, lounging now against the wall at the head of the bed. "Your little girlfriend says her daddy isn't home very much of the time—that he travels for some big company."

"It's General Electric. He finds places to build factories." What does that have to do with anything?

"But what's important is that he's away. The girl hasn't got a man in her life." She points the bottle at him and winks. "It's your golden opportunity," she says. "You should step up. Be the missing man."

"She won't even look at me," David says. "Not after last night."

"You'll both get over that," Sherrie says. "So you struck out. You scared her off, but she'll sit home and think about it, about how maybe she should have tried to meet you halfway, and finally she'll forgive you."

"I hope so."

"Anyway, why is it so important? What's the big rush?"

"I don't know." He looks at the floor, linoleum in a pattern of rectangles that never seems to repeat. "I guess I want us to be like Tom and Shirley."

"Who's that?"

"Friends."

"And what's so special about them?"

"They're sort of the class lovers. They've done everything—and they don't try to keep it secret." Is that what he wants? To do it with Kate and then broadcast it to the whole school? "I don't mean they blab about it. Just that they aren't ashamed."

"Do you think it's something they *ought* to be ashamed of? Having sex?"

"I would be," David says. It's true; even at this moment he can feel himself blushing.

Sherrie gives a funny little laugh and gets up from the bed. She sets the ale bottle—it looks to be empty—on the kitchenette table, then crosses back to the closet behind her bed. She slips out of the chenille robe and hangs it inside the closet door. "You're an odd one," she says, her back turned to him. "Why would you try so hard to do something with a girl that makes you feel ashamed?"

It's a complicated question, made all the more complicated because Sherrie is standing not ten feet away and she's wearing nothing but a pair of fluffy pink slippers. He tries to look away, but of course he doesn't quite succeed and in this flustered state his mind struggles after an answer to the question.

"I don't know," he says. His voice cracks on the words. "I don't understand things. Sometimes I think I don't belong in this world." He's thinking not only of how he has embarrassed himself and offended Kate, but of the persistent coldness in his father's manner toward him, of his mother's sweet ineffectualness, of how even his few friends make fun of him. If only another world existed.

Sherrie meanwhile is doing some sort of limbering-up exercise. She stands on tiptoe with her arms raised high over her head, half-facing him, the movement raising her breasts so that she looks like the *Esquire* girl with her tight clothes stripped away. Now she does three knee-bends in quick succession, thighs parted and her hairless crotch exposed to his watching. And now she stands and with fingers straight bends to touch her toes, left then right, three times each.

David tries to focus his gaze on the anklet she wears, the one that reads *Love*. "You know what I ought to do?" he says desperately. "I ought to quit school and join up with a carnival like this one."

She ends her exercises and turns to the closet, taking down the costume she wears in her performance. "Did you just this minute think of that?" she says. "Do you really want to run away from home?"

"Sometimes I do." He watches her dress, the harem pantaloons, the embroidered vest that won't entirely hide her nipples, the gold slippers with curled-up toes. "I'd work hard. I could learn to run a concession."

Sherrie smiles. "If I didn't have a show in ten minutes, I'd give you a thousand reasons not to do such a thing." She faces a mirror set inside the closet door and begins to put on makeup. "But for now," she says, "don't think about what you'd be running *to*. That's daydream stuff. Think about what you're running *from*."

"I do."

"You run off, and after a while the work makes you mean and hardhearted. You get so you look at the marks like they're all your enemies, and you don't care what you do to them. That's not a nice boy like you."

"I don't know what a 'mark' is," David says.

She looks at him, sad-eyed, a gold lipstick tube poised in a tripod of her fingers. "You are, baby," she says. "You and everybody who buys a ticket at the carny, or plays a hanky-pank or a flat, everybody who comes onto the grounds. You're all marks, suckers, somebody to steal from."

"Nobody's stolen from me."

"Oh, baby David—" Then she does something David knows he will remember for the rest of his life. She puts the lipstick aside and sits on the edge of the bed in front of him, taking both his hands in hers. "You don't know what I could steal from you," she says. "What I'd like to steal." She reaches up and pulls his head down to her. She kisses him ferociously. "But I'm not going to steal it from your sweet little girlfriend."

"Let me come with you. Please." His mouth is numb from her kiss. In this instant he would give up everything for Sherrie's attentions. "You could teach me."

She looks up at him. Is she crying? "I tell you what I'll teach you," she says. "Be nice to the girl. She's as good as you. Be nice. Don't treat her the way you'd treat somebody like me."

She kisses him again, this time gently, and brushes the lock of hair back from his forehead the way his mother does.

"That's why I wrote *love* on my bracelet," she says. "To remind myself there is such a thing, no matter what."

She stands and goes back to her mirror. "Go on now. Back to your folks, your school chums, the world where you belong."

Before David can protest again, someone is pounding on the trailer door.

"There," she says. "Get out of here. I've got to go to work."

Then the trailer door swings open and Coggio is standing there, the light behind him canceling his features. "We g-going to do a show or n-not?"

"Hold your water," Sherrie says. "David was just on his way out."

17.

When Kate gets home from school her mother isn't home, but a piece of notepaper on the table in the front hall explains that Longfellow School called and needed a substitute for one of the fourth-grade classes. The note ends, *I made cookies. Help yourself but don't leave crumbs.* Then there is a p.s., written in more of a scrawl than the information about the school assignment, as if Mother was in a hurry: *Daddy just called. After class I have to drive to the airport to pick him up.* Finally, she thinks, a promise kept—though she wouldn't be shocked if Daddy called at the last minute to say GE was making him fly to Timbuktu.

The cookies are a lovely surprise, considering that Kate left her cafeteria food uneaten to avoid David, and now her stomach is growling. The warning about the crumbs is an unkind reminder of the times her messiness has attracted ants—a lot of them. Mother never lets her forget the ants, and Kate will never understand how so many of the darned things can congregate so fast.

The cookies are oatmeal, the healthy snack as opposed to the indulgent Toll House kind she prefers. She pours herself a half glass of milk and eats two cookies, thinking as she chews that she should have eaten her lunch at school—that it isn't fair that she should have to starve herself, just because David did something out of character and stupid. It's one more case of the female knuckling under to the male, as if it was her fault that she was pushed to her knees in front of him. And what if that man, Frank Coggio, hadn't come to her rescue? What then? She remembers Darryl's dirty pictures, she'd heard the sound of David's zipper, she knows in a secondhand way—mostly from Edris—what boys want, either hands or mouth or, worst, *intercourse*. That fifty-dollar word. Had David meant for her to do that too? And without Coggio, how would she have defended herself? You could dress up like a boy, but you couldn't put on his strength.

Which reminded her of what Daddy had said to her mother when he gave her the shiny revolver and she'd protested that she could never shoot anybody. "You'd be surprised how easy it is." So now Kate knows what he meant; in last night's worst moments, feeling the cold of the ground at her knees and the coarse dirt under her hands, catching the first odor of David's exposed skin—yes, if she'd had a gun, how easy it would have been to use it.

* * *

She rinses the milk glass under the kitchen faucet and sets it in the dirty-dish side of the double sink. It's only a little after two o'clock; elementary schools don't let out until after three, so Kate is at loose ends until then. Under ordinary circumstances—when was that? she asks herself—she'd telephone David and they would go for a walk or play cards or invent dialogues. No more of that. Not this week, anyway.

She drifts upstairs and tosses her notebook and the first textbook of the new year, *French 3*, onto her bed. French is the only foreign language they teach at Scoggin—not counting Latin—which is probably a concession to the French-Canadian population that years ago came down from Quebec to work in the mills. The only trouble is that when she hears those people talk, in the street or on a bus or coming out of the movies, they don't sound anything like Monsieur Casavant or Mademoiselle Tondreau. It's the difference between "Canadian" French and "Parisian" French; she knows that, but it doesn't make studying it any more reasonable.

Having disposed of the book, she wanders into her mother's room. She has no business there. It's really her parents' room—they sleep together in the same bed—but he was away so many years during the war, and now he's away so much on business, Kate has never given up the habit of thinking of the room as Mother's. Probably it was the question of defending herself against David that nudged her here, thinking of her mother's defensive weapon, all silver gleam and pearl shine, and when she slides open the nightstand drawer, there it is, the first thing she sees, and alongside it the little yellow box of bullets that are meant to fill the empty cylinder.

She lifts the revolver from the drawer and pretends to shoot the picture of herself on the dresser, the one with Daddy taken the day before he went into the army, Kate all pigtails and pinafore. Eleven, was she? Or ten, going on eleven. The gun isn't heavy, but heavy for its size. Loaded, you'd probably have to hold it with both hands. She wonders why her mother doesn't keep it loaded, at least one bullet, ready to be fired. If she really needed to defend herself, think of the time it would take to open the drawer, take a bullet out of its little box, and put it in the cylinder. By the time you did all that, whatever was going to happen to you would have happened. Burglary. Rape. Murder. You name it.

She is about to return the gun to its proper place when she notices a piece of paper, notepad size, half-tucked under the yellow box. When she takes it out, she sees that it's a small brownish envelope with a window, and inside it some sort of letter. She slides the letter out—it's folded once, and the fold looks worn—and opens it. *Dearest Carrie*, it begins. "Carrie" is what Daddy calls her mother.

Kate thinks probably she shouldn't be reading this, but it doesn't entirely seem to be a real letter; the writing is too small and looks more like one of Daddy's business Photostats than genuine handwriting, though it could be a shrunk-down version of Daddy's real penmanship. *Dearest Carrie*. The page has a date in the upper-right corner: *12/28/44.*

> *Dearest Carrie,*
>
> *Christmas wasn't easy, even though the English civilians here in* ▬▬ *really bent over backwards to make us feel at home, and they kept reminding me that a lot of the xmas customs we're used to originated in England, and that we owe them a debt of gratitude in spite of the Revolutionary War unpleasantness. You have to admire the way they use language.*
>
> *Well, as you know (I hope) things are going well here in Europe and I hope we won't have to be here much longer. We hear that there's a big dustup in* ▬▬ *with a lot of troops involved, but my guess is that in the end it won't amount to much and may be the last stand the Germans are making. We still send out the daily round of* ▬▬ *on their way to* ▬▬ *and* ▬▬ *but they rarely lose a single aircraft.*
>
> *I hope you and Katie had a nice holiday. I don't know if my presents reached you or not, but if they haven't arrived, they soon will I'm sure.*

Now, I have to say some things that will probably make you unhappy, and this is the main reason I'm writing you tonight. Right up front I want you to remember that I love you dearly, and that there's no other woman on earth for me. I hope you feel the same about me, and that you'll be generous to me. I wouldn't hurt you, or Kathryn, for all the world. Do believe that. Please believe it.

Xmas eve I was invited to a private home near the base, to celebrate with an English family. I'd met this old guy at a pub near here—oh, months ago—and a week before the holiday he invited me to his home. Long story short, there was a daughter, mid-20s, and after we'd all had plenty of what they call "wassail" I woke up the next morning with Lilian beside me. Carrie, it wasn't serious, it wasn't even intended. It was a guy a million miles from family, lonely and drunk, and I'm profoundly sorry. I'll never see her again, I swear.

I'm running out of space on this Vmail sheet, but I had to confess to you. I love you, Carrie. Nobody else.

Donald

By the time she finishes reading the letter, Kate is crying.

* * *

Kate dries her tears and replaces the horrible letter in its envelope in the nightstand drawer. She has no particular plan, though there has been plenty of time to devise one. The airport is four miles away in South Scoggin, a small landing field carved out of the Naval Air Station that was used to train English pilots during the war. By the time her parents arrive home from the airport, she only knows that

Daddy has to be confronted, and when the black Ford pulls into the drive, her father behind the wheel, she is already out the back door, waiting.

Her father gets out of the car, smiling, ready to accept the welcoming hug she knows she won't give him. Instead, she screams at him and runs at him, blindly, fists clenched, seriously intent on hitting him as hard and as often as she can.

"How could you?" she says, the tears starting again as he catches her wrists in self-defense. "How do you dare to come back?"

He holds her away from him; he really is strong. "What's wrong?" he says. "What kind of a question is that?"

Now her mother is out of the car, hurrying around it toward her. "Katie, what's the matter?"

"You know what kind it is," she says. "It's the question Mom is afraid to ask. Why do you come back every time when she knows you've been with the others?"

"What others?"

"Katie, baby. Please." Mother is behind her and takes her shoulders, trying to pull her away from this fight she obviously doesn't understand.

"I found the letter," Kate says. "You don't have to pretend." She pulls one arm free and takes a swing at her father. "God damn you, Daddy. What do you think I am? Daddy's little girl who's too fond to see through you?"

He recaptures her arm. "What others?" he repeats. "I asked you a question."

"Other women. Who else?"

He holds her, hard. What is it about men, the way they use their strength? "You're making a scene," he says.

"I know about the woman in England," she says. "She has a name, *Lilian*, and she doesn't even spell it properly."

"Please, Katie," her mother says. "Let's take this inside."

"You act so damned nice and thoughtful and patient with Mother; but you might as well have the woman in the room with you, hiding under the bed."

"Kathryn, that's a crazy thing to say."

"Well, it's true." Though at this moment she isn't at all certain what's true and what's not. The smothering rage that possessed her when she first attacked Daddy has lifted somewhat, and she sees that Mother doesn't seem to share her anger, but is instead sending a perplexed and helpless look in Daddy's direction.

"That was three years ago," he says. Now he has both her wrists contained in one of his hands, and with the other he opens the car's back door and pulls out his suitcase. So. Is this what she wanted? He's angry, probably because Kate has found him out—though he hasn't admitted anything except the woman in the letter. But who knows how many women he's known over his years in the army, the traveling since he became a civilian, the weeks he spends away from the marriage?

"Come in the house," her mother is saying. "Let's not put on a performance for the neighbors." And Kate allows herself to be steered inside and into the kitchen.

"Sit down, sweetie," Mother says. "I'll get you a lemonade."

An offer so absurd under the circumstances that it's almost funny.

"Look," her father says. "This is all a long way behind us, your mother and me. I wrote that letter because I was ashamed and guilty and I needed to be forgiven. One slip. One foolish mistake. There haven't ever been any others. Your mother knows that, and you should too."

"Maybe I'm not so easily fooled," Kate says.

Now her father is laughing. "Oh, Katie. You're my best reason for loving the very idea of having a family."

This throws her. What's the difference between "family" and the "idea" of family? Does he really love her mother, really love Kate, or does he just love the idea of loving them both? Where does he draw the line, and is it a line anybody can *see*?

"I don't understand it," she says. "Why would you even keep a letter like that? Why wouldn't you just tear it up and set it on fire?"

Her mother gives Kate a gentle kiss on the forehead. "Maybe it's as well you found it."

"But why keep it?" *Damn parents anyway.*

"I don't know. Maybe to remind myself what forgiveness is."

"That's dumb," Kate says.

"You're young," her father says. "You'll understand in time."

"No," Kate says. "I don't think I ever will."

* * *

And it nags at her. She feels—what does she feel? Anger, double-edged, on behalf of her mother and herself; frustration, that her mother's excuses won't make sense and what Daddy has done cannot be undone. The woman he was unfaithful with is even now going about her life in England, probably remembering Donald Meredith, that Yank soldier, the fond lover in and out of her life like an unexpected Christmas guest, probably wishing he could have stayed on, divorced Mother, begun a new family that spoke English with a fancy accent. And what if she were already a mother? What if Daddy made her pregnant, then left her? Would he even have known? If he *had* known, would he have told his wife? Was there another Vmail letter, better hidden, confessing his fatherhood? Or did he know and not tell, is secretly sending money to support the accidental child? *The bastard*, because that's what it is—if it is.

When her mother has gone upstairs to bed—"All this fuss has given me a headache"—she can't help reviving the discussion.

"How could you have done such a thing?" All the emotion invested in that sentence! Kate thinks she might choke on it.

Her father is calm. "Kitten," he says, "let it go. You're making much too much of this."

"What if you got her pregnant?" Because it has to be said out loud. "What if I've got a little brother or sister I don't even know about and I'll never meet?"

"Katie—"

"How do you know I don't? Things like that happen."

"In books and movies," Daddy says.

"In real life," she insists. What is the matter with him? Does he think she's stupid?

"I mean it's in the movies that a man and a woman—" He hesitates. "—that they get together once, only once, and the woman conceives. It's a plot contrivance. And I was careful," he says, "if you understand what I'm saying."

"Yes, I understand." She can feel the tears starting. "It means you knew ahead of time what you and this woman were going to do. You planned it. Mother was home with me, two women scared you'd get killed in a war thousands of miles away, and you were *planning* to be unfaithful. To her. To both of us."

He reaches to take her by the shoulders, but she pulls away.

"Katie," he says, "my god, do you think I'd ever do anything so cold-blooded to you two? Do you think I'd even have gone to Lilian's house for Christmas dinner if I'd imagined I was going to drink too much and fall into bed with a woman who wasn't my wife?"

"How could anybody drink that much? How could you forget everything? You were married—and if you ask me, you're lucky you still are."

"I know how lucky I am," he says. "And I felt guilty for what I did, God knows. Sometimes I still do. Sometimes I fret about how that one bad action of mine might forever have damaged the life your mother and I share—and if I could undo that Christmas away from her, don't you think I would?"

"I don't know," Kate says. Her frustration has changed to sullenness, a mode in which she can nurse the emotion without using it up.

"It's hard for you," her father says. "You're young. There's a world waiting for you that you can't yet imagine, and it's a world where good and bad aren't as simple as you want them to be. You want absolutes, and that's good, because we build our practical morality on a foundation of absolutes. The foundation is important, but it's like the basement of a house: you can't live in a basement; you have to build the house above it, and it's the house where you live, with all its different rooms and different values. And we're always redecorating and remodeling, because experience changes us—all of us."

"David's father would say you're just rationalizing. David's father would say you're only making excuses for doing something sinful."

"Harvey Willard is no paragon, as far as I'm concerned. He's rigid and humorless—and if his boy is anything like him, then you ought to be careful." Her father shifts uneasily in his chair. "No, I shouldn't have said that. I'm sure David is a good kid, and I know you like him."

None of this is going the way Kate expected. What started out as her intending to call Daddy to account for his betrayal of Mother has now become by some parental sleight of hand an analysis of her own relationships. She's beginning to see that she has precious little control over the behavior of others—as if David hasn't already taught her that. And Daddy—Daddy's starting to seem wise and, worse, forgivable.

"None of all this talk can make a wrong thing right," Kate says. "Some houses just aren't very well built."

"The houses built on sand," her father says. "That's the classic sermon topic, and it's what I meant by foundation. Anyway, what I did, thoughtless and wrong as it was, didn't wreck the house."

"How do you know? You weren't here when she read that letter."

"But I know why she's kept it."

"Why."

"To remind us both that we're strong enough to survive what I did. We're maybe even stronger because of it."

"That makes no sense," Kate says. And it doesn't. It makes it seem as if Daddy is some kind of saint, that by *doing it* with the English woman he was only spreading love across the world.

"Your mother knows my flaws," her father says, "and she loves me in spite of them. And I love her all the more because she forgives me. That's all I'm saying."

Kate lets that pass. There doesn't seem to be any point in pursuing the matter, especially since Mother is so strongly on Daddy's side.

"Anyway," she says, "maybe it's true that David isn't as good a kid as everybody thinks he is."

18.

Pedaling home, David hears what he said to Sherrie repeated over and over in his head, and now he is embarrassed by the words, even more embarrassed by Sherrie's trying to take him seriously when of course she must have been secretly laughing at him. Run away with a carnival? What a dumbbell he must have looked to her. And touching her breast. As if he had the slightest idea of what he was supposed to do next. She saw that, all right: he was only a child, and she was used to grown men. What was the matter with him? Dumbbell.

All the way to his driveway he hears himself, watches his performance in his mind's eye, relives making a fool of himself in front of a real woman who's practically naked—no, *really* naked—and who puts calendar and catalogue pictures in the shade. Dumbbell, dumbbell, dumbbell.

He wheels the bike into the garage and leans it against the tool bench that never gets used. The car is here, meaning his father is home from his charity rounds and will want to know why he's so late getting home. Ma will do her best to stand up for David, and then before you know it the two of them will start in on each other. It's as if she's sacrificing her own peace to protect his.

But today is different. His father is standing on the backdoor landing, fists against his hips, his face grim.

"Where the devil have you been? You have to drive me to North Berwick."

"Why? What's the matter?" He comes into the kitchen. His father's suitcase is sitting in the hall doorway. His mother is at the table, and it looks as if she's been crying, her handkerchief—one of two or three she owns with a pink tatted border—squeezed in her hand.

"Your Grammy Willard," she says. "There's been a terrible accident."

His father takes him by the elbow and steers him back toward the door he's just come in. "I'll tell you on the way. We can just make the evening train to Boston if we don't dawdle."

"Let me make you a sandwich, for the train ride," Mother says.

David is already at the door when his father says, "Deuce of a time to think of *that.*" And as his father catches up, carrying the suitcase, he says, "I hope you've got your license with you."

"I do," David says. He always has it with him; what does his father think? He practically sleeps with it under his pillow.

*　*　*

"It's an awful thing," his father is saying. "An awful, tragic thing." They're in South Scoggin, headed toward the station in North Berwick, and David still doesn't know what's going on with Grandma Willard. Not that he's likely to care much; he's met the woman only twice in his life, and she's the grandmother the family hardly ever visits—or even talks about. He guesses that whatever the reason for this trip, his father is doing it from a sense of duty. It isn't something he *wants* to do, and so far he's more interested in being critical of David's driving than anything else. *Don't hug the shoulder so. Didn't they teach you the proper way to take a curve? Watch out for that dog!* It's a wonder he didn't drive himself and leave the Chevy at the station.

"I could have driven myself," his father says now, as if he'd read David's mind. "But I'll be gone several days, and I didn't want to leave your mother high and dry."

"I can be her chauffeur," David says.

"That's the general idea."

They motor on in silence. The sun is low in the sky behind them, and as the road bends, the trees cast elongated shadows ahead. There's hardly any traffic; the roadside vegetable stands along the way have no business at all. You wonder why they stay open so late.

"I expect your grandmother will be dead by the time I get to the hospital in Springfield," his father says. The word—"dead"—comes out of the blue.

"What happened?"

His father sighs. "Carelessness. She was heating water for her bath—you know she has to make a fire in that old pot-bellied stove in the cellar—and the flames caught the shawl she was wearing."

David didn't know about the stove—how could he?—but he can imagine the woman on fire, the wreath of flame around her neck. It's a horrible image, and he puts it out of his mind.

"The next-door neighbor heard her screaming," his father says. "That was one piece of luck. Otherwise she might have lain there till we visited at Christmas. What a mess we'd have found then."

"Yeah," David agrees.

"She's in her late seventies. I've been saying for years that she ought to be in a nursing home, where someone could take decent care of her."

* * *

What stays with him after he's dropped his father at the depot is the word "luck"—meaning, apparently, that it was lucky for the Willards, who wouldn't have had to see the old lady's rotting corpse.

But what's genuinely lucky for David is that now he's able to have the use of the family car—within reason; he knows his father wrote down the mileage before he got out. It's a rare event, and though it's a shame that someone has to be on the edge of dying before it happens, driving the Chevy is pure joy. Maybe he can impress Kate, give her rides to school until his father comes home, make her see his maturity. If you have a car, you can do almost anything, especially with a girl. Even David's father, "before you were born"—which is how he almost always begins stories about the past—used to take Sunday drives with Ma, going to the beach for picnics or to the lake where they could rent a canoe.

This car has a history. After David's father gave up being a track star and went to school in Troy where he got his divinity degree, he moved the family to Scoggin and took over the Congo church. That was the same year they got the gray 1937 Chevrolet with maroon fenders. David's father bought it from the Chevy dealer in South Scoggin, even though Ma said she thought it "might be too racy for a minister." That was also the year the Japs bombed Pearl Harbor and the United States declared war on Japan and Germany and Italy.

David was ten that year. One of the things he remembers about those days was that his father shaved off his mustache because people told him it made him look like Hitler. David supposed it was a smart thing for his father to do. How could you sit in church listening to a sermon if every time you looked up at the minister you thought of Adolf Hitler making a speech to a bunch of Nazis yelling *Sieg Heil?* Though it took a while to get used to the change. Mother said it made his face look naked, and that at first she was embarrassed to be seen with him in public. This was a joke, David knows. Now it's as if his father never did have a mustache.

For a few months after the Chevy came into their lives the family went for Sunday drives—out to the countryside or to the Wells or Ogunquit beaches, or down to Portland. There was always ice cream at the end of every drive, and chicken for dinner. One long trip was to Boston, a holiday drive to see a ball game and to stay overnight at a hotel.

Gas rationing ended the pleasure drives. They got an A sticker, though his father argued he should have been entitled to a B because he was a reverend. But Mother said he should count his blessings; the church might not entitle him to more gasoline, but it earned him a draft deferment, and wasn't that more important to the family?

But to this day David's father grumbles about the irony that let him finally buy his first auto and then took away the gas that would have allowed him to drive it. All David cares about, now that he has his driver's license and gas rationing is over, is that the Chevy is in better shape mechanically because it wasn't driven that much.

* * *

David's mother always said that every cloud has a silver lining, that sometimes events that seem bad turn out to be blessings in disguise. For David, the blessing of not being able to freely drive the car during the war was having to take the train for the annual trip to Boston to see a ballgame and—for his parents—go to the theater. They drove only as far as North Berwick, parked the Chevy at the depot, and rode the Boston & Maine to North Station.

The train was a thousand times better in its way than the automobile. On the train you could get up and move around; you could walk all the way to the end of the train's last car and watch the tracks grow smaller and smaller toward the horizon, like a lesson in perspective. If you wanted to take a nap, the rhythm of the iron wheels rolling over the track would lull you to sleep. You could even eat on the train if you wanted to; there was a dining car with table-cloths and a little vase of flowers on every table, where you could sit and eat and watch the scenery go by. Unfortunately, his mother always brought a box lunch for the three of them to share at their coach seats, so David had never gotten the chance to have a meal in the dining car.

What he did have was the countryside flowing past his window. What he did have was his imagination. Between the two, he was a happy traveler. He saw places where he would have liked to live— big houses well away from the tracks, with white fences and horses, white and red outbuildings for chickens and goats, neatly laid out victory gardens with rows of pole beans and tomato plants and green leafy things David couldn't identify because they grew so low to the ground. He saw miles of forests, pine and birch, oak and maple, with corridors of light and shade where he could imagine playing, looking in spring for lady's slippers and violets to bring home to Mother, or in fall for milkweed pods to break open and spill behind him like a trail of snowflakes. He saw open spaces that led his eye westward, where—this was one day, one crystal-clear morning in mid-September—he saw the snowy crests of Mt. Washington and Mt. Adams, a hundred miles away in the blue haze of New Hampshire.

As time went on, and he was eleven, twelve, thirteen, he saw best of all the ideal hiding places where he could imagine going when school and chores and the demands of his parents were more than he could bear. They were hollows and gullies, cavelike bushes and small trees shaped like fountains, hedges and tumbledown stone walls

where serious boys could practice being snipers and play out the strat-
egies of war. There were small streams and grassy banks for having
picnics, and ponds so still that a surface barely brushed by a darning
needle could ruffle the water all the way to the farthest shore.

All these sights and thoughts came and went in moments as
the train swept past, and soon enough the rural scenes David found
so peaceful were replaced by the cities north of Boston—streets
and cars and tenements with laundry hung on porch railings and
clotheslines made of wire. The closer you came to the city, the more
crowded the streets, and the tenements huddled closer and closer to
the tracks so you could look into their windows, spying on the lives
of the people inside, wondering how they could stand the noise, the
soot, the absence of privacy. Much as he liked the excitement of
coming to Boston—the ballgames, the wonderful hotel where you
could order food brought right to your room any time you wanted
it—David was happy to be traveling back down to Maine through
the countryside that looked to offer such variety, such a change from
his ordinary life in Scoggin.

The older he got, the more he began to populate the world of
the train ride with girls, seeing places where he could run away,
perhaps with Priscilla Hansen, perhaps with any one of several
long-haired, giggling girls who traveled in packs down the corridors
of Scoggin High. Just this spring, when he had already found and
started noticing Kate Meredith, the Boston trip for a Memorial Day
doubleheader preoccupied him with hideaways where the two of
them could kiss and touch and do things he would never dare in the
real world to suggest to her. There, beyond that row of lilacs, in that
meadow where a slant of hillside made a bed of wild flowers—far
enough from the tracks as to be anonymous, but close enough to

provoke the jealousy of riders watching, traveling without any idea of love. Someday, David had thought, someday he and Kate would do everything together.

Now, he thinks, perhaps *someday* has come. His mother willing—and he's sure he can persuade her—the car is his at least until the weekend. By then he and Kate will have made up. By then they can drive to the country: one last picnic while the weather is good, hidden away in just such a meadow, a hollow, a secret grove where anything might happen.

* * *

When he has parked the car and pulled the garage doors closed, Ma is waiting for him in the kitchen. She embraces him and gives him a peck on the cheek. Her eyes are still red from crying.

"I couldn't get in touch with your father," she says. "The hospital in Springfield called. Grammy Willard passed away before the ambulance got there. Now your dad will have to make the funeral arrangements."

"Poor grandma," David says. But he's thinking it's another "piece of luck" for his father, who won't have to sit at his mother's deathbed and be bored.

19.

Third period, Wednesday, David is on his way to the library. He has a study hall—though this early in the school year he can't imagine what he's expected to study. He and Kate discussed the matter a couple of weeks ago, before all the horrors of their visit to the carnival, and they decided the most likely, and most responsible plan was to start memorizing the lines of the parts they hoped to try out for in the fall play. The play is "You Can't Take It with You" and David wants to be Tony Kirby. Kate wanted to be Essie Carmichael, but David thinks she could play Alice Sycamore. There's an old movie of the play, but neither of them has seen it. Nobody's sure who's going to be the grandfather, but Kate thinks probably Miss Samways will argue that one of the teachers—maybe Mr. Ambrose—will have to do it. "My students can grow up one generation," she told Kate, "but I'm not sure they can skip two." None of this may matter now: Kate might not even want to be on the same stage with him, though there's nothing he can do except "soldier on"—as his father likes to say. What saves his mood in the face of another day of watching Kate avoid him is that he's been permitted to drive the Chevy to school—"but don't tell your father." So what if Kate doesn't speak to him.

Kate's mother has already bought her a copy of the playbook, but David is planning to use the library copy this period. When he'd suggested to his father that he'd like to own the play, his father had postponed him. Instead, he'd opened the Willard family Bible and shown David the source of the play's title.

"Timothy six, verse seven," he said. The verse read: *For we brought nothing into this world, and it is certain we can carry nothing out.*

David isn't sure this qualifies as a source. The verse is a far cry from *You can't take it with you,* though there's no arguing with a man who went to divinity school. "Your father could have been a biblical scholar," David's mother once told him. "He just decided he'd rather be a family man."

As if "family man" was an occupation.

He is just turning the library doorknob when he feels a hand on his shoulder. It's Tom Gowen, who steers him away from the study room.

"Get a c.p.," Tom says, "and meet me in the boys' room."

"What for?" David says, but Tom is already walking away.

David has an uneasy feeling in the bottom of his stomach, provoked by the expression on Tom's face, which is serious, even scared, in a way David has never seen. He puts his books on a desk near the windows and goes right away to the front of the room. Coach Clarke—Kate's homeroom teacher—has charge of the study hall; when David asks for a corridor pass, Clarke scrawls a signature and gives him the slip of blue paper, barely looking up.

* * *

In the boys' bathroom at the end of the north wing, Tom is sitting on a windowsill, feet dangling, schoolbooks stacked on the sill beside him. He's smoking a cigarette in an agitated way—short puffs, the cigarette cupped in his hand. When David appears, Tom drops the butt on the floor and slides off the window ledge to grind it out with his heel.

"I need a favor," he tells David. "A serious favor."

David waits. Tom is nervous. It's as if he doesn't want to say what the favor is. He paces a step or two toward one of the room's two sinks, leans his palms on either side of one of them, looks at his face in the mirror above.

"Shirley's pregnant." He watches himself say the words, then straightens up and faces David. "Her period's two weeks late."

"Jesus," David says. It's the last thing he expected to hear. It's only a few days since Tom bragged about how Shirley couldn't get pregnant, even though he'd never used a rubber. "You told me you always pulled out."

"Well maybe once I didn't. Anyway, there it is." He pulls a mangled pack of Camels out of his shirt pocket, finds and lights another cigarette. "I need your help."

"How?" He can't imagine what use he could be in this situation, and in fact he's thinking more about himself than about Tom Gowen. What if he'd done that to Kate? Not just made her touch him, but forced her to take him inside—pushed her onto the ground on the pitch-dark edge of The Meadows and torn off whatever underthings she wears, pried her knees apart. . . . But she'd have fought him, and in the dark of that night he couldn't have seen any of the body parts that excite him when he's in his own bathroom with the door locked and the picture pages opened before him, so how could he know if he'd have been hot enough to actually come into her? None of it is like his imaginings across the street from the church, picturing Tom and Shirley on the Trojan Club couch. But *pregnant!* The word doesn't fit any of his fantasies.

"There's a doctor in Wells Beach," Tom says. "He can do an operation to take care of the baby. But we don't have any way to get there."

Killing the baby—maybe it makes sense. When Betty Lowe got pregnant a couple of years ago, when she was a sophomore, her parents yanked her out of school and sent her away. She never came back to school; everybody said that she went to a home in Bath where she could have the baby, and that she did have it. Nobody is sure what happened to it. One of her friends said she gave it out for adoption, but another friend said she kept it and when her parents sold their house on East Street and left Scoggin she and the baby moved in with them. Betty never said who the father was, but everybody knew it was Harold Watson, who the very next year went away to a military school in Indiana. Going to high school is like being in one of those soap operas on morning radio.

"I don't know what you want me to do," David says.

"You've got your license, don't you?"

"Sure."

"Then you can borrow your dad's car," Tom says. "You can drive us to Wells Beach, and then drive us back after she has the operation."

Does Tom know he got Ma's permission to drive the car to school today, and that because his father's mother died, David has what Mr. Casavant would call *carte blanche* with using the Chevy? If Tom already knows, then David won't be able to say he can't help him out.

"It isn't legal, is it? The operation?"

"What does that have to do with anything?" Tom says. He takes a long, angry drag on the cigarette. "Will you do this for us or not?"

"I don't know if they'll let me have the car," David lies. It isn't that he has any definite plan for the car. It's that he has hopes that involve Kate forgiving him and letting him take the place of her missing father, the way Sherrie suggested.

"Jesus Christ," Tom says. "Give me a fucking answer."

"When? When are you doing this?"

"Tomorrow afternoon. I already called the doctor, and he expects us to be there at five-thirty. Come on, Dave. Can you do it?"

"I'll try," David says. Friday his mother will have to go to Springfield for grandma's funeral, and David will have to drive her to the train. He can't go with her to the funeral because of school. Nothing prevents him from driving Tom and Shirley to Wells Beach tomorrow. If worse comes to worst, if his father checks the odometer and finds out what he's done, he'll just have to face the consequences. "I'm pretty sure I can do it."

"I'll buy the gas," Tom says. He grinds the second cigarette under his shoes, then stoops to pick up both butts, which he throws into the toilet in the nearest stall.

"I appreciate that," David says.

"Shirley's supposed to be going to the dentist. That's what she's already told her folks. I'm going to meet her downtown, so you can pick us up in front of the State at, say, four o'clock."

"Okay."

They leave the boys' room together. Tom has physics lab in one direction and David's study hall is in the other, but just as they are separating Tom seizes David's hand.

"I won't forget this," Tom says. "You're a real friend."

"I hope I am," David says. "I hope I'm a friend to both of you."

* * *

He wants to tell Kate what he has promised Tom. It is the sort of promise that makes him feel older, almost adult, because it involves him in a serious act that will rescue others from a crisis situation. If Kate knew about it, she would think him noble and she would admire him, and perhaps she would forget what he did at the carnival. But Kate is having nothing to do with him. In the cafeteria—they're both assigned to the ridiculously early 10:45 lunch period—she lets him catch her eye only once, and she does that so she can look away with an expression on her face that tells him what she thinks of him. She thinks he's contemptible. Then she carries her tray to the other side of the room and sits with Trudy Sawyer. David happens to know that Kate doesn't even like Trudy Sawyer.

20.

Sherrie isn't exactly in pain. What was done to her by the men in the tent has mostly been done to her before, but only by one man at a time, off and on over all the years of her adult life. This time she feels both abused and aroused, and as she lies on the bed at the rear of the trailer it is as if she is floating just above the mattress, light-headed, suspended somewhere between waking and dreaming. She isn't bleeding—or doesn't think she is—but she's certain there will be bruises all over her when she studies herself in tomorrow's mirrors, and the chafing between her legs—once the numbness wears off—means sitting will be unpleasant and uncomfortable.

When Frank comes back, he'll soak a washcloth in hot water with Epsom salt and bathe her gently from head to toe. That will be genuine pleasure, a human relief from what she can only think of as an animal mauling. Probably she has suffered some kind of shock, the shock a part of the barrier between the hurt she ought to be feeling and what she in fact does feel. She has smoked reefer, and that gave her a similar sense of being separated from herself. A blessing, she thinks, like saying that what the body doesn't know can't hurt it.

Animals. It isn't so much that she didn't invite an animal attention from the men who watched her perform. The performance itself, the last one before teardown, was calculated to be just such an invitation. But the expectation was that the public nature of the setting, and the social connections among the men of the town, would make impossible any genuine violence, any unrestrained, cave-man brutishness. At first she had accepted, even *wanted*, the touches, the caresses, the intrusions of fingers and hands and tongues. But then things went haywire. Now there were teeth and nails, her body rolled and dragged and all but dismembered. How many men were there, on and around her? How many had only stayed to watch? She had no way to know; the light was on the stage, the area around it unlit, dark, a limbo where there could have been dozens of watchers. Onstage, one man entered her, and then another, and then there were two at once. Her body contorted impossibly. She might have replaced the rubber man's act and drawn a different audience. When Frank finally stepped in, punching and kicking until the last half-dressed man was off her, she lay on her back, lame and exhausted, her breasts aching, sex raw, mouth bruised from kisses that smelled of beer and cigarettes and were never affectionate.

"What's the m-matter with you?" Frank said. "Why do you m-make them want to d-do this to you?"

And so she lies in bed, looking up at the ceiling of the trailer, where the metal reflection of objects from below shimmers into shapes as crazy as her mind. When she hears the trailer door open, she closes her eyes. Now she'll be touched by hands that love her, and now the world will be healed.

"Dear Frank," she says—the words so soft, she can barely hear them herself.

"It's Joe," a man's voice says. "Did you think I'd never find you?"

* * *

She hasn't seen him in nearly three years, but all it takes is the sound of his voice to bring back the trials and terrors of the marriage. His stocky body, and the way he holds himself inside it—always leaning slightly forward, elbows out from his side—belongs to a man on the defensive, ready to strike back at any real or imagined threat. He still wears his scowl, the expression of a man who looks at the world and sees neither virtue nor pleasure nor reward. He comes into the trailer, door slamming behind him, as if it is his, and he surveys Sherrie—speaks to her, too—like a man who has never given her up.

"Where's your nigger waiter?" he says. "Where's your sweet stuttering Lochinvar?"

"Frank's working. The show's leaving town tonight."

"And what's the matter with you?" He approaches the bed. She can smell him, his sweat the odor of whiskey. "You sick?"

"I did three performances tonight," she says, thinking *And the last one damn near killed me.* "I was taking a little nap."

"Wore yourself out, did you?" he says. "I saw your fancy sign-board. Nice horny picture. I bet the yokels really love you."

"We do a decent business."

Joe laughs. That dirty laugh she'd never gotten used to. "Decent," he says. "That's a hot one."

He sits heavily on the bed, his hip against hers, forcing her to give way. Now she can smell his breath as well.

"What do you want, Joe?" she says. "Say it and get the hell out of my life."

He smirks and reaches for her. "I see you've still got this ratty pink robe," he says. "You look like a wilted flower garden." He parts the lapels of the robe and bares her poor hurt breasts. "Nice," he says. He opens the robe to her waist and strokes her breasts, thumbs pushing the nipples upward and chafing them into stiffness. "Real nice."

She feels helpless under his big hands. Is it going to be the tent all over again, one more man bruising her, violating her, teaching her humiliation—as if she didn't already know it well enough?

"Don't, Joe." She grips his wrists but can't move them. "Don't."

He pushes her breasts together, forces them apart—once, twice, setting a rhythm, handling her as if she is a thing with unfeeling movable parts. "Nothing else feels like tits," Joe says. "Nothing in the whole world."

"Please, Joe."

"And it's nice how this one's healed," he says. "I can hardly see my brand on you. We'll have to freshen it up, won't we?" Now he is sliding a coarse hand across her belly, trying to probe between her legs.

"No," she says. She crosses her left leg over her right, twisting away from him, shutting his hand out. God, where is Frank?

Joe sits up, draws his hands back. As a parting gesture, he flips one lapel of the robe so it covers her chest. He stands up and rubs the swelling below his belt.

"All right, Mrs. I'm-too-fucking-good-for-you. Get up and put some clothes on. We can be home by morning."

"I'm not going anywhere."

The hand that has affirmed his arousal flies toward her. It whips her, palmflat, across the forehead and snaps her head into the pillow, then it comes again, backhand, and strikes her across the mouth. "Get into your goddamned clothes," he says. He grabs her left arm and drags her off the bed. "Now!"

* * *

This is what Coggio sees when he opens the trailer door and steps inside:

A large man wearing black trousers and a black leather jacket has hold of Sherrie by one arm and is dragging her off the bed she shares with Coggio. Her pink robe is open to the waist; the way her legs are flailing, Coggio can see everything she has. The man is yelling, "Now! Now!" and swearing a blue streak. Sherrie is screaming, saying words that are unintelligible—probably they are swear words too. As Coggio watches, Sherrie is rolled off the bed and falls to the floor. Now the man—Coggio never sees his face—tries to lift her to her feet, his hands holding both her wrists.

All this takes a couple of seconds. They don't see Coggio, they don't hear him, and he himself says not a word, doesn't make himself known, eases the trailer door closed and makes a beeline for his truck. Running to the driver's side, he yanks open the door and reaches inside the map pocket. He takes out the gun, a .38-caliber pistol he bought when he drove for Railway Express, and carries it back to the trailer. He has never fired the pistol, but he keeps it loaded—a box of cartridges sits at the back of the glove compartment—and knows that all he has to do is slip the safety off and pull the trigger.

Perhaps this is what Frank Coggio has lived for, these past three years: Sherrie, the carnival, the gun, all part of a calculation that will put the lid on the past—like a destiny, so that when he once more opens the trailer door, he does it boldly and noisily and with no fear.

The two faces turn toward him. Sherrie's is pale, tear-stained, her eyes frightened. Joe's—and this is the first moment that Coggio *knows* who the man is, though the knowledge hardly surprises—is angry and defiant; he has been interrupted in the act of being himself.

Joe speaks first, saying, "Well lookie who's here." He pushes Sherrie aside. She stands unsteadily, wearing a lacy beige slip and a white blouse not yet buttoned, beside the open closet. Joe draws himself up to his full height and hooks his thumbs in his belt. His jacket is unzipped; under it he wears a plaid shirt opened far enough to display his black chest hair. "What can we do for you?"

"No, Joe," Sherrie says.

The gun is in Coggio's right hand, safety off, but he holds it behind him, out of sight, the muzzle alongside the back of his thigh. Jesus, who'd have imagined the man Sherrie has described to him—the one in his twenties, the smooth dancer with the rubber legs and the windmill arms, the handsome Valentino with the slicked-back hair and the pouty mouth made for kissing the girls—would turn out in his forties to be this coarse ape with a beer belly and a face like a wrestler?

"G-get out of here," Coggio says. "Sherrie's been through with you for a l-long, long t-time."

"Says you."

"That's r-right. S-s-says me."

"You puny little twerp," Joe says. He takes a step toward Coggio, both hands raised into fists. "By the time you get the words out to beg for mercy, you'll be out the door and on your ass."

Before Joe can take a second step, the pistol is out. "Stop," Coggio says—one sharp syllable, no stammering.

Joe stops. "Let's get this straight," he says. "Sherrie's still my wife. Legally. I'm here to take her home. You and your gun aren't going to stop me, even if you had the guts to use it—which I'm damned sure you don't."

"T-try me," Coggio says.

"Finish dressing," Joe says to Sherrie. "I haven't got all night."

Sherrie begins buttoning the blouse. Joe folds his arms; he contemplates Coggio and Coggio's weapon.

"I think I'll smoke a cigarette," he says. "Isn't that what the condemned man does in front of the firing squad?"

He takes a pack of Camels out of his shirt pocket, taps one out, puts it in the corner of his mouth. He finds a book of matches in a jacket pocket and lights the cigarette.

"She's n-not leaving with you," Coggio says.

Joe takes a long drag from the cigarette. He holds it the way movie gangsters do, between the thumb and middle finger so the curve of the palm shields it. "We'll see," he says.

Sherrie has stepped into a black skirt that zips up the side. She adjusts the blouse at her waist so it's tucked in evenly. She takes a pair of low-heeled shoes from the closet and slips her feet into them, holding the edge of the door for balance.

"Don't pack anything," Joe tells her over his shoulder. "We'll go shopping in Hartford."

"I'm w-warning you," Coggio says.

Joe takes Sherrie roughly by one arm and drags her with him toward the trailer door. "Get the fuck out of the way," he says.

The first shot catches Joe in the shoulder away from Sherrie, the force of it turning him half around. He lets Sherrie go and lifts the freed hand to touch the wound, the blood. "You little shit," he says.

The second shot hits him in the stomach, which is where Coggio had thought he was aiming the first one, and his knees buckle. The third grazes the side of his head and imbeds itself in the floor in front of the icebox. The fourth enters his neck and tears into his throat, so that when he tries to talk, the only sound is a harsh wheezing noise.

By this time Joe is face-down on the floor of the trailer; Sherrie is cowering on the bed, hugging a pillow to her chest; Coggio is standing over the fallen man, firing and firing. Five. Six. All the men in Sherrie's life, all the liars and takers, all the thieves of her attentions; every man Coggio knows about and every man he's ever imagined, they're all lying dead in front of him.

"Sweet Jesus, Frank," Sherrie says. "Dear sweet Jesus."

She drags herself up from the bed and kneels beside the man who abused her more than any other in her entire life. In spite of that, she is sobbing.

Coggio is amazed. "Are you s-sorry for this evil s-son of a bitch?" he says. "He m-made your life hell."

"And he's dead. Everything paid for." She wipes the tears from her cheeks with a knuckle of her right hand. It's a child's gesture, Coggio thinks. As if all this time Sherrie is a little girl and he has been her guardian.

Now he looks down at the gun in his hand, seeing it as if for the first time. He tucks the weapon into his belt.

"I have to go for the cops," he says. "You'd better come with me." He doesn't want to leave her weeping over a man who doesn't deserve it.

* * *

Looking back, what Frank finds most surprising is that the pistol fired at all. It was an old Smith & Wesson he'd bought at a gun shop in Boston, off Scollay Square, while he was driving for Railway

Express and thought it might be wise to have protection. You never knew what was in some of the bags and boxes RE carried; if they had value, and if someone knew about the value—well, there was still a lingering Depression after all.

So he'd bought it, along with a box of cartridges he'd loaded into the weapon's six chambers, and for years he'd carried it in the pickup, tucked down in the pocket of the driver's door behind the maps and the winter gloves. Until Joe Connors showed up, Frank had nearly forgotten the pistol existed, and when he fetched it out of the map pocket, his hands shaking because he was so angry, he could feel the coarseness of rust along the barrel and the spine of the grip. *God,* he'd thought, *what if I pull the trigger and nothing happens?* And then of course *everything* happened.

He has no particular recollection of the shooting. It's as if his mind has to reconstruct it—*this* must have happened, and then *this,* and then I must have done *so* because of whatever it was he said to me—because the moment itself is all shadow and a noise like a railroad train. He's heard the expression "blind rage", and he thinks this must be what he experienced at the time: an overwhelming darkness that appeared between himself and the man he was killing—not like a curtain descending, but a wall rising all in an instant, the sound of the pistol shots barely audible through the thunder throbbing in his head.

When he is told how many times he fired, all six and only one of them a miss, he finds the information difficult to believe. But it must be true. Joe Connors is dead. Not only did Frank Coggio do the deed, but he then drove to the center of town, asked directions to the police station, and turned himself in. He doesn't even remember if Sherrie was with him.

21.

At first Kate thinks they are a part of her dream, the succession of light knocks that seem to come from a great distance, and it isn't until she is awake enough to read the face of the clock on her nightstand, its hands pointing to a few minutes past three, that she realizes the knocking is at the front door, the loudness of it diminished by the expanse of hallway and stairwell. Now it stops. Kate has almost drifted back to sleep, convinced she was dreaming all along, when it begins again—this time only three sharp raps that echo in the silent house.

She gets out of bed and puts on the white terry robe Daddy brought last Christmas from Chicago. The noise from downstairs apparently hasn't roused her parents, whose bedroom is at the back of the house, so it's for Kate to discover whoever is at the door at this small hour.

As she switches on the porch light and opens the door, Sherrie says, "Thank the Lord it's you. I wouldn't know what to say to anybody I don't know." She looks frazzled and pushes a fallen lock of hair away from her forehead. "Can I come in? Can we talk?"

For the moment Kate can't find words, simply opens the door wider to let Sherrie in. She's never seen the woman really *dressed*—in a black skirt that just falls to the knee, a simple white blouse, and a dark red cardigan over her shoulders. Her shoes are plain and black, with a short heel, and a round black straw hat is perched on her head. She's carrying a purse that looks to be make-believe alligator hide.

"I didn't ring the bell," Sherrie says, "because I didn't want to wake up the whole house. I thought with your young ears you might hear what your folks wouldn't."

"You were right."

"I looked you up in the phone book—you were the only Meredith in town—and asked them to bring me here."

Kate turns on a table lamp in the front parlor and steers Sherrie to a seat on the couch. Who is "them," she wonders, and why is Sherrie here? "Have you been crying? Can I get you a tonic? I think we have ginger ale and Orange Crush."

Sherrie wipes her cheeks with the back of her fists—that answers the first question—as for the others, she says, "If you had something stronger..."

Kate knows there is whiskey in the dining room sideboard, "for medicinal use," and she guesses that whatever is bothering Sherrie will qualify. She gets a juice glass from the kitchen and pours an inch or so of liquid from a pint bottle of Old Mr. Boston rye. When she brings it to the parlor, Sherrie has taken off the hat and slumped into a corner of the couch as if she is exhausted.

"Well, it happened," she says. She takes the glass from Kate and sips from it. "Joe found me, just like I knew he would someday."

"Oh dear," Kate says. "Is he following you?" If that's even a remote possibility, she should go upstairs and wake Daddy.

"He's dead," Sherrie says. "Frank killed him."

"God!"

"That's why I'm here. The police arrested Frank, and they won't let me stay in the trailer until they're finished investigating. You were the only person I knew in this town." She downs the rest of the whiskey, puts the empty glass on the table, beside the lamp. "I know your boyfriend too, but his dad is a preacher; I didn't believe he'd take kindly to the likes of me."

"But are you all right? Were you hurt? Tell me what happened." Now that she's wide awake, all sorts of ideas and questions are buzzing around in Kate's head. Oddly, she wishes David were here, knowing how much he wants to be a reporter, imagining how excited he'd be that the story of Sherrie and her husband is honest-to-gosh news. Kate wants to know exactly what happened at the trailer, who said what to whom, and what did Frank kill him with. What did the police do, where was Frank now, and was it self-defense?

"Frank had a gun in the truck. He brought it in and shot Joe with it. I was scared half to death."

"Oh, Sherrie." Kate sits on the couch beside and squeezes Sherrie's hands in hers. "My goodness."

Kate is so engrossed in Sherrie's story, the appearance of her father startles her. It's as if he's all at once materialized in the parlor doorway.

"I heard talking," he says. "What's going on?"

* * *

By the time Kate has made the introductions and Sherrie has told her story, and Daddy has been persuaded that everything that can be done has already been taken care of, the clock in the front hall has struck four. The sound of the chimes seems to energize Sherrie.

"Lord," she says, "the time. I should let you nice people go back to bed and catch up on your sleep," and she reaches for her purse as if she's on her way.

"Where will you go?" Daddy asks her.

And that's a good question, because Sherrie has already told them that the police haven't finished doing whatever it is they're doing with the trailer and with Frank's truck, and she doesn't know anybody else in Scoggin, and nobody in town would even dream of staying at the Belvedere Hotel—rumored to harbor fleas and bedbugs—so where *will* she go?

"I guess I haven't given it any thought," Sherrie says, "with all the excitement. Maybe I should go to the police station and have them put me in with Frank."

"Can't she stay here?" Kate gives her father a pleading look. "Just for tonight?"

"Well..." Daddy says.

"She can have my bed, and I'll curl up right here on the couch."

"No, no," says Sherrie. "The davenport'll suit me fine."

And so the matter is settled. Before she drifts back into sleep, Kate hears Daddy talking to Mother, and though she can't make out the words, she knows he is explaining why a man has been murdered and why a naughty dancer from the carnival is spending the rest of the night—and probably the morning—on the couch in the parlor.

* * *

Kate wakes up with the daylight, the events of the early morning reforming themselves in her mind's eye. She gets up, puts on the white robe and bunny slippers, and goes down the front stairs as quietly as she can. The living room couch is unoccupied, the linens Kate used to create a makeshift bed are folded neatly and stacked at one end. Sherrie must not have slept at all.

22.

Thursday morning at school, everyone is talking about what happened at the carnival last night. A man murdered, the man rumored to be the husband of the kootch dancer—the way the *Tribune* described her—and David can imagine the pleasure Mr. Godwin took writing the phrase. Not much happens in Scoggin, and the idea of printing words like *murder* and *kootch dancer* and *scene of the crime* must have thrilled him, not to mention his readers.

David heard about the shooting while he was eating breakfast, sitting across from his mother and eating Shredded Wheat, which he hated because it has no taste unless you drown it in sugar and milk. His mother lowered the *Tribune* and clucked her tongue.

"You remember your dad warning you about that carnival that's out on the edge of town?"

"Sure."

"Well just in case you thought he was talking through his hat, they say a man was murdered there last night."

"No kidding? Who?"

"I don't think it would be anybody you know." His mother turns to the society page and goes on reading. David has all the information he's going to get from this particular source. When she finally leaves the table, all she says is, "I do wish your father were here." As if that would change anything.

David finishes his cereal and pulls the newspaper toward him. He reads about Sharita and a man "believed to be the woman's husband," and about Frank Coggio, who is "alleged" to have pulled the trigger of the gun that killed the husband. The husband doesn't have a name, because the police haven't released it. The *Tribune* story describes the trailer where the shooting happened and talks about Sharita's performances at the carnival.

David feels an odd thrill as he reads the story. He was there, inside that trailer; he knows who Coggio is, and he is closer to Sharita than anybody knows. What would have happened if he had been with her when the husband appeared? Would he have risen to her defense? And then what? The newspaper story doesn't say if the husband had a gun, or maybe a knife. Maybe a struggle would have taken place and David would have been wounded. Maybe someone outside—yes, Coggio—would have heard the struggle and burst into the trailer. Then Coggio draws his gun and shoots the husband. Same outcome, but when the police arrive, Sharita has her arms around David, telling him how brave he is.

* * *

Tom Gowen is the first person he talks with when he gets to school. When he finishes parking the Chevy in the school lot, Tom is across the street, smoking a cigarette, and when he sees David he waves him over.

"Did you get it?" David knows he means the car. In the midst of the morning's news he has almost forgotten his agreement to drive to Wells Beach, but of course that's what he'll be doing this afternoon.

"I drove to school," David says. "Did you hear the news about the dancer we saw at the carnival?"

"I heard something. Is she dead?"

"It wasn't her that got shot. They're saying it was her husband."

Tom scowls. "She had a husband?"

"So they say."

"Christ, who would marry somebody who made her living showing the world her cunt? Would you?"

David shrugs. "I suppose not." But he's never thought of Sharita in that way. Tom is making her into something ugly and dirty, and David knows she isn't like that.

"Anyway," Tom says, "we've got problems of our own." He takes a last drag on the cigarette and flicks the butt into the street. "Don't forget," he says, walking away, "four o'clock in front of the State."

* * *

Wells Beach is where David's Uncle Willie used to have a souvenir shop. When he was young—eight or nine years old—David had trouble figuring out all the family relationships. At first he thought Uncle Willie was *his* uncle, but finally he came to understand that this jovial, bald man with bad teeth was his mother's uncle—her father's older brother. As time went on, Ma had filled in details: when her father—David's grandfather—had his heart attack and died, Uncle Willie had "joined the family." "I think he tried to replace Daddy," Ma said. "He'd take me for ice cream, or to the movies, or he'd read to me at bedtime, even though I was perfectly able to read for myself. I was six when Daddy went to his reward; by the time I was twelve,

I'd almost forgotten him. We were so grateful, my mother and I, for Uncle Willie's coming into our lives. He wasn't nearly as smart as Daddy—so my mother told me—and he wasn't much to look at, fat and bald and red in the face, but he had a good heart. And he sang to me. My favorite was 'Froggy went a-courting, he did ride.'"

Much of this she told David after Uncle Willie's funeral, three or four years ago. Today, driving with Tom and Shirley down these same roads, passing the motor courts and motels on Route One, most of them already putting out signs that read *Closed for the Season*—because "the Season" was Memorial Day at one end and Labor Day at the other—then turning at the Howard Johnson's onto the Mile Road that leads to the ocean, David remembers Uncle Willie with something like pleasure. He remembers the cluttered shop, the crocodile, how happy he felt to be the center of attention in a grownup world. The souvenir shop isn't here anymore; now its location has become a fried-clams restaurant. Too bad, David thinks. Today he'd have chosen the most expensive toy in the shop.

Along the shore road, many of the cottages are already shuttered, some with windows boarded up against the Atlantic winter, a few with ropes stretched across driveways, the ropes hung with *No Trespassing* signs. The cottages are without exception wood-framed and clapboard-sided. All of them have porches that face the sea; all have single chimneys for fireplaces. None of them looks anything like a doctor's office or a clinic.

"What's the number of this place?" David is watching the mailboxes, driving slowly past the long row of houses.

"Thirteen-thirty." Tom is holding a creased slip of paper. "It's a yellow house with white trim."

"I can't make out the numbers," David says. "It must be raining."

"It doesn't rain anymore," Tom says. "That's from the wind blowing in from the ocean."

"There's twelve-fifty," Shirley says. She leans across Tom so she can read the mailbox numbers. "You should slow down."

"I'm not going fast," David says. Now that the three of them are about to reach their destination, the enormity of what he has done—is doing—comes to the front of his mind and hangs there like a headache not quite arrived. He has lied to his parents; he has stolen his father's car; he is helping to murder a child. The fact that the child is a mere embryo—it probably doesn't even look human, for God's sake—is beside the point. It's a life; he can hear his father using words like "precious" and "sacred" and "holy" to describe the thing Shirley is carrying inside her, though in the same breath his father would call the act that produced the thing "vile" and "profane" and "an insult to God."

"Here it is."

Tom points across David's field of vision at the house. It's an ordinary summer cottage painted mustard-yellow, and the trim is dirty white.

"It doesn't look much like a doctor's office," David says. He pulls into a driveway—two dirt tracks through unmowed grass—and shuts off the engine. Another car, a black Packard coupé, is parked facing him.

"He said to come in through the side entrance," Tom says. He takes Shirley's hand and opens his door. "Let's get this over with."

"I don't want you to come in," Shirley tells him.

"Why not?"

"I just don't."

"I have to pay the doctor."

"You can give me the money." She frees her hand from Tom's and holds it in front of him. "I'll pay him."

Tom hesitates. Watching Tom's reflection in the rear-view mirror, David thinks he can read what is going through Tom's mind, whether he can afford to give up control over this event and let Shirley be responsible for her own body in a way that hasn't been possible while the two of them were going to bed together, whether it means that killing their baby is killing their love—setting them free of each other.

But Tom doesn't insist. He puts the money in her opened hand and stands outside the car, holding the door for her. As she crosses in front of the car, David sees her jaw set, tears shining on her cheeks. She pulls open the side door of the cottage and goes in. A small white plaque at eye level reads *Clinic*.

Tom slams the rear door shut and gets into the front seat beside David. "I wish she hadn't done that," he says. He finds a cigarette and lights it with a silver lighter. David knows the lighter was a gift from Shirley; both their initials are engraved on it. "It's my money."

"How much?" David wonders. He rolls down his window so the smoke has some place to go.

"Two hundred and fifty."

"Golly. Where'd you get it?"

"Bank. I dipped into my college fund."

"Your folks know?"

"The account's in my name," Tom says. "It's my money."

David ponders this fact. He too has a college fund, at Scoggin Trust, but it's in his name and his father's. If he wanted to withdraw money, his father would have to sign the withdrawal slip—not that he ever would.

"How'd you find out about this doctor?"

"Jack's cousin Leo."

"He the one at Northeastern?"

"Yeah. One of his frat brothers got a girl in trouble last summer when they were working at the beach. He says this guy is really sharp, really safe."

"That's good for Shirley."

"His real practice is in Boston. He just comes here in the summertime."

The two sit quietly, Tom smoking, David staring out the windshield at the small surf rolling up the sandy beach he can see toward the southeast. The fine mist carried on the wind cools his face.

"You should roll down your window too," David says. "My Dad will raise Cain if he smells tobacco in his pride and joy."

"Sure." Tom cranks the window open, makes a show of blowing cigarette smoke outside.

"How long do you think it will take?" David says.

"The procedure?"

"Is that what they call it?"

"I don't know how long," Tom says. "It's supposed to be pretty simple."

A *simple procedure* is what they ought to put on the baby's cemetery marker, except there won't be a cemetery marker—no headstone, no name on the family crypt like the one at Oakdale that already has three Willard names on it, with birthdates and hyphens.

David sits in silence, thinking about Shirley and what sorts of things the doctor might be doing to her. He can't help remembering all the times he's envied girls because it's so much easier for them to masturbate, the world being so full of penis-shaped objects, and he thinks of Vernon Wiley's cucumber lady. Then it's all right for David to be preoccupied with sex; so is Jack; so, obviously, is Tom. Maybe girls are too—except cautious Kate Meredith. *Just my luck.*

The procedure seems to be taking a long time. The clock in the Chevy dashboard reads half past six. Out beyond the white furls of surf a fog is beginning to settle. Mist blurs the windshield and beads on the surfaces of both cars.

"You believe the Bible?" Tom says.

It's a strange question, and it comes out of nowhere. "What do you mean?" is all David can think to answer.

"Do you believe that everything they tell about in the Bible really and truly happened?"

"Not everything," David says. "I don't believe Jesus Christ went up to heaven, body and all."

"That's New Testament," Tom says. "What about Old Testament. You believe that?"

"I don't know. Like what?"

"Like the Adam and Eve story."

David knows what his father thinks—that the Genesis stories are full of *metaphors*, which means what they say happens stands for something else. "You mean the woman being made out of Adam's rib?"

"No, the later part, where they eat the forbidden fruit and get thrown out of Paradise."

"I never thought about it," David says.

"I was thinking how if Shirley and I were those two people, we'd be the only people in the whole wide world, and you and I wouldn't have to be here today. We'd just go ahead and have a baby. Nobody'd give a shit."

"That's true."

Tom lights a new cigarette, his third one since David asked him to roll down the window. Now, if this mist turns into the first real rain since April, David will have to choose between wet upholstery or the reek of tobacco smoke. Either way, facing his father gets more complicated.

"I don't know what's going to become of us," Tom says out of the blue.

"Us?"

"Shirley and me." He sucks on the cigarette, lets the smoke roll heavily from his nostrils. "She's Catholic," he says.

"What difference does that make?"

"She doesn't look at things the same way we do. This abortion business. She calls it a sin."

When Tom says "we," he means Protestants, but David thinks his father—and probably other denominations—also considers it a sin. But if sin is so important, why did Shirley do what she did to get pregnant in the first place?

"How do you suppose it happened?" David says. "Her getting pregnant."

Tom shrugs. "The old story," he says.

"So did she want to have the baby?"

"She says not."

Then, thinks David, she's not such a hot Catholic. "How do they get rid of it?" he says. "I mean I know it's simple, but do they scrape it out of her, or what?"

"I don't know the details," Tom says. "I'd just as soon not know what they do."

"Probably messy." Though the jars at the carnival hadn't shown any blood.

"Probably."

"But she'll be fine in the end."

"Positively," Tom says. "This doctor couldn't stay in business if it hurt the girl."

* * *

It's dusk when Shirley finally emerges from the beach cottage, the horizon already turning a deep purplish gray ahead of the eventual night, the shoreline a thin and changing pale line where the waves break on the sand. She lets the screen door bang shut and slides into the back seat. The cottage is dark; no one was in the doorway behind her as she came out.

Tom is already out of the car and getting in back to sit beside her. "Did you give him the money?" he says.

"Of course I did. What do you think?"

She lets Tom put an arm around her shoulders and give her a kiss just above her eyes. "You all right?"

"I'm swell," she says in a tone that means sarcasm. "He gave me a shot of something to kill the pain, but it still hurts." She slips a hand under her skirt. "I think I'm bleeding a little."

When she draws her hand out from under the fabric David thinks he can smell blood—as if blood had an odor. Now he has something new to worry about: blood on the seat of his father's Chevy. How will he get *that* out?

"What did the doctor say?"

"He said I should go home and lie down, and rest as much as I can."

"That's easy," Tom says.

"He says you can't come into me for a while."

"Maybe never."

"Yes," Shirley says. "Maybe never." She wipes her hand on her bare knee. "I wish I'd stop bleeding."

"Dave?" Tom says. "You got a handkerchief?"

"Don't you have one?"

"I forgot to put one in my pocket. Lend me yours."

"You're going to get it all bloody."

"For Christ's sake, David."

"My ma will be mad," David says. "How am I going to explain blood?"

"Tell her you had a nosebleed. *Will* you?"

David hands over his clean handkerchief. Shirley slides it under her skirt and holds it against her. "Can we go?" she says.

David starts the car and turns on the headlights. Directly in front of them the Packard's radiator-grille chrome glitters; off to the right is a sudden flash of white ribbon, small waves vivid against the dark. When he backs out of the driveway onto the shore road, the lights sweep across the rear of the cottage.

"Somebody's looking out the window," Tom says.

"The doctor," Tom says.

"Or his wife," says Shirley.

"His wife is there?" David says.

"She stood beside me," Shirley says. "She held my hand."

Well, David thinks, that's sensible. If you were someone who did this kind of operation, you wouldn't want to be alone in the room with a high-school girl, doing whatever you had to do between her legs, killing her baby, making her bleed. You'd have to have a woman there, to be on your side, to make you feel as if it was reasonable, the thing you were doing.

23.

When he makes the turn onto the mile road leading back to Route 1, the rear tires let go for just an instant and the car skids to the right. It's not much of a skid—David brings the Chevy under control in an instant—but it tells him that he shouldn't drive so fast. It isn't raining—there's been scarcely any rainfall this year—but that mist, drifting onshore from the ocean, coats the asphalt and makes it slick. Once they're away from the coast the road will be dry and perhaps David can find out how fast the car can go if the accelerator pedal is pushed to the floor. He needs speed. Shirley's procedure took longer than anyone had imagined, so long that by the time David walks into the house to face his parents, his excuse for taking the car won't hold water; the concessions and games at the beach will have shuttered long since, and what on earth could he and his friends have been doing *at this ungodly hour*? A piece of his father's last sermon, something about the foolish things people do in spite of God.

> *The God we worship in this church is always and eternally an amazing and wondrous Deity. And yet the multiplicity of His interests on our earth seems sometimes bizarre, perhaps perverse,*

as if He were a hobbyist of creation, as if He were an amateur
who refuses to take us humans seriously.

But if his father thinks that's the kind of God He is, then what's
wrong with being late? David is one of God's hobbies. How can he
be blamed?

In the rearview mirror he can make out the shadowy figures
of Tom and Shirley huddled together in the back seat. It looks as if
Tom still has his arm around her, and her head is on his shoulder.

He says to the back seat, "How's Shirley?"

"Not so good," Tom says. "She's crying."

"What about the blood?"

"I can't tell."

"I think it's not as bad as it was," Shirley says. Her voice is small,
broken.

Consider the butterfly: fragile, beautiful, a masterpiece of intri-
cate design and pattern. Yet its life spans a matter of weeks,
sometimes mere days. As if God thinks life is so commonplace,
it can be squandered on a trivial insect.

That's Shirley, David thinks. Fragile and beautiful, though it's
not her life that spans only weeks, but the life just taken out of her,
and a commonplace life at that, squandered on a high-school kid.

Now he's at Wells Corner, the Greyhound bus stop, the hard left
toward Scoggin. The road unreels ahead of him, dry now, the white
centerline endless in the headlights. He wonders what Kate would
think of what has happened tonight. Would she think he's done a
good deed? He knows she doesn't like Shirley, considers her cheap,
slutty, but wouldn't she have a little sympathy after tonight? If you

love somebody, shouldn't you make allowances for their mistakes? But of course he's thinking more about himself than about Shirley. Shouldn't Kate forgive a mistake he made because he loves her?

> *On the other hand, consider the serpent. It is a creature offensive to us all, a creature renowned for its evil, its subtle treacheries. We say to one who betrays us: 'You snake.' We refer to an untrustworthy person as 'a snake in the grass.'*

Yes, the mistake was a betrayal. If Kate loves him—let's say she does, because that's what David wants—then he has offended her and made it difficult for her to go on loving him.

Damn it! he thinks. He and Tom are both in the same boat; they've both done damage to the girls they love, and they'll both pay a price—David is sure of it. How long will it take for Kate to forgive him? How much longer before she trusts him? And how long will it be before Shirley lets Tom touch her secret places? How much longer before she is ever again open to him?

The town is behind them now, open country on both sides of the highway, and David jams his foot angrily on the accelerator pedal. The Chevrolet, even ten years old, lunges ahead. The shoulders of the road—a rural mailbox here, a farmhouse turnoff there, a highway sign, a hedge—are a blur, and patches of fog rise up and vanish in an instant. He has heard ignorant classmates call the accelerator an "exhilarator", and it rings true: he has never felt so exhilarated as he does now, racing through the night at an impossible speed. The speedometer needle has just touched 85 miles an hour, and David has just come in sight of the overpass that carries the new Maine Turnpike between Kittery and Portland, when a tire blows out.

* * *

What's amazing about the ensuing accident is how slowly it happens, and how his father's voice is like a commentary all throughout—a tribute to David's memory, and to his listening to his father rehearse his sermons out loud. *Genesis tells us it is the serpent who tempts Eve to partake of the forbidden fruit, a fruit which in olden days may have been an apple, or may have been a pomegranate, or may have been some antique fruit for which the modern world has no name. But what do the facts matter?* The fact is that in the instant David is aware that a front tire has blown, the same instant that the car lurches toward the ditch and the overpass beyond it, the very instant that the steering wheel forcibly yanks itself out of his grasp—in that instant, time slows to a crawl. He finds himself leaning toward the center of the car, the gearshift pushing against his right knee, his right arm swinging outward in a slow arc that encounters first the top edge of the dashboard and then the bottom of the rearview mirror and then the headliner on the passenger side—a brush of fabric like the way the back of his hand felt against Sherrie's pink robe, except this time there is no breast under the cloth and no illicit thrill or hope that the woman doesn't realize what he's trying to steal from her—and finally the pillar between windshield and door, a hard but painless blow. At the same time he's watching the world outside the car, through the windshield, the night that is slowly turning, like the Earth itself, counterclockwise, the headlights illuminating this unexpected revolution of himself and the machine he was supposed to be driving: the ditch, its tall plants—is it milkweed?—white with dust; the low wall of loose stones some farmer put together not to keep anything in or out but only to mark a boundary—*my territory, separate from* the State of Maine's right of way; the bushes with the orange berries the robins eat that stain the walks and steps in town; the tall yellow grasses, no doubt a parched hayfield, that stretch into the night out of sight; and the overpass, the raw concrete abutment that carries the new turnpike safely over State Route 109—the abutment that is like a gray iceberg in a cold black ocean, stolid, unmoored, adrift beyond any human control, and toward which the Chevrolet is slowly gliding, rolling, tumbling at a pace that is all suspense, all anticipation. And at the same time—is it truly the *same* time, or another time that's running parallel to what David sees, parallel to what he feels?—his father's portentous voice. *What is important is the imagery, the symbolism, the actions of the first woman and the first man seduced by the attractions of sin. Whether that attraction is called knowledge, or pride, or merely the lust by which we define sex. It is ever the evil hiss of the serpent. It is ever shameful, ever and always a revulsion.* He couldn't possibly be taking all this in: the motion, the noise, the details seen over the hood and fenders of the car, the speed of his thoughts registering small things, big things, dumb things. What's it about? Is it the evil of Sharita's dance, or his jerking off with Ray's *Esquire* magazine, or wanting Kate to put her hands on him, her mouth? Now it's noise that's all around him: the engine—his foot is hard on the accelerator, when the blowout flung his right hand off the steering wheel, he grabbed it with his left and floored the foot pedal as if the car's wheels could find purchase on the air they're flying through and steer them safely back onto the highway—the slap of bushes on the underside of the machine, the whistle of wind in the opened driver's window, the voices from the back seat.... Shirley is crying, not words, not even syllables, but interruptions of breath that seem to be trying to imitate speech. Tom is swearing, shouting: *Jesus. Watch out! What are you doing?* And David is answering, so eloquent: *The tire. The tire!* Now his arm is over the seat back and Shirley is grabbing his wrist, pulling him away from the wheel, but he's still watching the iceberg looming larger, brighter as the headlights come closer, a relentless—but still slow, still ungodly slow—approach.

And at last they meet, the airborne Chevrolet and the eternally grounded overpass abutment, with a shock that David could never have predicted, considering the painfully slow progress of the car between the instant of the blowout and the final instant of the crash. The sound is deafening; it smothers the cries from behind him; it even drowns out his father's pompous voice. The impact tears metal, shatters glass, crunches bone and muscle, and the last thought David has as he breaks through the windshield that framed his summary view of the world is how foolish it was to drive so far to end the life of Shirley's baby, when this momentous event would have killed it anyway.

24.

Kate hears about it the next day; it's all over the radio and the Friday morning *Press Herald* and the corridors of Scoggin High School. What's interesting is that everyone at school is talking about Tom Gowen and Shirley Kostas—what a lovely couple they were, what a bright future Tom had with his dad's business waiting for him, what wonderful children (Shirley's beauty, Tom's brains) they would have had—but hardly anybody talks about David except as a peculiar afterthought. Oh, yes, by the way, David was driving his father's Chevy—but more importantly, what were Tom and Shirley doing, riding with him to Wells Beach on a school night?

And the stories Kate hears. One version is that Tom and Shirley—always Tom and Shirley, but never Tom and Shirley and David; poor David—had decided to elope, and got David (finally he's important!) to drive them to the Greyhound station in Wells, and the two lovers were going all the way to Maryland, where there was no three-day waiting period. One story says their suitcases were in the wrecked car; another says the bags were thrown clear and haven't been found yet. But why were they coming back to Scoggin? They got cold feet, changed their minds. Maybe David, being his father's son, persuaded them it was a wrong thing to do.

Now David is in the spotlight, the bad guy, the driver who talked the golden couple out of their happiness, and then he killed all three of them.

Another version of the fateful day is that it was all a lark, that on the spur of the moment the three of them decided to skip school and go to the beach: play the arcade games, eat clams and fries, run on the beach, make the most of the end of summer before the start of the daily grind. Probably that was Tom's idea, and David—everybody knows how David followed Tom around like a puppy, how he'd do anything in the world to call Tom his friend—David said he'd get Daddy's car and drive them. Then why wasn't Kate Meredith with them? Wasn't she going steady with David? Well, that was another story, wasn't it?

As the day wears on, Kate pieces together the puzzle of the three classmates' last day, mostly from overhearing gossip in the girls' room. Sophie knows that Shirley missed her period. Amanda thinks Shirley has been depressed for the past week. Edris agrees and says she knows Shirley has been "letting herself go," hasn't washed her hair or taken a bath in at least week. "Haven't you guys noticed?" she says, and holds her nose. Janie tells all of them she saw Tom and Shirley arguing in front of his locker. About what? She doesn't know; she couldn't get close enough to hear the words. Amanda says Tom walked out of hygiene class yesterday, right in the middle of Miss Cougle lecturing about the sanctity of marriage. What do you make of that?

It's clear to Kate what to make of *that*. There's not much chance Shirley would want to go away to have a baby, and probably an even smaller chance that Tom Gowen would marry her so she could. As for poor David, the gossip being perfectly right about his devotion—if that's the word—to Tom and to David's idea of their happy goo-goo-eyed state, he'd have been only too happy to help them out:

borrow his father's car and drive the couple to one of those "back-street butchers" Miss Samways was always preaching about. If she'd known what was going on, you can bet she'd have talked him out of it, but to do that, she'd have had to be on speaking terms with him.

* * *

She doesn't want to blame herself. It's not as if she could have made herself into some kind of guardian angel sitting alongside David in his father's Chevy, her hand on his to turn the wheel away from his death. Death was his fault, not hers. It served him right to be punished for what happened at the carnival, exposing himself, pawing her, things even Darryl Jenks on his worst day would never have dared do. What did he think? What kind of weak person would she have had to be to forgive him so soon?

But how terrible. It would have been better if the punishment had fitted the crime—and what form would that punishment have taken? Weighing the insult and embarrassment to Kathryn Meredith against...? An accident, all right, but not fatal; not a life ended in a red cross painted on the road inside a yellow circle. A headline in the paper: *Teen Dents Dad's Fender.* Stupid.

Sitting in English class while Miss Folsom goes on and on about Robert Frost and Edwin Arlington Robinson, Kate feels sick. She has to close her eyes and press her lips hard together, begging her body not to betray her, not to spew vomit onto the desk. David is dead. Truly dead. She'll never see him again except at a funeral she knows she'll have to attend whether she wants to or not. He'll never be able to apologize—and he would have wanted to; she knows he would—and she'll never be able to forgive him except on the imaginary stage inside her brain where she rehearses all the undone

actions of her life: rescuing Carmody, lecturing her father, reforming the carnival dancer, even playing the lead in "You Can't Take It
With You." An inner life is what she has; her outer life is miserable
and worthless. And David is dead.

What did he think? They say your whole life passes before your
eyes when you die; what did David see? What was there to see? In
seventeen years, how much life did he have? Did he see Kate? Did
he see the carnival? Did he see his father's anger? His mother's love?
Kate's contempt? Did he see the imaginary years ahead—the years
unused, the years left for somebody else to live? Did he see waste? Did
he see how friendship and envy and favors could undo everything
that was important?

She raises her hand. Miss Folsom goes on talking about Robinson, who lived right here in Maine, who viewed the world with a
jaundiced eye. Kate waves the hand; the teacher ignores it. But she
can't wait. She leaves her desk and runs to the door of the classroom,
into the hall, Miss Folsom's voice finally acknowledging her—her
name, "Kathryn," following her into the girls' room, where her per-
ceived responsibility for David Willard's death overwhelms her.

* * *

Eventually all the truths come out. Barbara Stackpole's father is
a doctor who works weekends for the medical examiner's office,
and Monday morning she confirms that Shirley lost the baby. Jack
Morrison admits he knew all along that David was going to take his
dad's Chevy whether he had permission or not, and there was no
grand scheme for Tom and Shirley to run off and get married, and
never would have been. Edris Bedford lets it be known that Shirley
confided in her that she didn't want to keep the baby—that she

didn't believe Tom would make a very good father because he was too self-centered and sometimes she had the feeling that Tom's only interest in her was the sex, and there were some things he asked her to do that were kind of disgusting.

The police report, picked up by the *Tribune* and the *Press Herald* both, is short and sweet. David Willard was driving the car; no evidence of alcohol or other drugs; one tire (right front) flat, though whether the cause of the wreck, or caused by it, not determinable; likely cause of accident: speed on wet pavement, lack of driver experience.

All this information disturbs Kate, like how does Jack Morrison know that Tom didn't really want to get married to Shirley, baby or not, because hadn't he confessed as much to David? And what was wrong with breaking the rules and taking your father's car if you were helping a friend? Wouldn't David's father see that his son was only being Christian, following the Golden Rule? Who were these people to take such pleasure in the deaths of three of their classmates?

* * *

Supper is quiet. Mother has made beef stew and scalloped potatoes and peas, and there's tapioca pudding for dessert, but nobody seems to be hungry. Daddy takes a bite of beef and chews it as if he's thinking about the mechanics of chewing, his gaze directed, apparently, out the dining room window—where the world is, Kate thinks; where David is dead and Sherrie is all alone and out of a job.

"Isn't anyone going to eat my nice supper?" Mother says.

"Yes," Daddy says. "Of course we are." But he just goes on chewing, the fork in his right hand nowhere near anything on his plate.

"Katie?"

"It's very good," Kate says. "Especially the potatoes."

Her mother shakes her head. "I give up," she tells her family. "I really do give up."

"It's been an awful week." Kate takes a sip from her water glass, as if she is about to make a speech—and in a way she is. Somebody has to make sense out of the thing that's hanging over all their heads, out of *death*. Kate pronounces the word. "Death," she says. "Our minds are all full of it—David, that guy who was married to the dancer, even David's poor grandmother."

"Such a gloomy Gus," her mother says.

Daddy puts up his empty hand, a gesture Kate realizes is intended to head off an argument, but that doesn't stop her.

"I'm not a gloomy Gus." She practically shouts at her mother. "David meant something to me. Just because you don't think high school kids have real feelings." She lets the sentence hang.

"Sweetie." Now her mother is all apology, reaching out to cover Kate's hand with hers, pressing it. "Certainly you have feelings. We know what a big part David played in your life." Daddy raises an eyebrow, then looks away from Mother and down at his plate. "But life goes on."

"But life isn't the same." And that is probably the truest statement Kate has ever made. *Life isn't the same.* "It won't ever be the same."

"People put things behind them," Daddy says. "Humans have a marvelous capacity for forgetting pain."

"Oh, yes," Kate says. "Leave it to you to believe that, with all you've left behind."

The silence is sudden and total. Mother puts a hand to her mouth, as if to stifle any possible words. Daddy lifts the napkin from his lap and lays it on the table beside his plate.

"You'll excuse me," he says, rising. "I've got paperwork waiting for me in the den."

* * *

Kate is in her room, looking through the day's school notes, wondering if she feels like doing homework, when her mother looks in.

"Busy?"

"Not really," Kate says.

"I thought you and I ought to have a talk." Mother comes into the room and sits on Kate's bed.

Kate pushes books and papers aside. "Sure."

"I know what a terrible week this has been for you," Mother says, "but I think you're upsetting your father—and maybe yourself—unnecessarily."

"And I think you're being too kind to him."

"I know you do. But perhaps somebody needs to give you a refresher course on recent history. A reminder of what the war has done to us all."

"Must we?" Kate says. "Must we have a lecture?"

"We must. Because the way you're acting upsets me, too."

"All right." Kate folds her hands in her lap and waits.

"Certain things you don't seem to realize," her mother says. "The war made everybody sort of *non compos mentis*." Kate knows what that means; it's what her father usually says when she does something stupid. "We were all a little bit crazy; it wasn't just our boys in the service, like your dad. Look at yourself, how you started hanging around that arcade on Main Street, out at all hours with those ragamuffins from across the river."

"They were perfectly nice kids," Kate says.

"Well I worried about you," Mother says, "and the later you got home, the more worried I was."

"You should have worried about Daddy."

"But he was three thousand miles away. I could miss him and pray for him, but I couldn't be responsible for him—and besides, he was an adult. You were barely in your teens."

Kate turns away and catches sight of her reflection in the dresser mirror. She's still in her teens, but she can already see herself looking older. David's car wreck has done that. Daddy's misbehaving has done it. Sherrie Adams and her dead husband have done it. This whole stupid week has stolen years from her life.

"It seems to me," she says, "that if Daddy had been one-tenth as grown up as I was at the time, he'd never have hurt you the way he did."

"If you knew him," her mother begins, and then stops. When she starts her sentence over again, her voice is softer and she won't look Kate in the eye. "If you knew," she says, "you'd realize that he hurt himself much more than he hurt me. He had to wake up to it, and live with it, and worst of all he had to confess it to me." Now she meets Kate's gaze, and her voice strengthens. "That's grown up, my darling Kathryn. I hope whoever you marry is half the man your father is."

"You're too forgiving," Kate says.

"And you're too smug."

"You're just thankful he came home alive. You'd let him get away with anything."

Kate finds her own words shocking, undaughterly. But her mother seems to absorb them without anger. "That's probably true," Mother says. "It's what I said before: war skews things, and people who love each other recognize how the war corrupts us, and *why*. Your father was in charge of a ground crew, the men who worked on the B-17s in his squadron. He watched the bombers leave, day after day, carrying not just the bombs to be dropped on Germany but the crewmen you father knew—men he joked with and drank with—"

"Drinking," Kate says. "Of course."

Mother ignores her. "And when one of those planes didn't come home, it meant it was shot down. It meant a crew of nine or ten men were either dead or prisoners. It meant your father would get to know a new crew—joke with them, and yes, drink with them—and watch them take off day after day, and worry himself sick until they were back on the ground in England." She sits straighter and pats the back of Kate's folded hands. "I understand why he did what he did," she says. "And I forgive him. And so should you."

25.

This Sunday the Congo Church is full. Probably most of the adults are regular members of the church, but Kate can see that much of the crowd is made up of high school kids who knew Tom and David—Shirley's services are at Holy Family Church, across the river—or were friends of Tom's, David not having close friends except herself and possibly Ray Sevigny, who dropped out of school to work full-time at Fein's Furniture. She wonders what David's father will have to say to so young an audience, he has such a reputation for not liking kids. It's a miracle he endured his son as patiently as he did. Kate wonders if David's death is a relief to him.

She tries to put these mean thoughts out of her mind. It's possible that the Reverend Willard won't even conduct the service, that he is so genuinely affected by the tragedy, he wouldn't be able to deliver a sermon without breaking down. These things happen. She can only wait and see.

The church is warm. She is sitting beside the Krauss memorial window, and through its glass she can see how the weather outside is clear, blue-skied, the world drenched in sunlight. This is what some people call "Indian Summer," although Kate's mother has taught her that the real Indian summer comes—if it comes—in October or November, when the Indian tribes were already huddled against the cold, and against what Mother calls "the elements." "We live in houses year-round," she explained when Kate was in fourth grade. "We never have to deal with the elements, so an unusual mild spell doesn't mean that much to us. It meant a lot to savages."

But it means something to us today, Kate thinks, because the warmth in the church has a lot to do with an atmosphere that is beginning to smell like the bodies that fill it—of sweat, and of the perfumes some women wear to smother it. If this ceremony doesn't begin soon, the Congregational Church will smell like a high school gymnasium.

Such are Kate's thoughts. Not of the loss of the boy who made her laugh, the boy she might someday have fallen in love with, the boy her mother approved of because his father was a minister. No, Kate is concerned with her surroundings. And what of it? This is a memorial service, not a funeral. There is no casket at the front of the church, no shiny black hearse waiting outside, no horror-movie attendants standing at the rear of the church wearing black suits and gray gloves. The casket is at Morse Funeral Home, where people went yesterday evening to pay their respects to David and the family surviving him, and the casket wasn't even open. Jack Morrison told everybody at school that David flew face first through the windshield of the Chevy, and his face was so mangled, "like raw hamburger," there was nothing old man Morse could do to make him look even halfway human.

And Jack is here, only a part of this young audience. Kate can see him—the other side of the church, the row ahead of hers—looking around, saying something to the boy next to him, his mouth just slightly twisted, as it always is, so that he looks as if he doesn't believe anything he sees or trust anybody he listens to. What will

Jack do now? He and Tom were practically brothers—lived next door to each other, had gone to the same schools since kindergarten, even had the same home rooms at Scoggin High. Poor Jack. He'd be a lost soul without Tom, nobody to clown around with, nobody to share secrets with. Kate wonders if he'll give her a call—not that she *wants* that, but they did date for a while. She doesn't especially like him, the way he looks down his nose at everybody, but at least he never tried to humiliate her the way David did. Tried to kiss her, of course—boys had to try, it was like a code of masculinity—but didn't try to force her. The story went around school that Jack and Harold Armitage gave a ride home to Edris—so many stories about Edris!—and when they were in front of her house, Jack held her so she couldn't move while Harold kissed her and put his hands under her sweater. Edris swears the story isn't true, that nothing like it ever happened, but with Edris you never could tell.

Kate wonders if anybody in this whole place is thinking about David, the reason we're all here.

*   *   *

It finally begins. The Reverend Harvey Willard appears almost magically through a door behind the pulpit. He wears a white robe and carries a white book that might be Bible or hymnal. He steps into the pulpit, braces himself with both arms against its railing, and begins. He has no notes, and speaks without hesitations.

THE SERMON

"I should commence by submitting my gratitude to all those of you whose condolences in the matter of my mother's death have lightened the considerable weight of my grief. She lived a long life,

and the Lord in his wisdom considered that life sufficient unto the day. As the Lord's servant, I dare not contend with the fact of my mother's passing.

"But we are met today for a similar, though different, occasion of sadness. If you were in my church last Sunday, when my sermon topic was 'The Serpent and the Butterfly,' you already know something of my feelings today. You know that I am a man who lives between the two poles of Beauty and Ugliness—as do we all—and that I am drawn irresistibly to Beauty—as, alas, some of us are not. I have devoted my religious life to the exploration of that disjunction, that discrepancy of wisdom, which draws some of my fellows irresistibly to Ugliness—or to Evil, as it is otherwise, and more intimately known. I have devoted my secular life, the day-to-day, the endless quotidian that rouses us each morning and sends us to sleep each night, to a parallel study. Both my religious and my everyday searches lead me to the same question: Is it in the nature of the sinner that he is so attracted? Or is it in his nurture?

"You may now feel a double sympathy for me and for my helpmeet, that we have lost our only son in a senseless wreck on a dark highway. And you may mourn with the parents of the other two children called to the Lord from that same wreckage. We may weep over the graves of all three, lay flowers, build monuments to the lives never fully lived. We may stand as models of grief and remembrance. But will we ask ourselves if these deaths were not deserved? Will we entertain the possibility that their deaths were only to be expected? That perhaps death was an invited fourth passenger in that automobile that carried them off the road and off the earth?

"*I believe we must ask these questions, if only so that when the time comes for us, we sad survivors, to meet our Maker, He will judge us as honest, and ruthlessly so, even in our grief over the loss of our loved ones.*

"*Let us consider these victims. One was a young woman who dishonored her womanhood by her promiscuity, her hedonistic pursuit of sexual satisfactions, her willingness to commit murder in order to conceal the depths of sin into which she had sunk. One was a young man, her partner in depravity, who first seduced her, then got her with child, then willingly became complicit in the destruction of that child.*

"*Lastly, one was my son, a young man with no moral compass, who for seventeen years under my roof and under my tutelage resisted, ignored, and mocked the teachings of the Lord whose presence informs this house of worship. David was a lamb who would not allow himself to be shepherded. He was a rebel whose cause was license to choose the wrong friends, the wrong books and magazines, the wrong music, the wrong behavior. He gloried in self-pollution, in material envy, in disrespect of his elders, in deceit and thievery. Of the three who died, surely he had earned death the best.*

"*I'm sure you have heard it said that the good die young, that they may not be corrupted. I say to you, now and in this holy place, that these three young people were not taken in order to preserve their virtue and their innocence. They were taken in order to punish their collective lack of that self-same virtue and innocence.*

"*It is not easy for me to condemn my own son. No doubt some of you will think it unchristian of me to do so. But truth is truth, evil is evil, justice is justice. The preacher's child shall not be spared an honest entry in the book of judgment. My son was shown every upright example, exposed to every text of morality, offered entrance to every form of Beauty and Goodness. He resisted, turned away, and paid the price.*

"I did my best with David; I absolve myself. I taught him the lessons of temptation and saw him unmoved; I absolve myself. I surrounded him with the joys of Nature, to no effect; I absolve myself. I loved him more than he deserved; I absolve myself. Of all blame, all failure, all grief, I absolve myself now and forever."

* * *

After the service is finished and the Reverend Harvey Willard has stepped away from the pulpit to vanish through a doorway beside the choir loft, there is a momentary suspension of time in the crowded church—a hush, an immobility, the words of the sermon, if that is what it was, sinking in, or dissipating, or never having been pronounced at all. It is this last—the minister's harsh attack on his own flesh and blood not real but only imagined—that Kate wishes for. How could he? What good did it do? If some remainder of David has been hovering in the unpleasant and odorous air of the church as witness to his father's outrage framed as a eulogy, what must his reaction be? To be dead is awful enough, Kate thinks. Never to have been loved is a thousand times worse.

When movement comes at last, the congregation stirring and picking itself up, shuffling and coughing, filing in broken lines up the three aisles, through the carpeted vestry and down the steps to the sun-beaten sidewalk, Kate is among the last to leave the building.

There is no sign of Mrs. Willard, David's mother, and Kate wonders where she is, what she is thinking, how her life will change. She is halfway down the steps, descending slowly because she is reluctant to join the milling below her, when she hears a woman's voice, off to her right and behind her.

"So angry a man!"

When she turns, Sherrie Adams is already approaching her, shaking her head and holding out her arms as if to embrace Kate. And embrace her she does, warmly, the way long-lost friends embrace after years apart.

"I never thought," Sherrie says, "to hear a father carry on so about his very own child. You'd've though the boy was Judas himself."

"It was awful," Kate says, and hugs back in spite of herself.

"And I can't say he seemed terribly fond of his own mother."

Kate can agree with that as well—but what is Sherrie doing here? Kate knows the carnival pulled up stakes three days ago, and she imagined Sherrie left the parlor couch so early because she was with it. Kate watched trucks and trailers and wagons parade down Hospital Hill, through town and up the highway past Mount Hope in the direction of New Hampshire. She watched thinking, sadly, "There goes Sherrie," and that scarcely a week earlier she and David had ridden their bicycles to The Meadows to see the tents and sideshows and concessions set up. How quickly life changed. How distant that arrival. How unfair it all was.

"I had to come," Sherrie is saying, standing back now, arms at her side, the alligator handbag dangling from the fingers of her left hand. "That sweet boy," she says. "He wanted to run off, he told me. Wanted to join the show and see the world. I couldn't understand that foolishness until today, seeing the father—hearing what he had to say about that poor child."

"But how can you be here?" Kate says. "The carnival—it's gone. Mustn't you be with it?"

Sherrie looks around at the others who've attended David's service, then takes a step closer to Kate as if not wanting to be overheard.

"You know the latest about Frank?" she says. "How they've moved him?"

"It was in the papers."

"He was locked up in the basement of your Town Hall. But that was temporary. Now they've transferred him to the jail in the county seat."

"That's Alfred," Kate says. She's driven past the county jail—red brick with black-barred windows—on family trips to Portland for shopping. "What will happen to him?"

Sherrie takes her arm and steers her away from the church. They walk down Main Street, past banks and a babershop, in the direction of the post office.

"I don't know," Sherrie says. "The local cops were terrible to Frank, rough and rude. I told them he was only standing up for me, defending me. I showed them the bruises on my arms, where Joe'd grabbed me, and I showed them the bruises where the men ganged up on me after the last show—but I didn't tell about that. I just let them think Joe had done it all. They said not to worry, they'd get it sorted out."

"And they will," Kate says. That's what the law did: it sorted things out until the truth came clear.

"I told them Joe didn't have any business with me. I told them there was a court order in Hartford that said he was forbidden to come anywhere near me."

"What did they say about that?"

"That they'd check up on my story, but in the meantime Frank would have to cool his heels." She gives Kate's arm a hard squeeze. They are standing at the corner of Main and Washington, waiting for the light to change. "They were hard on him, wouldn't listen to his side of it. Called him 'K-K-K-Katie'—you know: that old World War One song."

Kate knows. Her grandfather used to sing it to her.

"Then they shoved him into the back seat of the cop car and drove off with him. I've only seen him once since."

They cross Washington Street, arm in arm, like two old friends consoling each other. Kate wonders what people think. Do they think Sherrie is her mother and wonder why the woman wears so much rouge and lipstick? Do they think Kate takes after her? Her real mother would be—what? First, horrified. Then, amused.

"What happened to Joe?"

"Put him in a hearse and took him away. To the nearest garbage dump, if it was up to me. They wanted me to answer a lot of questions about him. How old he was, who were his next of kin. I told them to go through his pockets, and I suppose that's what they did."

"What about you?" Kate wonders. "What will you do now, with no job?"

Sherrie smiles a smug little smile. The two women are walking through the park in the center of town, and Sherrie leads them to sit on one of the wooden benches, as if sitting down to rest is part of the answer to Kate's question.

"That's where Frank has it all over Joe—why I should never have left Chittenango to hook up again with Joe. Frank is a saver, socked his money away for a rainy day—an emergency, if one should come up. He's got eleven hundred dollars saved up, all in a cigar box in the trailer. He's told me the money's mine, to keep me going till I find something worthy of me. Isn't that lovely? That's just the way he said it: 'Find something that's worthy of you.'"

"He's a good man." In some ways better than Daddy, Kate thinks. Loyalty and devotion and sacrifice. She likes to think of her father in those words, but after what she found out, that yes, there was another woman in his life, what can she do but admire Frank Coggio more?

"Of course I don't intend to use up all his money," Sherrie is saying. "I'll earn my keep, find any kind of job that lets me stay near him."

"I'm sure you will."

Sherrie sighs. "We'll see. I was always a whiz at tending bar, so here I am in a dry town, where there's no call for bartenders."

"But that will change," Kate says. "My father says that now the war's behind us, people are getting more relaxed and liberal. He says he's already hearing that liquor by the drink will be on the ballot in the next election."

"That's sensible," Sherrie says. "Why should the Elks and the American Legion be the only lucky ones?"

Was it really *lucky* for people to be able to drink in public? Darryl Jenks was killed, like David, in a one-car accident, and afterward a state trooper told the newspapers Darryl's blood-alcohol level was "sky-high." People said that old Doc Johnson, the vet who'd put Carmody the cat to sleep, drank himself to death. It seemed likely there'd be worse things than living in a dry town.

Sherrie hefts the handbag into her lap. "I'd best be going," she says. "Your folks'll be wondering why you didn't come straight home from the so-called eulogies." She stands and draws the strap of the bag up over one shoulder. "You can tell them there wasn't a wet eye in the house."

"Where are you staying?" Kate asks.

"Way down on south Main. You know where the drive-in is? Across the road from it is a trailer park where I've rented a space for the Airstream. I wasn't sure at first that they'd let me have the trailer—it being a scene of the crime and all—but they said they were done with it, but I'd better not leave the state of Maine. The park's not a bad place. They've got hookups for water and sewage and electricity. At night I can sit on my steps and watch the movie across the way. I can't have the sound, but I can try teaching myself to lip-read."

"I bet the carnival misses you," Kate says. "You always had a crowd."

Sherrie laughs—not the way you'd laugh at a joke, but the way you'd laugh to be sarcastic. "You can be damned sure they've already replaced me. The woods are full of Sharitas itching to take off their clothes and show off their goodies. They won't even have to change the posters."

26.

A week after David's father has shocked the town, the Portland *Press Herald* reports that Frank Coggio has been transferred to the York County jail in Alfred to await trial in the killing of Joseph Connors of Avon, Connecticut. The charge is murder in the second degree, and Coggio is being held without bail.

When the morning mail comes, Kate is in her room, reading. Her father climbs the front stairs and taps on her bedroom door. The door is half open, and he comes in.

"You've got a card," he says, handing her a penny postcard, "and a real letter."

Kate turns the card over and reads:

> Katie—
> Don't forget—Theres Sharitas around every corner—and Davids too.
> Your friend, Sherrie (Sharita) Adams

Kate reads it twice. She already knows that there's no sign of Coggio's old pickup truck and the silver Airstream in the trailer park Sherrie told her about, and she is happy to imagine they must already be hooked up at a new trailer park in Alfred. It will be a place near the jail, where Sherrie will visit Frank whenever she can.

Kate thinks that from this day forward the place where her dreams commence will be in a palace-like interior, high-ceilinged and glittering like kaleidoscope glass, where small birds and butterflies flicker and glide over her head—or, more properly, over the head of the dreamer in the dream, whoever she may eventually be. And everything that happens in this fairy-tale version of Sharita's silver Airstream will swim in that distorted ceiling like fish under a glass-bottomed boat. Maybe it will all be like the Xanadu poem they studied in English class last year, the one that might have been an opium dream, a trance, a hallucination the poet's mind transformed into a *pleasure dome*. That might even please Sherrie.

She slips the card between the pages of her book, perhaps to keep her place. She will look forward to dreaming in her pleasure dome, though she can't say she envies Sharita's living conditions in the waking world.

Her father has stayed in the room, awkward in the doorway, watching her.

"What's that about?" he says.

"Nothing," she says. "I don't think you'd understand."

"Aren't you going to read your letter?"

"Daddy?" Not a whine exactly, but a protest on the side of privacy. The postcard was available to any snoop; the letter, sealed, is not.

* * *

When her father has left the room—sheepish, she thinks—she closes the door and curls up against her pillow. The letter is in a smallish envelope that carries a *Boston Mass* postmark alongside the three-cent stamp. The letter is a long one, three pages of cramped handwriting in blue ink:

Dear Katie,

Harvey and I met you only the once, last year after the school play both you and David acted in, but I remember how sweet you were and how pleased I was, that summer, that you and David were spending time together. I know how fond of you David was, and although I don't know what sort of little misunderstanding you and he had been having, I do know that David would have done anything to please you. I'm sure that if God hadn't intervened, you might someday have been my daughter in law.

It's because you were so important to David that I'm writing this letter to you. I so much want you to know that Harvey showed me his eulogy, and that what he is going to say at the funeral is a million miles away from what I think. I didn't know the other two children, but I'm sure their parents loved them as deeply as I loved David, and I'm sorry for the hurt Harvey's sermon may have caused them. I know it hurt me when he made me read it Friday morning.

You understand why I couldn't bring myself to go to the church, to the funeral ceremony, and I didn't go to the viewing the night before. I'd already gone with Harvey to identify David's body. They'd taken the children to Portland, because Scoggin doesn't have a morgue, so we had to borrow a car and drive all the way to Portland and go down into the basement of Maine Medical. I was hoping and hoping that there'd been a mistake, that it was somebody else's Chevrolet and it only happened to be the same colors as ours, but of course that was a poor mother's wishful thinking. It was David, and I wish I hadn't gone there either.

We didn't see the others, the girl and the other boy, David's friend, but David was the saddest sight ever. Not just that he was dead, but the way he looked in his death. He was so terribly damaged. I'd never go through that experience again. And maybe that's the good thing, that I can't go through it again because I only had the one child to lose.

Harvey didn't make things any easier. He was mad all the way to Portland, raving about its being bad enough that he had to borrow a car from Stanley Johnson, a car dealer he hates, but to have to drive forty miles in the dead of night to confirm that your posterity's been taken away from you, and then, after you'd arrived, complaining about how cold the place was where they showed us David's body. But you don't need to hear about the awful scenes he made at every step we took that night.

The worst was the next morning when he made me go with him to look at the car. The police had towed it to an auto shop in Alfred. The car was in a big field with a lot of other machines, all of them wrecked to a fare-thee-well. Ours, Harvey's pride and joy, you wouldn't have recognized. It hit a concrete bridge support, you know, and the state police said David was driving fast, probably 80 miles an hour when the car impacted. That was a word, 'impacted,' I'd never heard used that way.

Anyway, if Harvey was upset about losing his son and heir, he acted twice as upset about losing that damned car—excuse my language. He went on and on, even while we were driving home, about how much he'd paid for it, how much money he'd put into it for upkeep, how there was no way it could ever be set to rights and where was he going to find the money for another automobile as good as this one had been.

And then he started in on David and David's choice of unsuitable friends. You never knew who he was hanging out with, you always had to nag him a hundred times to do the simplest chores, he ought never to have been allowed to get a driver's license, him being so obviously irresponsible. And what in God's name were the two of them, two underaged boys, doing with that girl from the wrong side of the tracks?

I heard about it afterward—how upset people were over the terrible things he said in church about the three of them, about his own flesh and blood. I should have warned you. I should have said that he'd been saving it all up, all the venom, all the resentment, all the envy toward a person he couldn't a hundred percent control. I was the easy one, he could control me, but David was something else. David was quiet, you couldn't tell what he was thinking, and then there was always this contention between David and his father.

Anyway, I've had enough of it. I'm writing this in a hotel room in Boston, listening to the traffic under my window and wondering where I'll go next. I can't go home to Harvey after all that's happened, all that's been said. I remember there was one day when I looked out the kitchen window and saw our dog, Brownie, playing with something I couldn't make out. David was just coming into the house, and when I asked what Brownie had he said it was a snake. Then he said I shouldn't be upset, because the snake was dead.

It was so strange, but what came into my mind the day David passed away was the Genesis story, and Brownie's snake, and at that instant I thought We'll never again see Paradise. And I thought how sad it all was, the worst of it not having known the terrible way we would lose it.

Be happy, dear Katie.

Yours truly,
Florence Willard

* * *

The letter is upsetting, not so much because it raises once more the possibility that she and David might someday have had a life together—a possibility that she knows will wake her from those inevitable Xanadu dreams and nightmares—but because Kate has no specific memory of David's mother, no face to put with the name, no recollection of her voice, and so she can't see or hear the sadness that must inform every word she has just read. Yes, they must have met after a school play, but among so many parents milling backstage, hugging their kids and saying their pride, who can remember them all? It means Kate can't give a shape to what life will be like for Florence Willard, going it alone, her son dead, her husband cast aside. And then Kate sets that beside Sherrie and Sherrie's solitary sadness, and she wonders: Why would anyone want to grow up and be a woman in this world?

27.

The fire begins on a windy Friday afternoon, under a sun too bright, too warm for October in Maine. Someone driving the two-lane blacktop south of Scoggin finishes his cigarette and tosses it out the window of the car, where the wind catches it and carries it into the dried yellow grass of a pasture so withered no animal could graze there. The cigarette smolders only a few moments before it kindles a patch of surrounding grass, the easy tinder of this driest of autumns. The patch of small flame widens, the encouraging west wind pushes it toward a cluster of low bushes, the flames climb the thin branches with a sigh of hot mischief. In a half-hour most of the pasture is blackened, all its vegetation reduced to ash, while the flames move on to a modest windbreak of cedars, which it devours in a flash and crackle of orange. Still windblown, the fire burns through the adjoining fields, spreading and accelerating, through brush, juniper and small fir, headed for a grove of pines. It disposes of the pines, one at a time, in a swift fountain of sparks and flame, its heat so intense that if you were facing it, even at a distance of fifty yards, you would have to turn away to protect your face from burn.

On it travels, this accidental fire making ash of whatever waits ahead of it. The gray smoke rising in its wake dims the sun, the smoke casts a warning shadow eastward, toward civilization, toward barns and farmhouses, racing across the blueberry plains until it reaches the highway. This is the same road where David Willard lost control of his life in a September fog, where Tom and Shirley ended their romance, where the wreck of the old Chevrolet revealed the Reverend Willard's true soul. The fire dithers here, rambling through the ditches north and south until it finds a single pine tree. Streaking up the trunk it ignites the low branches, explodes to the treetop where the partnering wind carries a shower of sparks to the far side of the road, and almost before you can describe it the flames are moving again, pushing toward the ocean, knowing now that the ocean is the only force that can arrest it.

*　*　*

When Kate walks to school on Monday morning the smoky air stings her lungs and makes her want to sneeze. Even at three-thirty, when she walks home after play rehearsal, the sun is no more than a perfect white disc in the smoke-clouded sky. The radio this morning has told the story of hundreds of acres burned and fire departments from as far away as Massachusetts coming to Maine to help contain the fire. Her father has hooked up the garden hose in case flames come close to their house. Mother is perplexed.

"Oh, George," she said. "Surely the fire is too far away. It won't affect us." And then she had hesitated, as if she might be misunderstanding the threat. "Will it?"

"In this wind, better safe than sorry," he said.

Fire or no fire, Kate is deeply involved in rehearsals for the school play. The cast meets every afternoon in the school gymnasium, a place that has a stage at one end and smells of floor polish and male sweat. Some days Miss Samways walks them through one or another of the play's scenes, other days they try on the costumes they've scavenged from home or from local merchants, or sit in groups of two or three running their lines—first reading from the playbooks, then laying the books face down, to say the words without looking. Kate is playing Alice Sycamore, not the part she wanted, but the one David thought she should get because Alice is the only normal person in the play. Jack Morrison is Tony Kirby, the part she's sure would have gone to David. Amanda Burgess got the Essie Carmichael part.

Poor David. He's been dead only a little more than a month, but already it's as if he never existed. Nobody talks about him. Nobody says what a shame it is that David couldn't be here to play Tony—he was so believable, and he'd already memorized most of his lines.

Worse than that, it's as if the whole Willard family never existed. Their house sits empty, with a *For Sale* sign nailed to the front porch. She wonders what happened to David's stamp collection, his father's butterflies. If fire comes into the town, who will pour water on the Willard house? Not Fred Leach, the realtor whose name is on the sign. Everybody knows Florence Willard is divorcing Harvey. As for Harvey, nobody even knows where he is, though naturally there are all kinds of rumors. The Congo Church skipped a couple of Sunday services, but last week a minister from Biddeford filled in, and next week another substitute, this one from South Portland, is listed on the church signboard. "Fire and Brimstone" is the announced sermon, a topic that sounds more Baptist than Congregational.

Or perhaps the subject is simply appropriate.

* * *

This morning a northbound Boston & Maine freight train—a long one, a hundred-thirty-three cars drawn by a pair of steam locomotives—is making its slow way from Rochester to Gorham. Under smoky skies it has made a stop in Scoggin to take on water, and now, near Waterboro, the lead locomotive throws off cinders that ignite the brush alongside the tracks. In the train's wake, this fire, like its sister to the southeast, gives itself to the steady west wind and travels its own path toward the distant Atlantic, turning pine and spruce into skeletons that look like stick figures at prayer, blackening the yellow meadows, leaping small stream beds, broadening its reach with amazing speed. All the secret hollows where David Willard would have imagined himself embracing Kate are merely ash.

But now there is opposition. Firefighters from small-town departments have come to the scene, and volunteers who prowl with Indian pumps on their backs or carrying pine branches soaked in any available water source—a lake, a stream still running—stand at the edge of an evergreen woods, waiting to meet the flames when they drop from the trees into the field. The sound of the approaching fire is like small animals walking across twigs, but if the waiting men and boys are confident of stopping the fire, their confidence vanishes when the flames burst out of the woods in a wall of yellow and orange. The heat is unbearable, and a cascade of sparks blows over the men's heads to seed the meadow behind them. The line breaks in an instant, everyone running to a safe, cool distance while the reckless wind sends fire racing across the unguarded field.

At the end of the field is a farmhouse, a barn, a shed for tools and equipment. The volunteers make their stand between fire and buildings; they manage to save the house, spraying water on its roof against any sparks borne upward, but the shed is destroyed and the barn is lost when the hay stored in its loft catches and burns. These are the first structures to be devoured, but hardly the last. By the end of the month more than a hundred-fifty houses will go up in smoke.

* * *

Fire is everywhere now, and one Thursday morning when Kate arrives at the high school she sees a flat-bed truck is drawn up at the front entrance. A half-dozen boys are sitting or standing in the back of the truck and others—she recognizes Jack and Jimmy Sanborn and Rick Lowe—are climbing on.

Edris Bedford appears beside her, smelling of soap and perfume. "Isn't it exciting?" she says.

"What's going on?" Ordinarily, she wouldn't get into a conversation with the likes of Edris, but curiosity wins out.

"The guys are volunteering to fight the fires. It's so brave."

"They're letting them skip school to do that?"

"And they'll get paid too. Harold Armitage says he heard the state of Maine will pay them $70 a day."

"That's incredible," Kate says. And it is. Seventy dollars is a month's pay for some people. Even seven dollars a day would be generous.

"It's dangerous work," Edris says. "You have to pay people to risk their lives."

* * *

No one is certain how the third fire starts, near Newfield, a couple of days later, and by the time more volunteers can reach it, a hundred acres are blackened and the flames are in forest, dancing eastward through the pine treetops. It seems unstoppable, this force of nature let loose by a summer of drought. Houses, outbuildings, fence lines, the fire eats them all. Farmers cart their livestock to safety in trucks and vans, or lead them where they hope fire won't find the frightened animals. Vain hope for some. The flames are relentless in their hunger, spreading across the pine-needled ground through small towns at a dozen crossroads, lakeside cottages and boathouses, roadside stands displaying the season's meager crops, leveling everything in their path. Bare chimneys and foundation walls are all the fire leaves behind. The Hansen cottage, where David Willard watched while Priscilla's boyfriend applied suntan lotion to her shoulders and breasts—that's gone now, nothing left but the stones of the fireplace. At the foot of Mousam Lake, where Kate and David rode their bikes on an August Saturday, the picnic tables where they ate the sandwiches Kate's mother made are charred black. Wherever the fire has been, the world is colorless.

* * *

Jack Morrison is full of stories. A week has passed, the fires across the state are mostly contained, so there is no further need for high-school boys dreaming of earning $70 a day—wages never to be paid—and Jack stands across the street from the school, smoking a cigarette and regaling his friends with his experiences in the front lines.

"First they sent us to Shapleigh Corner," he says. "You know where I mean? We always drive through the place on the way to the lake, stop at the general store—which by the way doesn't exist anymore—and sometimes put gas in the car. Anyway, it's just the store with one gas pump, and a sort of farmer's roadside stand, and a couple of houses.

"When we got there, it was already dark and the fire was still a mile or so away. But you could see it, like this orange glow in the sky with every so often a kind of fountain of yellow sparks above the treetops, and you could hear it, chewing up the woods and getting closer.

"What we didn't expect was that before the flames had even gotten to us, the wind—and boy, it was windy—blew the sparks over our heads and set fire behind us. You got to picture that: half-a-dozen of us standing between two fires and wondering how we were going to get out of the way."

He stops and takes a drag on his cigarette.

"Well you must have got out," some wiseguy says, "because here you are, talking about it."

"But it was scary. The general store went up like it was made out of paper, and so did the houses on the other side of the road. Then somebody said we'd better get out of there, in case the underground gas tank blew up, and just about then the truck came back for us. I swear we drove like a bat out of you-know-where through real flames and we were all coughing from the smoke."

"So you were no help at all," somebdy else says. "Jack Morrison goes off to save the world, but he can't save shit."

Jack flings his cigarette into the gutter. "Fuck you," he says, and crosses the street to the high school just as the outside bell starts ringing for classes.

* * *

At second lunch period, Jack is still telling his stories, about how a few days after Shapleigh he and his crew were sent east of town to The Meadows, where the carnival had been, because a wind shift had turned the fire toward Scoggin and everybody was afraid the hospital might burn.

"We had to help move the patients outside," he says, "just in case. Some of them could walk, and we just led them to places where they could sit down and wait for buses to come for them. Rick and I were pushing people in wheelchairs. We put them in that circular drive in front of the building and told them to stay put. Did you know wheelchairs have brakes?"

"Where did the buses take them?" somebody wants to know.

"Nowhere," Jack says. "The buses never showed up." He put an unlit cigarette behind his right ear and stood up to carry his tray back to the kitchen window. "But neither did the fire."

28.

When the fires are under control at last, Kate remembers that at the height of the burning the male prisoners in jails at Alfred and Thomaston were let out to help the firefighters. She thinks of Sherrie, and of the chance that Frank will have managed to slip away from whatever guards were watching; that the two have been reunited; that even as she is imagining it, the pickup truck with the cracked windshield is hauling their shiny silver trailer—through a clarified air that carries the last odors of smoke, through the desolation of naked chimneys and burned cars and stripped trees, running toward a promise that she and David have lost forever. But that's a romantic notion; David would have made fun of her. He would have said, *In the real world, Sherrie would be visiting Frank at the jail, and while she was there the wind would shift, and when she got back, the trailer and the old pickup would have gone up in smoke.* Kate can almost hear his voice, talking from beyond the grave.

* * *

On the last Sunday of the month she rises early, finds a warm jacket in the front-hall closet—the weather has turned cold, and snow is promised—and lets herself out the front door. Her bike is on the porch; she wheels it down the steps and vaults onto the seat.

She heads for The Meadows. What for? Other carnivals leave in their wake a litter of candy wrappers and popcorn boxes, crumpled cigarette packs and paper cups, soiled napkins and—how is this possible?—condoms grotesque as white snakes. The concessions vanish. The trucks and vans drive away to other ends of the earth.

But this is different. True, the paradise that was Sharita's is likewise carted away, the World of Pleasures a company whose actors will never again perform—some of them dead, all of them unnecessary. But this time no trash from the departed shows and concessions swirls about Kate's feet in the raw winter wind. What Jack told her is true: the field before her is black from fire, and what the wind stirs are eddies of gray ash that may have been litter, may have made a connection to forgotten pleasures, but more likely are only what remains of one dry summer's bleached and brittle abandoned pasture. Next month a town meeting will take up the question of whether The Meadows should be used for such disreputable carryings-on in future.

It seems a hundred years since she and David rode up Hospital Hill to watch sweating, swearing men put together this World of Pleasures where her life changed. She thinks of Harvey Willard, who humiliated his wife and cursed his only son before God and the town; of Joe Connors and all the nameless men who teased and abused Sherrie Adams to satisfy who knew what; of Tom Gowen, David's idol, who carelessly ruined silly Shirley Kostas; of her own father, betraying Mother because it was Christmas and he happened to be a million miles away; and David—poor innocent David, begging Kate for something she wouldn't have known how to give.

All the hungry, selfish men. *When I am a woman, what pleasures should I expect in a world like theirs?* And yet Sherrie will stay by Frank as long as she must, whether waiting within sight of the Alfred jail or fulfilling Kate's daydream of their escape from October's firestorms—a devotion Kate Meredith can only marvel at as she coasts down Hospital Hill toward the shelter of home.

Robley Wilson is the author of three earlier novels: *The Victim's Daughter* (Simon & Schuster, 1989), *Splendid Omens*, and *The World Still Melting* (St. Martin's/Thomas Dunne Books, 2004 and 2005, respectively). He has also published three books of poetry, and six story collections, most recently *Who Will Hear Your Secrets?* (Johns Hopkins, 2012). His second story collection, *Dancing for Men*, won the 1982 Drue Heinz Literature Prize, and his first poetry collection, *Kingdoms of the Ordinary*, won the Agnes Lynch Starrett Prize—both from University of Pittsburgh Press. Wilson has been a Guggenheim Fellow in Fiction, a Nicholl Fellow in Screenwriting, and was for 31 years the editor of the *North American Review*. He and his wife, novelist Susan Hubbard, live in Florida with three indolent cats. Visit him online at www. robleywilson.com.